C000217556

Cover design by
www.catherineclarkedesign.co.uk

9781915887054

Williams & Whiting (Publishers)
15 Chestnut Grove, Hurstpierpoint,
West Sussex, BN6 9SS

Also by Marilyn Pemberton
from Williams & Whiting

The Jewel Garden

The Grandmothers' Footsteps Series:
A Teller of Tales
A Keeper Of Tales

Also by Marilyn Pemberton

Out of the Shadows: the life and works of Mary De Morgan

Sold For A Song

by

Marilyn Pemberton

For my own two, Thomas and Maria

Preface

Let me say first and foremost that this is not a history book but is a fictional account of events triggered by something that actually *did* happen in seventeenth and eighteenth-century Italy, this being the act of castrating young boys in order to preserve the purity and innocence of their unbroken voices for the entertainment of others. I learned this startling fact when listening to a Radio 3 programme a few years ago and the seed for this novel was sown.

The story I tell deals with the castration itself at the start and thereafter explores the ramifications of this single act and the ripple effect of the consequences on the players in this human game of chess.

Castration - that is the removal of a male's testes - has been practised since records began, and probably before. In Deuteronomy 23:1, for instance, it references men who are 'wounded in the stones,' and condemns them to never being able to 'enter into the congregation of the Lord.' There are characters who are castrated in both Greek and Egyptian mythology and Roman law goes so far as to differentiate between those who have had their testes pressed, crushed or completely removed, the latter being known as *castrati*.

The reasons for castration were many-fold but one reason was the belief that it would cure leprosy, madness, epilepsy or gout. One cannot but feel sorry for the poor man who not only lost his manhood, but also still suffered from the original illness, as castration will not have been the hoped-for cure. Another more successful reason was because the removal of the testes resulted either in significantly reducing the male aggressive and sexual drive or completely removed his ability to procreate. Castration

1

was therefore often used as a form of punishment or constraint, either to prevent criminals from reproducing, to reduce the sexual drive of soldiers and rapists or to diminish the aggression and fighting spirit of prisoners of war. The eunuch being the 'guardian of the bedchamber' in the Eastern harems is well known, their purpose to ensure the chastity of the sultan's wives whilst being themselves no sexual threat.

The physical changes of a castrato described in this book are accurate: there is an absence of an Adam's apple; minimal body hair; a tendency towards obesity and having female physical attributes such as breasts, fatty hips, thighs and necks. The combination of the larynx not dropping and the rib-cage expanding into a more rounded shape and therefore becoming an excellent sounding box, meant that the trained castrato had the voice of a child with the power of a man. In the early seventeenth century it was realised that the sound made was exquisite and for two centuries it became much sought after. The rest, as they say, is history.

Chapter 1

The deed

Merlo, Italy - 15th May 1756

We waited in silence. *Il Barbiere*, the barber, sat with his eyes closed, taking swigs of wine from his flagon. His white apron, stretched tight across his ample belly, was patterned with red drops. He looked more like a butcher of meat than of hair; I hoped it was not an omen.

I felt too nervous to drink.

Il Barbiere's house was beyond the outskirts of the village of Merlo; I assumed because it offered him the privacy he needed for this second, more lucrative occupation. The window was open as it was a warm May evening and despite its isolated location I could still hear the church bells tolling Compline, reminding us all to reflect on the day just finished and the night to come. I too closed my eyes and offered up a prayer for a successful outcome of the night's activities. It was, I tried to convince myself, ultimately for the glory of God.

The building that the boys and I had been put into, and in which we were now sitting, was separated from Il Barbiere's family home by a long piece of land, in which he kept a penned herd of pigs. The sound of their snuffling and grunting as they foraged for food was carried into the room by the gentle breeze, along with their unwholesome stink. Didn't they ever sleep?

Il Barbiere suddenly banged his flagon down onto the table, making me literally leap out of my chair. His eyes

3

were open and he glanced at the three boys who were lying on their beds along one wall. Not one of them stirred.

'Right, Philippe, they're ready. Bring one of them to the other room.' He stood, swigged the remains of his wine and left.

Which one to start with? The nearest was Fabio, a serious little boy, already more pious at eight years old than I was, some sixteen years older. Next to him was his cousin, Roberto, who I had already taken a great liking to, for his spirit, sense of humour and optimism. At the end of the row was Luigi, who I knew didn't understand why he had been taken from his family and wanted nothing more than to go home. They had all been given enough drugged wine to keep them comatose during the procedure. I decided to start with Fabio. He offered no resistance and it was like lifting a rag doll. I carried him easily out of the bedroom and into an adjoining room, where Il Barbiere was bustling around, checking over his instruments. He glanced up as I entered and pointed at a wooden contraption placed in the centre of the room.

'Put him in there and fasten the straps, just tight enough so that he can't lash out.'

It was not a normal chair. It had all the necessary parts but it was so made that anyone sitting in it would be in a semi-lying position and his legs could be spread wide apart. There were leather belts attached to the arms and the two front legs and I buckled them loosely around his wrists and ankles. Fabio didn't stir although I was ham-fisted in my nervousness and kept knocking his limbs against the hard wooden frame.

I suddenly had an appalling vision of him waking up in the middle of the operation. 'Should we give him more of the wine? Just to be sure?'

'No. He's had just enough to keep him unconscious until morning. Any more of the opiate and he will sleep permanently, and we don't want that, do we?' He grinned, revealing black gaps in yellow teeth. 'Lift his night shirt.'

I did so, revealing Fabio's scabby knees, skinny thighs and his cock curled like a little pink maggot.

Despite it being a warm night there was a fire burning fiercely in the grate, making the room almost unbearably hot. Il Barbiere crouched before it, holding a metal contraption in the flames. He looked over his shoulder at me. 'Are you squeamish?'

'I don't think so. But I am the secretary to *il Conte*, not a soldier; my work doesn't usually involve large quantities of blood.'

He smiled at my poor attempt at humour. 'Hold the lamp up high above his stomach then look away, just in case.'

There was little to see inside the room other than the reclining Fabio, the squatting Il Barbiere, a small table by my side upon which stood a pile of clean linen squares and the shadows dancing on the rough, whitewashed walls. The window was open in here as well, but this one faced away from the house, overlooking, I guessed, the open countryside. The nearly-full moon was shrouded by cloud and when I looked out I could see nothing but the absolute blackness of night.

The smell of pigs still permeated the air.

Il Barbiere suddenly stood up, walked the short distance across the room until he was standing in front of Fabio and placed the metal contraption over the boy's genitals. There was a hissing sound and a smell that made me gag. I saw Il Barbiere pluck something from between Fabio's legs and throw it into a bucket.

I put the lamp down on the table with deliberation, slowly walked to the window and spewed out my evening meal. I heard Il Barbiere chuckle behind me.

I was squeamish after all.

I took deep breaths of the cool night air until my head stopped spinning then turned cautiously back into the room. Il Barbiere was just finishing binding some of the linen squares around the wound. Thankfully I could see no blood.

Fabio slept on.

'Take this one back to his bed and bring me another one.'

I undid the straps, lifted Fabio from the chair and carried him carefully back to his bed. I know it was my imagination but he seemed to weigh less. I lay him on his back and covered him with a sheet. He mumbled in his sleep and gave a little burp.

I went to the next bed. Roberto had taken his night shirt off and was lying spread-eagled on his front. Even though he was in a deep, drugged sleep, I could sense the energy waiting to be released and I could imagine him leading a company of soldiers into battle. But that would never be now, of course.

I secured Roberto into the chair and stood holding the lamp high in the air to provide as much light as possible.

'Lizzy can help, if you'd rather?'

6

Lizzy was his twelve year old daughter.

'No, I'll be alright. It was the smell. But I'll know this time. I'll be alright.'

He laughed and I smelt the wine on his breath.

The mutilation process was repeated. I still looked out of the open window into nothingness but I was better prepared and I breathed through my mouth to avoid the smell of burnt flesh. I managed to stay in position although the sound of Roberto's balls landing in the bottom of the bucket made the bile rise in my throat.

I watched as Il Barbiere wiped Roberto's wounds and then bind him as he had done Fabio. I carried the boy back to his bed and lay him on his back but he immediately turned onto his stomach, sighed deeply and slept on.

Whereas the two cousins' colouring was dark, Luigi had blonde hair and blue eyes, as had all of his family. He weighed so little; I felt a wave of apprehension as I buckled the straps around his twig-like arms and legs.

This time I watched.

Il Barbiere was quick and in literally the blink of an eye Luigi was unmanned. But it hadn't been so quick that I hadn't had the time to see that the barber's hands were shaking as if he had the palsy. I breathed through my mouth again and braced myself for the sound of his balls being dropped into the bucket, at which I only swayed slightly. Il Barbiere dampened the fire as I released Luigi from the restraints and he followed me as I carried the boy out of the room. He locked the door, gave me a conspiratorial wink and told me to catch a few hours sleep whilst I could.

Once I had put Luigi back into his bed I lay down on my own. I was exhausted and hoped that sleep would come quickly. I did not drift off to sleep, however, but rather back to the morning that this ill-conceived journey had started.

Davide and I had arrived at Montalcino just as the sun's nascent rays were casting out the night-time shadows, revealing the rough, ill-repaired dwellings of the families I had come to break up. All the village was awake by now, preparing for another day working in il Conte's vineyards, but we approached the house from whence came a wave of sound: women sobbing, men remonstrating, children whining, babies wailing. I dismounted and as I walked tentatively towards the house the noise slowly abated into an eerie silence, broken only by the blood pounding in my ears. I couldn't yet see inside but the house itself seemed to be glaring at me, and having judged me, found me very much wanting.

I hesitated in the doorway. I could now see that the room was packed with people, all of them facing towards me, motionless, as if frozen by a sorcerer's curse. I searched the faces for one I recognised but in such a close community they all had similar features and I could not distinguish one from another. No-one moved but I felt as if they were all pressing onto my chest, stifling me. I stepped back outside and took a deep breath of the fresh morning air. This seemed to break the spell for everyone surged out and formed a circle around me, their closeness and hostility making me sweat.

I had to take control. 'Are the boys' fathers here?' I was ashamed to realise I didn't even know their names. There were murmurings and shufflings and eventually five men stepped forward. Not only were their faces akin, so too their expressions of distrust and disdain. I suddenly felt angry at il Conte for putting me in this position, at his arrogance and self-indulgence. My guilt made me harsh. 'You are here then, to exchange your sons, each for a bag of gold?'

They glanced at each other, then one spoke for them all, his tone defiant. 'Conte De Lorenzo promised they will have more opportunities and be able to earn good money.' He hesitated, 'And the gold will help to repair our houses, buy more stock and better our own lives. God gave our boys their voices and it would be sinful of us to waste that gift.'

I felt embarrassed that they were putting their trust in a man who I knew to be only interested in his own aggrandisement. I could have, should have, tried to dissuade them, but I wanted to keep my job and the security and life-style it gave. 'As il Conte explained to you, they will spend quite a few years in the conservatoire in Florence, where they will be taught to sing properly. They will certainly be well looked after there and if they work hard and it is God's will then, yes, they will have a better life and will earn good money.' More murmurs, shuffles and furtive glances. 'So, I have five bags of gold here, one for each boy.' The words tasted foul in my mouth but I swallowed them. I took a leather pouch and poured the coins into my palm, the sunlight glinting off the golden faces. A gasp encircled me and the five men, the five fathers, smiled and nodded. They each held out their hands.

'The boys first.' When had I learned to be so callous? The men called into the crowd, which separated as the five mothers led their boys to me. The women's eyes were red rimmed and as I handed a bag to the father, I had to tear the son from the mother's grip.

As Davide had driven the carriage out of the village I had looked back. The reflection of the sun off the gold that was already being eagerly counted had blinded me and the screams of the mothers had deafened me. The carriage had lurched round a corner and the huddle of villagers had been lost to sight. But I could still hear the screaming.

I woke with a start, realising I was in fact in my bed and that I could still hear screaming.

It was Fabio. He was sitting bolt upright in his bed, the sheet thrown to the floor. He was staring in horror at his linen binding and he screamed and screamed.

I rushed over to him, sat on the edge of the bed and took his hand in mine.

'Hush now, Fabio, it's all right. Everything went well. Are you in any pain? Are you thirsty?'

Fabio looked at me with his black eyes filled with panic. He stopped screaming but then leaned towards me and threw up all over me.

I heard giggling in the doorway. It was Lizzie, holding a jug of water and more squares of linen.

'Don't just stand there, come and help me clean this up.'

She may only have been twelve but she was a good and efficient worker. Whilst I changed my clothes she gave Fabio a drink, wiped his face and changed his binding. He was calmer when I returned to his side and he gave me a sheepish grin.

'Sorry, signor Agostini. I was dreaming I was in the barn with Roberto. I had forgotten about,' he pointed down to his middle section 'about all this. I am alright now. It doesn't hurt very much. Actually, I am quite hungry.'

'You're always hungry.'

It was Roberto, propped up on one elbow, his hair tousled, still stark naked. I smiled at his brazenness. 'How are you feeling, Roberto?'

'Good, thank you, signor Agostini.'

'I wish you would both call me Philippe. Are you hungry too?'

Roberto nodded then gingerly swung his legs over the side of the bed. He tried to stand up but gave a yelp of pain and sat back down again.

Il Barbiere's wife, Mathilde, stood in the doorway, holding a tray. 'Don't go rushing things, young man. Wait a moment and I'll help you.' She put the tray onto the table and then went over to Roberto's bed. She took hold of his upper arm then lifted him up. 'Try and stand upright, don't bend. The pain will pass.'

Roberto stood for a minute, his mouth a thin, determined line, then he gave a stiff nod and, guided by the wife, he walked with small, shuffling steps across to the table.

I similarly supported Fabio, and when he was seated they both fell onto the bread and cheese with great gusto. Whilst Mathilde poured out three cups of milk I went over to Luigi's bed. I could see immediately that things were not right. He was burning with fever. I wiped the sweat from his face with the red and white spotted neckerchief that he was so proud of, but I made no impression. His eyes were open but unfocussed; he looked through, not at me. He was mumbling the same thing over and over again.

'Mama, Mama, Mama.'

Mama, who had sold him for a bag of gold.

Mathilde came over and tutted when she saw him.

'I'll go get Frederico.'

Frederico, Il Barbiere, tutted also when he saw the state of Luigi.

'This happens sometimes, even to the best of us. I'll give him some more opiate, not too much mind, but enough for him to sleep some more.'

He lifted the linen squares and I saw his eyes narrow.

'It might be better if we moved his bed away from the others. Take the boy, signore, and Mathilde and I will carry the bed into the other room.'

I lifted Luigi into my arms and nearly dropped him, so great was the heat radiating from his little body. The two boys stopped their eating long enough to look quizzically at me.

'Luigi is not very well. We are putting him in the other room so he can sleep. I am sure he will be fine by tomorrow morning.'

I sat with Luigi all morning, wiping his whole body with a damp cloth, trying to cool him down. I managed to get him to drink some of the drugged wine by raising his head then stroking his throat to make him swallow. Eventually his feverish mumblings stopped and he fell into a restless sleep. I decided I needed to get away from the house for a while.

I popped my head round the bedroom door to tell the boys I was going out, but they too were sleeping, theirs natural rather than drugged.

As I wanted to get to the village I had to walk from our single storey annexe, across the piece of land and around Il Barbiere's family home. I gave the pigs a salute as I passed them; it was not their fault that they smelled so terrible.

As I walked by the side of the house I peered into a window and saw Il Barbiere busy about his daily business. A soldier of rank, possibly a captain, was lying back in the chair, his eyes closed, his lathered neck exposed to the razor that was about to descend. I noticed that Il Barbiere's hand was steady again, due, no doubt to his consumption of the product of the vineyards for which the region was justifiably famous.

The village of Murlo was much larger than Montalcino but nonetheless it didn't take me long to find the inn. It was mid-day and the place was full of tradesmen, soldiers, farmers, vintners, all partaking of either a solid or liquid lunch. I found an empty seat against the back wall. On one side there were three men huddled together, their bent heads almost touching, whispering as if they were plotting some nefarious deed. On the other side was a man well in his cups. He was staring into the distance, his face wet with tears. Perhaps he was a cuckolded husband, or his harvest had failed for a second year running.

A serving girl, her bosom barely contained inside a low cut blouse, came over, asked me what I wanted and winked at me suggestively. I smiled shyly at her sauciness and asked for a jug of wine, some soup and some bread. When she returned with my lunch she had to bend down to put the bowl and jug onto the table and in so doing one of her breasts broke free. She laughed boldly.

'It's always doing that! Do you want to put it back for me?'

I am a normal, hot-bloodied male but I was frozen with embarrassment and when she saw I wasn't going to make a move, she chuckled again, re-housed the recalcitrant breast herself and wriggled away, swaying this way and that to avoid the eager fingers that wanted to pinch and fondle her ample bottom.

I sighed. What was I doing in a place like this? How I wished I was back at the Villa De Lorenzo, doing my proper job, not looking after young boys. I wanted to be back working for il Conte; back with la Contessa Eleanora, his wife - my lover.

Chapter 2

What the night brought

I closed my eyes and remembered the last time we had lain together. The sheen of her satin nightgown, the swish as it had fallen to the floor, the smoothness of her flawless skin, the blackness of her hair as it lay fanned out on the white pillow. The little sounds she made as I stroked and aroused her.

'Join you?'

Il Barbiere jolted me out of my reverie. He was the last person I wanted to see but I nodded and he sat on a wooden stool directly opposite me. He lifted his mug of wine in a toast, his hand trembling slightly. '*Buona salute*!' He replaced the empty mug, his hand now rock steady. 'The little one won't last, you know. He's not looking good.'

'He has a name. It's Luigi.'

'Doesn't matter what his name is, he still won't last. It happens sometimes, even to the best of us.'

And he was one of the best. Il Conte had been given Il Barbiere's name by none other than Cardinal Christophe himself. I knew the Church openly denounced the practice of castration and when I had questioned il Conte about what he was planning to do, he had merely shrugged.

'About a quarter of the cathedral choir is made up of *castrati*; some of them are the best in Italy. They may condemn with their voices but they welcome the end result with open arms. Fear not, Philippe, what we are doing is ultimately for the glory of God.'

And your own, I had thought. I had baulked at the use of 'we' but fear for my own future had sealed my lips and kept any words of condemnation unsaid.

But there was nothing glorious about poor Luigi's condition.

'Is there nothing that can be done? He is only eight years old.'

Il Barbiere shook his head. 'Not in my experience. If he's going to go it will be early in the morning. That is the usual time, early in the morning.'

I remembered him crying for his Mama. I felt my cheeks flush with anger and I glared at Il Barbiere.

'He was, is, a sweet boy. He didn't ask for this to happen. He just wanted to go back home to his family.'

Il Barbiere shrugged nonchalantly.

'He has no home or family now, does he? I expect his parents were promised that he would have a far better life, even maybe become rich and famous? And were given a bag of gold to help persuade them?'

I winced at his insightfulness and nodded.

'Well, they should also have been told that it doesn't always work out quite as they expect. Even if the operation seems to have been a success, I have heard stories of boys whose voices still break or who aren't able to hit the high notes when they reach adulthood.' He shrugged. 'Even if their voices last, there is no guarantee that these boys will become rich and famous. In fact, there is only one certainty; these boys will never be able to lead a normal life.' He shook his head sadly. 'And, as we are now seeing, not every operation is a success. I am good at what I do, but I still lose some. It happens to the best of us.'

'Why do you do it? Surely there is a risk of you being caught?'

He shrugged again.

'I am a barber, a good one too. But cutting beards does not pay as well as cutting balls!'

His crude laugh turned into a cough that he eased with a cupful of wine.

'I learned both skills from my father. I have a number of clients in the Church. They know I am discrete but they also know I will name names if necessary.'

He finished the wine and stood up to go.

'Don't worry about the boy. We'll deal with whatever happens when it happens.'

I didn't want to follow him back to the house so I decided to go for a walk. I wandered the dusty streets and alleys, peering into dark rooms or chatting with old women as they sat in a shady courtyard preparing the vegetables for the family dinner. I came to the far edge of the village and decided to follow a track that sloped down to a stream. There was an enormous olive tree that provided me with shade and I sat against its gnarled trunk and closed my eyes. The stream chuckled and gurgled and soon lulled me to sleep. I dreamed of satin, smooth white skin, black hair and bloody balls in a bucket.

I woke a few hours later feeling refreshed but not yet ready to return to the house. I followed the stream for a while, just enjoying the solitude. I had always loved to walk alone; I found it gave me the time and space to just think. I often composed poems in my head, where they remained, for they were for my diversion only. I also wrote imaginary letters to Eleanora. I knew I could never put pen to parchment, so I was able to be as passionate, humorous or melancholy as I wished.

16th May 1756

My own sweet Contessa,

How I wish I could actually whisper these words into your ear. Perhaps whilst I am pushing you on the swing in our secret garden, or whilst I am brushing your hair as day breaks, or when we have just made love in the wood on a bed of autumn leaves.

Oh, how I miss you. Do you miss me, my darling? Or am I no longer in your thoughts, your dreams? It has only been three days since we last saw each other, but it seems a lifetime and more. I wish I knew when I was going to see you again. When I asked il Conte how long he wanted me to remain with the boys all he said was 'As long as it takes.' I dared not ask him how long what takes? Until they are settled into the conservatoire? Until we can be assured that they still have their singing voices? Until they have become successful? Il Barbiere - he's the man who did the operation on the boys - said that students remain at the conservatoire for sometimes as long as ten years. I am sure your husband only intends me to stay long enough to ensure the boys are alright and then I can revert to being his secretary again.

You don't think he knows about us, do you? No, he cannot know; he would not hesitate to kill me.

Do you recall when we first heard the boys singing? I will never forget that Sunday morning. We were all out riding, you, me, il Conte and Isabella. By the way, make sure Bella rides her pony every day; tell her I say 'practice makes perfect.' It was Bella who heard them first, do you remember? She asked if it was angels singing. We rode towards the sound and stopped on a little knoll overlooking the village church. There was a wedding and the boys were outside singing as the couple stood in the doorway, now man and wife. Do you remember how their voices soared so it was as if we were standing right next to them? It was a popular folk song but they made it sound like a hymn of praise.

'Oh heart, my own heart, fear not I'll forsake thee,
Let gloomy sorrow o'ershadow thee never;

Within my breast here for shelter betake thee,
For thou, thou only, shalt be mine forever.

I seek for slumber, yet still I am waking,
I think on thee still, each step I am taking.

So, tell me, darling, why linger we longer?
Can love unite us together yet stronger?

You said it was almost as beautiful as the Ave Maria you had heard sung by a castrato when your Papa had taken you to the cathedral in Rome. You told us how you had been moved to tears and almost swooned at the sheer sublimity of the singing. Do you remember also telling us that your Papa had said that Marco Vitali was honoured by the Pope and accepted in the highest social circles all because he had sponsored the castrato? It is this preferment that your dear husband yearns for and which prompted him to offer to purchase the five boys.

There was Fabio and Roberto the two cousins, Rafaele and Michel the two brothers, and little Luigi. Rafaele and Michel ran away, did you know? It was the night we arrived at Il Barbiere's. We all sleep together in the same room and I heard them whispering together during the night. I thought they were just comforting each other but when I woke the next morning they had gone. Murlo is only one day's ride away from Montalcino, so if they managed to get a lift on a passing cart they should be home by now. Have you heard anything about them? I expect il Conte will demand his money back. Luigi was the blond one, the one you said looked like one of Michelangelo's cherubs. I'm afraid to say that he is not well after the operation and Il Barbiere says he won't survive the night. I hope your miserly husband won't ask the family to repay the gold; that would be too cruel of him.

So, we are left with just the two cousins. Time will tell whether either one of them will be the means to achieve il Conte's ambition. I feel so ashamed of my role in this whole fiasco. But if I refused to do your husband's bidding I will lose my job and, far worse, lose the opportunity to be near you. Oh, my darling, darling Eleanora. How I yearn to steal away with you and start a new life, as we have so often talked of ...

I stumbled on a root and realised that the sun was setting. It was time to go back. By the time I re-entered the house the family and the two boys were sitting in the kitchen eating supper. My walk had given me a good appetite and I gratefully shared the meat stew and wine from the local vineyard.

That evening, after the boys had retired, I sat with Luigi. His face was deathly pale except for two bright red feverish spots on his cheeks. His blonde hair was dark with sweat and his whole body was covered in a damp sheen. He was shivering but when I covered him with a sheet he threw it off as if he could not bear to have anything touching his skin. There was a cloying smell emanating from the linen that still bound his mid-section. He moaned constantly and I hoped that Il Barbiere was still giving him drugged wine.

I had with me a small travelling case that contained all my writing paraphernalia. I got out a quill, pot of ink and a sheet of parchment and wrote a short report for il Conte. I didn't seal it yet; I would wait to see what the night brought.

It brought, as Il Barbiere had predicted, death.

I was disturbed in the early morning by bumps, whispering and what sounded like the squealing of pigs, but I did not fully wake up until the sun shone through the window and a cock crowed in a nearby farm. It came as no surprise, though, when I went into the side room and found the bed stripped bare. I said a prayer under my breath, made the sign of the cross and genuflected. Luigi was not destined for glory on earth and I fervently hoped he would receive it in Heaven instead.

The boys were still abed so I decided to break my fast at the inn. Il Barbiere was sitting by the front door sharpening a razor, whistling under his breath. He nodded to me in greeting.

'Young Luigi didn't make it, then.'

'No, but it's all sorted, as I said it would be. You don't need to fret about anything.'

It annoyed me that he thought I was fretting like some young maiden. Nonetheless, I wanted to be sure the other boys had not deteriorated. 'Fabio and Roberto, they are still doing well?'

'Oh, yes. They are as strong as mountain goats. I'll get them up and about today and they should be fit to travel in a few more days. You off to the inn?'

I nodded, fearing he would ask to join me. But just then his wife called to him from the kitchen and he raised his eyes to heaven, gave his habitual shrug and hoped I enjoyed my meal.

When I had satisfied my hunger I went back to our little annexe to find Mathilde getting the boys up. They still seemed to be in some pain but they walked with much more ease and were chattering away to her as if they had known her all their lives. They didn't ask about Luigi and I didn't have the heart to tell them, not when they seemed so happy. After they had left to have breakfast with the family I stayed behind and finished my report to il Conte. I sealed it and took it with me to see if Il Barbiere could find someone to take it back to the Villa De Lorenzo, located on the outskirts of Montalcino.

As I walked towards the house I stopped to lean on the fence separating me from the pigs. There were about six of the beasts, each almost as big as Bella's pony. They were rooting about in the mud with their snouts, snuffling and snorting. I remembered the sounds I had heard earlier in the morning; were they always hungry and so didn't sleep?

Il Barbiere came and stood by my side and threw a bowl of vegetable scraps into the pen. The pigs went berserk and before I could count to three there was nothing left but the echo of their frenzied squealing.

'Eat anything and everything, them pigs. Absolutely everything.' He chuckled and walked away.

I turned to follow him but stopped dead in my tracks when I glimpsed a small piece of red cloth sticking up from the mud. It had white spots on it.

They hadn't eaten absolutely everything then.

Chapter 3

Cause unknown

I felt sick and dizzy and clung to the fencing to stop myself falling. Then I vomited into the pen and was further revolted by the stampede of pigs as they rushed to devour my erstwhile breakfast.

'Are you not feeling well, signor Agostini?'

It was Fabio.

'Are you sad about Luigi? Mathilde told us he was very poorly and died in the night. They have sent his body home but we are going to the church to say a prayer for his soul. Are you coming?'

'Yes, yes, that's it, I'm sad about Luigi. Of course I will come.'

I tore my eyes away from the red cloth to find Fabio watching me curiously. He looked into the pig pen but I don't think he saw the corner of red neckerchief that was still sticking incongruously out of the mud like a flag.

When I got to the house I gave Il Barbiere the report, which I had managed to keep hold of. I could hardly bear to look at him but I forced myself to ask if he could arrange for someone to take it to il Conte. His laugh, which I had previously thought of as merely crude, now seemed full of malice.

Mathilde, Lizzie and the boys had already left for the church but they had had to walk slowly and I caught up with them just as they entered through the doorway. It was by far the largest and most ornate building in the village. The villagers lived in homes that were built from plain, rough

24

blocks and the only internal decoration was a wooden cross hung over the bed or perhaps a small piece of tapestry handed down through the generations. Each stone of their church, however, had some sort of carving, be it the head of a flower, beast or saint. Although made of the same material as the villagers' homes, the church seemed to be whiter and to sparkle in the sunlight. The whole effect was of an enormous cake covered in deep snow.

After the brightness outside the interior seemed as dark as a mountain cave until my eyes became used to it. Then I saw there were lighted candles placed around the nave and chancel, their glow reflected by the dull gilt of Mary's crown. I bent my knees before her and joined the others at a small table which held a pile of unlit candles. I placed some coins into a wooden bowl and each of us took a taper, lit it from one of the bigger ones, said a silent prayer and then placed it in a rack. The tiny flames pointed unwaveringly heavenward and I prayed that Luigi's innocent soul would similarly reach its final destination without any need for purgatorial cleansing.

Mathilde plucked at my sleeve and whispered, 'We need to get the boys back now, before people start arriving for the midday service.' I agreed; we didn't want difficult questions to be asked and I didn't want to lie, not in the House of God.

We walked slowly back, following a route that skirted the village. By the time we reached the house the boys had shaken off their dejection and were chattering away. At one point Fabio stopped suddenly and stooped to pick something up from the dusty path. He held it in his palm for us all to see. He spat on it and rubbed it to remove the

25

dirt and revealed a brass button that had obviously come from a military jacket.

'I like shiny things,' was his simple explanation. He put it in his pocket and we walked on.

The boys and I spent the afternoon in our room. I taught them to play the card game called Scopa and although they were still physically weak their vocal chords were not and they shouted and laughed delightedly as they quickly learned how to trounce poor signor Agostini.

That night I lay on my bed listening to the boys' rhythmic breathing, mulling over the events of the last couple of days. I must have started to doze off because I was suddenly awoken by a sharp knock on the door of our annexe. It wasn't locked and I heard someone open it and their quick footsteps as they hurried along the corridor and knocked again on the bedroom door.

'Signore, signore! Please, can you come? It's Papa. He's not well.'

'Lizzie? Is that you? Come in, come in.'

Lizzie flung back the door so that it banged loudly against the table, waking Fabio and Roberto. She was carrying a lamp and in its light I could see the boys sitting up, rubbing their eyes.

'What is it Lizzie? What do you mean your father is not well? What is wrong?'

Lizzie stood in the doorway in her nightdress, the material so thin I could see her budding nipples and the darkness between her legs. She had the body of a young woman, but she was sobbing like a child.

'It's Papa. He's sick. Mama asked for you to come. Please, signore. Please come.'

By this time I had pulled on my trousers and shirt and I indicated for her to lead on. I turned to tell the boys to get to sleep but they were both up and waiting to follow us. I didn't want to waste time trying to get them back to bed so I let them tag along. The ever-wakeful pigs poked their snouts through the wooden fence and sniffed at us as we hurried past.

We had to go through the back door into the kitchen in order to get to the main part of the house and I saw the scullery maid heating a big pot of water over the range. She looked as if she had been pulled out of bed by her hair and her dress was buttoned up all wrong. The boys decided to stay there, attracted, no doubt, by the bread, cheese and cold meats that they knew they would find.

It was as I climbed the stairs that I was almost physically struck by the sound of retching and the repellent smell of vomit. I followed Lizzie into what was presumably the master bedroom and found myself at the head of the bed, right next to where Mathilde was supporting Il Barbiere. His head was hanging over a bowl, which I could see was half full of a brown-yellow liquid with unidentifiable bits of solid matter and streaks of red, possibly blood. He must have spewed every morsel of food out already but his whole body went into spasm each time he heaved, producing nothing, not even spittle.

Mathilde looked up at me, her face shiny with sweat; Il Barbiere was a big man and difficult to grip. 'I will hold him, Mathilde. You empty the bowl and fetch damp cloths to wipe him down with. Oh, and some wine and dry bread, that may settle his stomach.'

Mathilde released her husband and allowed me to take the weight. She looked at me gratefully and took the bowl from Il Barbiere's lap. His stomach continued to exorcise the demon within, manifest now by a white froth that gathered around his lips. Mathilde returned with the victuals and as I held him she put a cup of wine to his lips and got him to take a few sips. Within seconds it had been ejected into the bowl. I could feel Il Barbiere's body shuddering continually, and then he started clawing at his throat, his nails scoring bloody lines. He made harsh grunting noises, not unlike his pigs, and his eyes rolled in the sockets.

Mathilde took a cloth and tried to wipe the snot and saliva from her husband's face but he screamed and turned his head violently away. Mathilde stood, wringing her hands. 'I don't know what's wrong with him. We have all eaten the same thing and Lizzie and I are fine. He had his cupful of wine as usual and then came to bed. But within minutes he was complaining of a bad stomach, then he was sick, then, well then he just got worse and worse. I don't know what to do.' She started to sob.

'You need to get a doctor. Mathilde, hush now, send Lizzie for a doctor. He will know what to do. Is there one in the village?'

She nodded and she had just turned to give Lizzie her instructions when Il Barbiere suddenly went very still. I could hear his shallow breathing and I was about to lay him back onto the pillow when he gave an enormous heave and a great fountain of blood gushed out of his mouth.

Someone screamed; I think it was me.

Then there was silence. I could no longer hear his breathing. I may only have been a secretary to il Conte, but I knew a dead man when I was holding one.

First Mathilde, and then Lizzie, started a low moan that increased in tone and tempo until it became a high-pitched, undulating wail. I suddenly wanted to get away, away from this house of death. I wanted to lie naked in a cold mountain stream and wash myself clean of the corruption that lay over me like an invisible skin. I stood up and rested my hands on Mathilde's shoulders. I shook her, gently then quite hard until she stopped her yowling. As she fell silent, so did Lizzie, as if they were one mechanical toy that had wound down.

'We, that is, the boys and I, should leave. Now. It would be better if we were not here when the doctor comes. You still need to send for him, even though, well, you should send for him.'

She stood stock still before me, her shoulders drooped in dejection. I heard Lizzie leave the room, I hoped to go and get the doctor.

'Mathilde, I'm sorry about your husband, but we must leave now.'

I turned to go but she put her hand on my arm to stop me. 'Frederico was a good man, you know. I don't know how I am going to manage without him.' I nodded as if I agreed with her

'I'll leave the money we owe.' As if that was the answer to her loss.

I went quickly down to the kitchen to find the boys both tucking into a plateful of food, as though they hadn't eaten for days. I told them what had happened and that we were leaving immediately. Fabio crossed himself and whispered something, a prayer most likely. I wrapped up a loaf and some cheese and we went to our annexe to pack our things. Within just ten minutes we were back in the house. I left enough money to cover the cost of the funeral at least.

We were still in the kitchen when I heard the front door open and close, and the deep timbre of a man's voice. I decided not to risk being seen or heard by the doctor, so I put a few coins in the scullery maid's hand and we slipped out by the back door. It was still the middle of the night but there was a cloudless sky and the moon, along with the light from Il Barbiere's bedroom window, was enough for us to see where we were going.

The smell of the hay and the gentle breathing of the sleeping horses were very welcome after the smells and sounds that had surrounded me over the previous days. I told the boys to go and wake Davide, whilst I roused the horses. I heard them clamber up the ladder to the hayloft and smiled to myself at Davide's angry shouts as they leapt on him and pummelled him playfully. The boys' recovery from the operation was nothing short of miraculous. I guessed that I was twenty years younger than Davide but I led a relatively sedentary life and I envied him his muscular and lithesome body. He effortlessly carried a boy under each arm as he climbed down, then stood them upright on the floor and gave them a none too gentle cuff around the ear.

'You're both ignorant peasants; you should show more respect to your elders.' He pushed them both towards me, his wink belying his harsh words.

The horses seemed confused at being woken so early but their ears soon pricked up when they realised we were on the move. They must have been bored and restless at being kept in the stables with no exercise. I gave the horses some oats whilst we had a quick meal of some of the bread and cheese and then, within less than an hour since Il Barbiere had drawn his last breath, we were on the road. We left the village of Murlo without a backward glance.

Chapter 4

Shiny things

The gentle rocking of the carriage soon lulled the boys to sleep and I was worried that Davide too would succumb, so I told him to pull off the road so we could all finish our slumbers.

When I woke it was to the chattering of the two boys as they helped Davide make a fire. Dawn had broken and the early morning mist was already dispersing in the heat of the rising sun. There were four eggs lying on the ground.

'Who went for the eggs?' Roberto raised his hand. 'How much did you pay for them?' He looked sheepish but said nothing. 'You didn't steal them, did you? Roberto? Did you?' He had the decency to blush. 'Well, we'll stop off on the way and give the farmer's wife some money. Now, let's eat, I'm starving.'

Davide had heated some fat in a pan over the fire and the eggs now sizzled as they fried. It was not cold, but we sat around the fire in companionable silence and enjoyed our breakfast, each of us tearing off chunks of bread and dipping into the hot, golden yolk.

'So, boys. Are you ready for the next part of the adventure? In a few days we will be in Florence!' They all looked blankly at me. 'Florence, the most beautiful city in Italy, in fact, in the whole world!' They smiled at my exuberance but they had never been anywhere other than Montalcino and now Murlo; they had no notion of how different a large city would be. 'Come on, let's move whilst it's not too hot.'

It was only later that I remembered we had not paid for the eggs. It was a pleasant day and I enjoyed watching the changing landscape as we slowly journeyed through the state of Tuscany towards its capital. The boys sat outside with Davide and took turns to hold the reins, although the horses didn't need any guidance. It was quite hilly and the villages were few and far between but we managed to find a way-side inn where we partook of lunch and had a few hours rest whilst the sun was at its zenith.

The inn-keeper had been more than happy to break the neck of one of his chickens and to exchange it for a gold coin, along with some bread, cheese and wine. That evening, just as the sun was setting, we stopped for the night in the shelter of a wood, by a stream that would eventually, I guessed, end up joining the sea. This time I built the fire whilst Davide plucked the chicken and the boys fed and settled the horses. I skewered the carcass and the boys took it in turn to rotate over the flames, which crackled and spat as the drops of grease fell onto them. The smell of roasting meat was almost intoxicating and once the juices were clear we tore at the flesh, burning our fingers and tongues in our impatience. Despite all the rich, varied meals I had had, especially with il Conte, this was one of the best. Afterwards, we sat satiated, staring into the fire, each with our own thoughts. I saw the face of Eleanora smiling coquettishly at me. I don't know what the boys saw, but Fabio suddenly spoke.

'Signor Agostini?'

'I do wish you would call me Philippe.'

He pursed his lips, then shook his head slightly. 'No, it is not polite for someone like us to call someone like you

33

by your first name. Signor Agostini, what was wrong with Il Barbiere?'

'I don't know, Fabio. His wife said he ate the same as everyone else. I don't suppose we ever will know.'

Fabio glanced at Roberto then said, 'We didn't like him. He murdered Luigi and so God punished him.'

I was surprised at the vehemence in his voice. 'Oh, come now. He did not kill him on purpose. It was an unfortunate accident. I am very sorry Luigi died, but it really wasn't Il Barbiere's fault. Luigi must have been weak; look at you two, you are fine and fully recovered.'

They shrugged in unison, their brows furrowed. 'God punished him,' Fabio repeated.

They remained silent and I had begun my day-dreaming again when Roberto suddenly blurted out, 'What if we can't sing any more?' They were both looking at me with their dark eyes full of fear and desperation.

'Why do you think you mightn't be able to sing?'

'What that man did to us. Il Conte promised it would make us sing like angels for ever, but what if it is the opposite and our voices are ruined and we will never sing again? What will become of us then?'

I considered for a moment. 'Well, there is only one way to find out, isn't there?' I am not a great singer but I could keep a tune and I started singing the song they had sung at the church; the song that had started this journey. I sang the whole of the first verse and then started the second. The boys looked at me tight lipped, then they looked at each other and, although they didn't speak or make any gesture to each other, they both joined in at the same time. To begin with they were a little hesitant, as if fearing what they would hear, but as they realised that their voices were unaffected they grew more confident and I stopped my paltry attempt and just listened, enraptured.

How can I describe the sound? It was as if a nightingale and a lark had come down to earth and were singing a duet. Even the birds in the trees ceased their evensong as the notes took wing and flew under the canopy of leaves until they found a gap and soared to the heavens, to give pleasure to God, sitting on His celestial cloud.

When they finished we sat in silence until Roberto asked another question that had obviously been worrying him. 'How long will it take for us to become famous?' Fabio tutted at him but Roberto leaned right forward, eyes bright, mouth slightly open. 'What we had done to us, that will mean our voices will stay like this for ever, won't it? Even when we are grown men?' Roberto seemed desperate for confirmation.

'Yes, I believe so but I don't know how long it will take before you are famous.' I didn't have the heart or the nerve to tell him he may never become so. 'You have to study at the conservatoire for a few years at least. You must both work hard and then, who know what you might become?'

Roberto seemed satisfied with my vague answer but Fabio frowned at him. 'You should not think about such things. We will learn how to use our God-given voices to praise Him, not to impress and seek fame.'

All the time we had been talking Fabio had been fidgeting with something in his pocket. He noticed me looking at him and smiled shyly. He took out a leather bag, undid the cord and emptied the contents onto his lap.

Roberto punched him playfully on his arm. 'These are his treasures. Look there is the button he found yesterday.' He pointed it out and then continued, 'Tell Philippe all about the others, Fabio.'

'I just like collecting shiny things. See this pebble?' He picked one from the pile, licked it and it was transformed from a dull brown to almost gold. He held it in the palm of his hand and moved it to catch the reflection of the flames. After a few seconds it had reverted to its former lack-lustre colour. 'I found this at the bottom of our river. Roberto and I went every day after we had finished at the vineyards. I often found beautiful stones there. Look, here are some more.' He picked out a few and after wetting them their colours were revealed: gold, emerald, ruby red. 'I know they are not worth anything, Papa told me, but I like them all the same.'

'And what's that?' I pointed to a piece of glass, the colour of a summer evening sky.

'It's a bit of stained glass. I found it at the side of the church after one of the windows got smashed last year.'

Roberto giggled. 'Fabio is the reason why poor Mary's dress has a patch of a different colour!'

I used my finger to sort through the collection of buttons, pebbles, pieces of broken pottery and glass, a jay's feather iridescent in the light of the fire and a small bottle with a glass stopper. 'And where did you get this from?'

Fabio pursed his lips, glanced at Roberto and lowered his eyes. 'I took it. From *La Strega*.'

'La Strega? The witch?'

Roberto took over telling the tale. 'Yes, there's a witch who lives alone in the woods outside of our village. The other boys told us she was over a hundred years old, all bent and crooked, and would turn us into frogs if she ever saw us.' I laughed as he hunched his own back, held out his hands like claws and made a hideous grimace. 'So, we had always been scared to go there, until this one day. It was at Agathea's wedding wasn't it, Fabio?'

Agathea's wedding, when we had heard the boys singing for the first time, when this whole chain of events had started.

'Yes, it was when everyone was eating and drinking, do you remember, Roberto? We saw our cousin Beatrice sneak off, looking really secretive, and we decided to follow her. We thought she was going to meet a boy; if we had known where she was going we would have stayed where we were.' Roberto nodded as he remembered. 'We followed her up the track, getting hotter and hotter until we came to the edge of the wood. The path disappeared into the trees but we could still see flashes of her white dress, so we continued. It was only when we saw a little house that we realised where we were, but by now we were so curious we couldn't turn back. Beatrice had gone in through the door so we snuck up to an open window and crouched underneath to see if we could hear.'

Roberto chimed in. 'She probably wanted a potion to make a boy fall in love with her. It would have had to be a strong one, she isn't very pretty.' He snorted with laughter.

Fabio grinned then continued. 'We waited and waited but couldn't hear anything, just low murmurings. Then the door opened and Beatrice skipped out clutching something to her chest. Thankfully she didn't see us. We were just about to crawl away when suddenly La Strega's head

37

popped out of the window and she asked us if we wanted a cold drink!'

Roberto nodded delightedly. 'She must be a witch because she could see through walls! Well, we didn't know whether to run away as quickly as we could or whether to risk staying.'

'She wasn't so very old. In fact she was probably about your age, signor Agostini. And she seemed to be very nice so we decided to stay. We were thirsty, anyway. She gave us a really refreshing drink made from honey and lemon and some biscuits she had just made.'

Roberto chipped in again. 'I let Fabio take the first sip of the drink and bite from the biscuit. I only took mine when I saw he hadn't been changed into a frog!' He threw back his head and laughed unrestrainedly.

Fabio frowned at this revelation. 'She had shelves full of bottles and jars. She explained that they were just herbs and potions she had made from plants and roots she had picked in the wood and at the top of the mountain. Roberto told her what the boys in the village said about her. She just smiled and said there was nothing magical about her potions at all and she had a good business helping the villagers with their aches and pains. She asked us if we wanted to go outside to see her animals; she has chickens, goats, pigs - not horrid big ones like Il Barbiere's, but little pink ones that were really sweet - ducks, a cat and a dog. I think that's all. Anyway, La Strega and Roberto went out first and I followed behind. I suddenly saw something glittering on one of the shelves and, well, I just grabbed it without thinking.' He held out the bottle and shook it. 'It's empty anyway and she had lots and lots of other bottles. I do feel bad about taking it but I'm sure she would have given it to me if I had asked.'

I saw there was still a small amount of clear liquid in it. 'It's not quite empty.' I took the bottle from him and tipped it up. A drop nestled on the pad of my finger. I lifted it to my nose. 'All I can smell is the chicken we have just eaten. It's probably just water.' I licked my fingers to clean them and handed the bottle back to Fabio, who looked at me intently before putting his treasures away.

'Let's get to sleep; we have an early start tomorrow morning.'

It was not to be, though. That night I woke with the most terrible stomach ache and I had to rush further into the woods to empty my bowels a number of times. I cursed the fact that we had been too impatient to cook the chicken properly. The boys slept through; they must have had bellies made of iron.

Chapter 5

Homesick

I was in no fit state to get up at dawn and it was not until about midday that I felt confident enough to continue our journey. We didn't travel far that day, even so by early evening I felt exhausted and so we stopped at a small farm on the outskirts of a large village and the farmer agreed to provide a meal and the use of a stable for the horses and us to sleep in. I ate the stew cautiously, but with no ill effects.

That night I sat outside after the others had settled down; though tired, I didn't feel like sleeping. It was a full moon and in its face I could see Eleanor's satisfied expression just after we had made love. Oh, how I wished I was back home. I continued to stare at the moon and Eleanora's face became younger and plumper than it was now, as it had been when I had first seen her. I smiled at the memory I could share with no-one but her.

'Can't you sleep either? Are you still feeling ill?' Roberto came and sat down beside me.

'Ah, Roberto. No, I am quite recovered, thank you. I am just not ready to sleep. I was thinking of home.' I regretted saying it even before the words were out.

'I miss home too, Mama, Papa, my brothers and sisters, even la Diavolessa.' I could see Roberto grinning in the moonlight.

'The She-Devil? Who is that?'

'La Diavolessa is the name I give to one of our she-goats.'

'Ha! Tell me about her.' I settled down to hear his story.

'It was always my job to milk the goats every morning before going up to the vineyards. I suppose someone else is having to do that now. Oh dear, I hope they cope with her better than I ever did.' His shoulders slumped and he looked quite dejected.

'I'm sure they will manage. Come on, tell me about her.'

'Well, all goats have the eyes of the devil, don't they, but this one, well sometimes I thought she really was the devil. She never played up for Fabio or anyone else, and some days she was no trouble for me at all. On other days, though, she would stand still until I was settled and had started pulling at her teats, then she would turn, look me in the eye, smile, I swear she smiled, and then step forwards, backwards or sideways as the mood took her, so that the milk sprayed all over the floor. She often knocked the bucket over which made me angry and I would scream and lash out at her. She would kick out at me or butt me until I ran away crying to Mama, who would come and find her standing serenely waiting to be milked. How I hated that beast! I told Mama we should eat her, but Mama always said she was too good a milker.'

His laugh turned into a sob. He put his hands to his face until he regained control, then he wiped his eyes and gave me a crooked smile. 'Signor Agostini? May I ask you something?'

'Of course, Roberto, anything at all.' As long as it wasn't how soon would he become famous.

'Mama and Papa agreed to let us come with you, to be cut and everything because they wanted us to have a chance of a better life? Not ... not because they didn't love us?'

41

Oh, how my heart went out to the little fellow. Before I could reassure him, Fabio sat down with us, put his arm around his cousin's shoulder and squeezed so hard that he squealed.

'Roberto, I keep telling you, Mama and Papa have let us go because they love us and because they love God. We have been blessed with beautiful voices, which we should use to His glory. Isn't that right signor Agostini?'

I nodded, though I found these words disconcerting coming out of the mouth of an eight year old.

Roberto sat upright and put his shoulders back. 'And we might, if it's God's will, of course, we just might be noticed and asked to sing in cathedrals, maybe even before the Pope himself! And because we sing so beautifully they will pay us lots of money and we will earn more in one day than Papa does in a whole year. And we will send it all home and they will be so happy and proud of us. Isn't that right, signor Agostini?'

What could I say? I knew that is what il Conte had said to persuade their parents. That, and a bag of gold. There was no point in sowing the seeds of doubt just yet. After all, it might all happen as Roberto predicted. 'That could certainly all happen, yes, as long as you work hard at the conservatoire. So, yes, Roberto, your Mama and Papa agreed to let you come because they want a better life for you, because they love you. Now off to bed both of you. Hopefully we will have a full day's travelling tomorrow. We should reach Florence by nightfall.'

The next day we made slow but steady progress. The track was rough and in places quite steep, so the boys and I often walked to make it easier for the horses. I took over from Davide in the afternoon and I was quite content to sit with the reins loose in my hands, and my thoughts in the bedchamber of la Contessa.

There was still quite a few hours of daylight left when Davide suggested we stop for the night. We had halted at a junction at the edge of a village. There was a steep track that went down to the valley and the other, the one we were following, would take us straight to Florence.

'But why? We must be nearly there, surely? We can make it before it gets dark'

'Si signor Agostini, but if we continue on this road we will have to go through a dense wood that is well-known for being the hide-out of *banditi e assassini*.'

At this Roberto whooped with glee, picked up a stick from the ground and started fighting with a less than enthusiastic Fabio, letting out a blood-curdling cry at each dummy thrust. I smiled at his enthusiasm but Davide shook his head and frowned.

'It is not a joking matter, signore. They are dangerous men and would kill us all in a blink of an eye.' He sliced his hand across his throat to illustrate his point. 'We need to go around the wood and that will take many more hours and it is a steep incline down. The horses need to rest first.'

I conceded to his experience and we started to look for somewhere to stop. We carried on deeper into the village but I could neither see nor hear any signs of life. There were no children running around getting under people's feet; no women sitting in their doorways preparing the evening meal; no men tramping along the road, tired after a hard day's work in the fields; no moving shadows; just a scrawny cat creeping along a wall who disappeared into a doorway so quickly I wondered if I had imagined it. All the houses were run-down and emanated a sense of forlornness and defeat.

'Where is everyone, Davide? Where have they all gone?'

'Moved to the city or become one of *i banditi*, signore. The land here is poor and not all land-owners are as good as il Conte. They probably couldn't grow enough to sell to pay the ever increasing taxes and still have enough to keep themselves alive.' He spat bitterly into the dirt.

I shared Davide's resentment. My father had paid his taxes as he aught, and got poorer and poorer each year until he had had to give our lands away to some member of the aristocracy who was not worthy to wipe the dust off my father's shoes. The day he handed the contracts over to the lawyer he hanged himself. I was sixteen.

Chapter 6

Reminiscences

We chose a house - no longer could it be called a home - that stood next to a brook that trickled sullenly down to the valley below. There was a patch of relatively green grass for the horses, so I hobbled them to a post that had presumably been put there for such a purpose. The boys explored, yelling and shouting pointlessly as only eight year old boys do. Davide disappeared to return a short time later clutching two rabbits by their ears.

After we had eaten, the boys' energy suddenly evaporated and they took themselves off to the house, rolled themselves in their blankets and fell fast asleep. Davide and I continued to sit by the fire in a companionable silence, sipping our wine. Davide gave a little cough to clear his throat.

'If you don't mind me asking, signor Agostini, how did it come about that you are working for il Conte? You are obviously a well-educated man of high birth. Please,' he hesitated, 'please, just tell me to mind my own business if you'd rather not say.'

I shook my head and stared into the flames, searching for the memories that I had kept locked away.

'No, it's alright Davide, it is no great secret. I did indeed come from a good family, though I would not say of high birth; we were not of the aristocracy. We lived in Siena in a large villa and had a reasonably sized estate with many people working on the land. My father was a good, fair man and a successful merchant. He was too good, really, because unlike other landowners he didn't demand extortionate taxes from the villagers and then pay nothing himself. No, instead he asked for little but gave what was asked of him until he had nothing else to give. My mother had died many years previously and we had lost my elder brother to the war in '46.' I stopped to swallow. 'I think he felt such terrible shame and honestly believed that I would be better off without him. So, at sixteen I was an orphan, alone with no home and no money. That was nearly eight years ago.'

Davide looked at me in sympathy. 'I am sorry, signore. That must have been hard on you.'

I shrugged as if it were of no matter. 'After I buried my father I joined a regiment with the intention of dying for my country.' I grinned at Davide. 'I was no soldier. I was more used to holding a book in my hand than a sword. But it didn't matter because the war ended before I could get myself killed, or indeed kill anyone.' I hugged my knees and cast my mind back to the day my life had changed. 'I was still a soldier as the regiment hadn't been disbanded yet but we were basically left to our own devices. I didn't know where to go or what to do so I just stayed in uniform, did as I was told and escaped to read whenever I could. One day we had camped near a large estate whose owner I knew vaguely. I also knew he had a wonderful library. So, when the others were eating I crept off and found a way in. Oh, he had the most wonderful books, Davide, you cannot imagine.'

Davide gave me a wry smile. 'It is true, I cannot imagine. I cannot read.'

I cringed at my insensitivity. 'Well, I found a book of poems I hadn't seen before and as I didn't want to steal it I settled down to read it in a large arm chair.' I wriggled on the hard, packed earth and sighed at the memory. 'It was very comfortable and I was tired. I don't think I had read one verse before I fell asleep. I must have dozed for a good thirty minutes before I was very rudely awoken by someone shaking me and shouting "who the hell are you?" in my ear. You can imagine my shock. Two men were towering over me; one was the man I knew and the other, it turned out, was il Conte.'

'Ah, so that is how you two met.'

'Yes, the owner didn't recognise me until I told him my name; even then I'm not sure that he did. Il Conte just picked up the book I had dropped and said, "this is a strange choice for a young soldier."'

'What did you say to him?'

'I just stood up, held my shoulders back, looked him in the eye and said something like, "I am Philippe Agostini, youngest living son of Alberto Agostini, recently deceased. I am well-educated but have nothing to my name. I joined the regiment to serve my beloved country but even that is now not possible." I must have seemed a real prick, but il Conte seemed to like me for he said, "there may be no need to serve your country any more, but you can serve me. I am looking for someone to be my secretary. Come back here tomorrow at dawn, I am returning to my own villa." He didn't ask if I was interested in the job. I was of course, so here I am, eight years later, still doing his bidding. How did you come to work for him?'

'I served with him in the war. I looked after the horses then, as I do now.' He smiled wryly. 'We both get on better with horses than people. How do you find him?'

I didn't want to sound disloyal but I also didn't want to lie. 'He is demanding but, as you said, usually fair to his employees.'

'And you agree with this venture we are on?'

I didn't know Davide well enough to share my real feelings, so I just shrugged and sipped more wine.

'But you have a good life.' It was a statement, not a question. 'And there are certain, well, perks that go with the job.'

I looked at him sharply. Did he know about me and Eleanora?

He winked at me knowingly. 'You have a room in a beautiful villa, a horse of your own, you eat with the family and get to travel, perhaps not always in style,' he indicated our less than salubrious surroundings, 'but even so, it is a lot more than most people get.'

I had to agree with him. I did not have my father's mercantile skills and I was content to live a reasonably comfortable life at someone else's expense. And, as Davide said, there were the perks.

A thought suddenly occurred to me. '*I banditi*, they won't come here in the night and murder us as we sleep?'

'No, they keep to the woods. We will be quite safe.'

After Davide had retired I sat by the dying embers planning the next day in my head but I found the silence oppressive so I followed him soon after.

The next morning we all woke early as the sun's rays found their way through the windows and tickled our eyelids. We only had some stale bread to eat so we just washed in the stream and then set off, nibbling the crusts as we went. We all walked, worried that because the track was so steep the horses might lose control and not be able to stop. I held one horse's head and Davide the other, each gripping the bridle and trying to stop the horses from hurtling down the track.

The boys ran on, sliding on the loose stones and raising a cloud of dust that filled our eyes, noses and mouths with grit. I tried to shout to them to slow down but they couldn't, or wouldn't, hear and careered on, whooping and laughing as they went. Eventually they were out of sight and earshot, though their passing was marked by the motes of sand that hung in the still air.

Holding the horses back was hot and tiring work. By the time we reached the valley floor, we all, men and horses, were covered in a mixture of sweat and dirt. We turned the final corner and saw before us a wide river, the sun reflecting off its surface, the leaves of the trees on its banks fluttering in a gentle breeze, seeming to beckon us in. The boys had already accepted the invitation and they had thrown their clothes off as they ran and were now splashing each other with great zeal.

'Leave the horses to me, signore. You go in and get refreshed.'

I left him with no hesitation, stripped, placed my clothes in a neat pile, and stepped cautiously into the water. I walked slowly away from the edge until the water lapped my waist, then I crouched until it came to the top of my chest. I rubbed the wonderful, cool liquid over my skin and when I felt human again I turned on my stomach and swam slowly along the bank. I was not a confident swimmer and I needed to know I could stand up if I needed to. The boys, on the other hand, were like little bronze water sprites. They darted here and there, fighting each other one minute then diving out of sight only to pop up further down the river to resume their boisterous tussle.

I saw Davide lead the horses into the river so I went over to help. They stood placidly whilst we poured water over them and rubbed them until their coats shone like polished metal.

As we lay on the bank, the water quickly drying in the heat of the sun, I realised I was prevaricating and that we should push on and get to the conservatoire. Despite the two deaths we had experienced in as many days, I had enjoyed the freedom from my master's impatience and bad temper. I realised I had become quite fond of the boys, although I still found Fabio's apparent godliness unsettling and unnatural.

'Come on, we need to make a move, and what's more I'm hungry. We'll stop for something to eat then get to the conservatoire before noon.'

The track followed the river for a while and then turned away and rose gently. As we neared the city we caught up with others going in the same direction: women and men walking with large baskets of wares balanced on their heads; donkeys laden down with heavy panniers plodding along slowly, heads hanging down dejectedly; whole families trudging their way up the incline, fathers carrying tots on their shoulders whilst the mothers carried babes in arms and the older children pushing barrows filled to overflowing with their worldly goods. I felt embarrassed passing them by but we could not give everyone a lift, so we gave it to no-one.

As we turned yet another bend we were suddenly presented with a panorama of Florence spread before us. It was breath-taking. My eye was immediately drawn to the red dome that towered over the city. I saw that the others were also transfixed.

'That is the cathedral of Santa Maria del Fiore, commonly known as *il Duomo*, for obvious reasons. It is magnificent, isn't it? It has stood there for hundreds of years; maybe you boys will sing there one day. Just imagine!'

There was an appreciative silence, then Roberto, ever the realist, wrinkled his nose.

'What's that awful stink?'

There was indeed an unpleasant smell that wafted up from below. I lowered my eyes from the lofty dome in the distance and saw that separating us on the hill from the river that bordered the city, was a settlement of hovels that stretched some distance along its banks. There seemed to be no sense of order; families must have just found themselves some open ground and built a shelter from whatever materials they had brought with them or, more likely, they had found nearby. I could see that some were trying to grow vegetables in the sandy soil, but the lack of greenness belied their success. There were columns of smoke where women were cooking breakfasts but the smell of bacon couldn't quite mask the stench of poor sanitation that had insulted Roberto's olfactory senses.

Davide indicated the buildings below. 'This is where the people from the countryside come, when they are driven out by the greedy princes. They believe it will be a better life in the city. Maybe it is. We cannot even begin to imagine what they had to cope with in their villages. There are not enough places to live in Florence itself and anyway it is expensive. So, they have built their own community. It will get better in time I hope.'

Fabio's brow was wrinkled. I could almost see his brain processing what Davide had just told him.

'We were poor and sometimes life was hard, but ...' He looked thoughtfully at me. 'If il Conte had not given Papa the money in exchange for us, might our families have had to leave and live somewhere like this?'

'I don't know, Fabio but I don't think so. Il Conte is a hard man but he is not overly greedy. He demands the rents from all his tenants, as is his right, but he only charges what is fair and I have known him to be lenient if someone cannot pay. No, I think your families and the other villagers are safe.'

Fabio seemed happy with my answer but Roberto continued to stare silently at the scene below us. He turned to me, his eyes full of anger. 'It is not fair, signor Agostini. It is not fair that some have to live like this whilst others take more than they need.'

I agreed with him but this was not the time to discuss the disparity between the classes with an eight year old. He didn't wait for an answer and we continued along the track, which eventually sloped back down to the river. The makeshift commune was behind us and we now drove through the outskirts of the city looking for somewhere to eat and to get directions to the conservatoire. The nearer we got to the centre of Florence the lower the boys' jaws dropped. I had some experience of the city but I could imagine how overwhelmed they must be by the sheer size of the place and the number of people going about their business. Their eyes were wide and their heads were continuously moving from side to side as they took in the different scenes: the pavements thronging with people walking from here to there; shops displaying their wares outside, protected from the sun by colourful awnings; dark alleys leading to goodness knows where; children playing tag in a park; large gardens fronting ever more lavish villas, where a solitary man hoed or pruned, a straw hat protecting his nut-brown face. I hadn't wanted the journey to end, but now I was here I felt energised.

I suddenly espied a tavern and shouted to Davide to pull over. Inside it was quiet, it being well past the normal time to break one's fast. We all ordered a hearty meal and I wondered whether it would be the last one we would ever enjoy together.

Chapter 7

I castrati

The first we saw of the conservatoire was a high stone wall, topped with broken bits of glass. I wondered whether it was to keep people out, or in.

There was nothing to break the face of the wall except a single wooden door, which, it turned out, was locked. There was no knocker so I banged hard with my fist, then harder and harder until the shutter behind the grill suddenly opened and a face peered out.

'Who is that banging as if *il Diovolo* himself was at his heels?'

'Excuse me father. I am signor Agostini bringing two charges from Conte De Lorenzo. Monsignor Mazzini is expecting us. I have a letter of introduction here.'

A hand was thrust through the grill, its empty palm waiting to be filled. I obliged by putting the envelope into it and waited, expecting to hear the lock turning, but instead heard the sound of footsteps receding until they disappeared altogether. I went back to sit in the carriage with the boys.

'I expect he is checking we are who we say we are. I'm sure we won't have to wait long.'

We waited for thirty minutes, during which time the boys became fractious and started pinching and punching each other. I got hotter and more irritable with each passing minute. Then the wooden door opened wide and a priest wearing a black cassock beckoned us in. Once we had alighted Davide trotted off, giving the boys a wink as he passed us by. I had already booked a room at the tavern where we had breakfasted and I had agreed with Davide that he should go there and I would meet him once I had made sure the boys were settled.

The priest said nothing, merely locked the door behind us, turned and walked across the flagstones towards the main building, which loomed above us. The best one could say about it was that it was functional. Its architect had obviously not been inspired by the beautiful buildings which surrounded us; it was simply a large, three-storey, undistinguished, stone box. There were wooden shutters at the windows, but any colour these may once have offered had, over the years, been bleached to a uniform grey. Despite the boys and I stopping to inspect the facade, the priest continued without slowing and disappeared into the dark interior of the conservatoire. We hurried through an imposing front door and across the cavernous entrance hall, just catching a flash of his cassock as he disappeared round a corner. We followed the sound of his footsteps down a long corridor that ended with a door, upon which the priest was knocking as we caught up with him, slightly out of breath.

'*Entra!*'

The priest opened the door for us then shut it again, standing in front of it like a sentinel. Did he think one of the boys was going to make a run for it?

Monsignor Mazzini remained seated; a round, hunched figure with bright, black, belligerent eyes that slowly appraised each one of us. He reminded me of a toad sitting on a lily pad waiting for a dragonfly to pass near enough for him to dart out his tongue and devour. He had been writing when we entered and he carefully put down the quill and held out a pudgy hand for me to kiss his ring. I have always considered myself a good Catholic, but I baulked at showing any deference to this Jesuit. I took his hand, nonetheless, and touched my lips to it, thereby acknowledging his authority over me.

'So, signore ...' He glanced at the letter that lay unfolded on his desk. 'Signor Agostini. You bring me two boys to transform from nothing into something. To bring glory to your master, Conte De Lorenzo.' Statements, not questions.

He was correct, of course. 'No, Monsignor, my master seeks nothing for himself. These two boys, for whose training you will be amply paid, are just a small offering to God, whom my master wishes to serve every day of his life.' Fabio nodded at my words. I gave Monsignor an insincere smile, to which he responded with the same.

'Father Stephen, show ...' He glanced at the letter once more. 'Show signor Agostini and these boys around and then take them to Father Guiseppe. I want to know if they can sing.' He dismissed us with a wave of a hand, then dipped his quill into the inkpot and continued writing.

Father Stephen closed the study door behind us and then, without a word, turned and walked briskly back down the corridor, leaving us standing in the gloom. I felt my face flush with anger.

'Father Stephen!'

The sound of his footsteps continued unabated.

I shouted as loudly as I could. 'Father Stephen!'

There was silence, apart from the boys shuffling in embarrassment. 'Don't fidget. I will not be treated with such disrespect. This is not the only conservatoire in Florence.' I said this loud enough for both the priest and Monsignor to hear. Father Stephen appeared out of the shadows. I lowered my voice slightly. 'Ah, there you are again. If you would be so good as to show us around at a reasonable pace so that I can have a good look. I will need to describe everything to Conte De Lorenzo in detail. He will want to know that his money is being well spent.'

Father Stephen had the decency to look sheepish as he mumbled an apology. The boys were standing close together, their backs ramrod straight, their eyes wide in bewilderment. I noticed they were holding hands; I felt a surge of pity for them. 'Come on boys. Let's take a look around.'

Our guide started off down the corridor again at a slower rate this time. The passage was dim, the only light infiltrating from the hallway we had come from earlier. I was determined not to be rushed so I stopped every now and then to study the paintings and etchings that hung on the wood-panelled walls. Unsurprisingly, as this was a Jesuit establishment, they were without exception of martyred saints. The boys seemed fascinated and studied each image intently. There were men being stabbed, stoned, garrotted and crucified. Roberto pointed to one and chuckled.

'Look Fabio, this one is being boiled in a pan like a huge vegetable. That must have hurt but he is still smiling!' He leaned closer to take a better look at another one. It was of a naked man stretched out on the ground in the shape of an X, each limb already pulled taut by the four horsemen eager to pull him apart. I could almost see Roberto's brain working as he realised what would happen to the hapless man in a very short space of time. He gave a shudder. 'He must have done something very bad, mustn't he, signor Agostini?' It was not my place to educate the boys in the horrors men inflicted on each other in the name of religion, so I just shrugged.

Fabio had moved on and had stopped in front of a large painting, framed in an ornate, gold frame. 'What are they doing to this poor man, signore?' I took a quick look then shrugged again and hurried them on to catch up with Father Stephen, who was waiting for us impatiently at the bottom of a flight of stairs. How does one explain to a child why one man would take such obvious pleasure in flaying another alive?

As we climbed it occurred to me that we had only seen the priest and Monsignor Mazzini since we had entered inside the conservatoire. 'Father Stephen, where are the others? The place seems empty; I imagined it would be teeming with boys.'

'They are in the refectory on the ground floor, signore. They eat at midday.'

It was lucky that we had had a late breakfast as there was no suggestion that we should also partake of some refreshment. Instead the dour priest led us up a second staircase to the top storey, which transpired to be the sleeping quarters. There were doors on both sides, all shut. The rooms that I calculated were at the back of the building all had a roman numeral neatly painted on the door. The rooms on the opposite side were, according to the labels, storerooms, bathrooms or individual sleeping quarters. When we came to the last door on the left, number IV,

Father Stephen opened it and beckoned us into a large dormitory. The room was square in shape, with the door through which we entered in the centre of the front wall. There was a row of ten simple wooden beds along the two side walls and another two rows in parallel head to head down the middle. Forty boys in each room, four rooms, one hundred and sixty boys in total - each boy there because of his musical potential. I wondered how Roberto and Fabio would compare. I suddenly felt worried that they would not be good enough, and then what would happen to them? It was il Conte's plan but he was a soldier at heart, what did he know about singing? I was only following his instructions and all I could do was make sure they were settled in and treated well.

There were ten wooden cupboards either side of the door, the storage place, I guessed, for each boy's worldly goods. Another twenty cupboards lined the far wall, which also had five small windows high up to provide light and fresh air, if not a view. The room was cheerless and without character. The only decoration was the occasional crucifix or icon above a bed. The boys, however, did not seem unduly disappointed and I reminded myself that they were used to sleeping in far more squalid places than this.

Father Stephen pointed at Fabio, but talked to me. 'This one goes there,' indicating a bed about a third of the way down one side wall, 'and this one,' now pointing at Roberto, 'goes there,' nodding his head at a bed on the opposite wall about two-thirds of the way down.

I saw the look that passed between the boys. 'Father Stephen, could the boys not be together? They will settle in far better if they could be close to each other.'

'No signore, Monsignor's orders. The boys should put their belongings in their cupboards. There is a number on the bed and a corresponding number of the cupboard. Tell them to be quick.'

I gave the boys what I hoped was an encouraging smile and walked with them to help them match the number on their bed with the one on their cupboard. I watched as they put their paltry possessions into their cupboard. There was no lock. I noticed Fabio slip his bag of treasures inside his trousers so that it was hidden from view. I wondered how long he would be able to keep it. I did not imagine that the other boys were great respecters of other people's possessions.

Father Stephen waited by the door, tapping his foot again. As soon as we joined him he wordlessly led us back down to the lower storey. As we descended I finally heard the sound of other people: the shuffling of feet, the murmur of voices, the opening and closing of doors. As we reached the bottom of the stairs I saw priests ushering boys along and into different rooms. We stopped and waited to let them pass. They varied in age from about seven to seventeen, but to my eyes they all looked very similar: underfed and pale with ill-cut hair, universally dressed in threadbare, none too clean shirts and trousers. Despite the priests trying to keep them quiet they were chattering together, the high-pitch of the younger boys, and the deeper timbre of the older ones.

Then I heard what sounded like the prattle of girls. A group was passing us by that moved with, but were separate from the rest. It was as if they had an invisible fence around them that prevented others getting close. I looked at them in fascination as did Roberto and Fabio. I could not gauge these boys' ages, but they were taller than average and their bodies looked odd, almost female in shape. They all had plump faces and even though they soon passed us by, I could see that some of them had rounded hips and thighs and some even had evidence of breasts. Fabio and Roberto stood, open mouthed. It was Fabio who voiced what I was thinking.

'Who were they? They looked .... different, and sounded silly.'

The priest looked at me and spat out the words '*I Castrati*. An abomination to God.'

Chapter 8

Two nightingales

The boys gasped and I felt such a surge of anger that I had to clench my fists to stop myself striking him. I doubt Fabio knew what the word abomination meant but he understood the sentiment behind the word and looked stricken. 'But, we ... I mean, is that how we ... Doesn't God ...' He couldn't get his words out.

I put a hand, now unclenched, on each of the boys' shoulders. 'Fabio, Roberto. This man,' I looked Father Stephen in the eye, 'this man is wrong in what he said, may God forgive him. *They* are not an abomination. *You* are not an abomination. You are still boys and God loves you. When you sing to Him with your beautiful voices He will be pleased. Now, Father Stephen, take us to Father Guiseppe.'

Father Stephen looked at me with animosity but then shrugged and led us into one of the rooms. As the door opened we were met by a wall of noise. The room was the same size as the dormitory and was inhabited by about forty boys standing or sitting in random positions in the process of making sound. At first all I could hear was a cacophony but as Father Stephen threaded his way through, I picked out individual boys practising their scales or singing psalms; yet others playing pipes, violins or harpsichords. They seemed to be practising individually with no attempt to produce a coherent, harmonious piece of music.

Father Stephen led us towards the only other adult in the room, who stood swaying, his eyes closed; he was obviously listening to something that pleased him, although goodness knows what. Father Stephen tapped him on the shoulder and Father Guiseppe, as I assumed him to be, opened his eyes wide and then scowled when he saw who had interrupted him. Father Stephen leaned close to the other man so that he could make himself heard. He looked at me, then at the boys as he spoke, then turned away and strode back across the room, without a backward glance.

Father Guiseppe had a very round body, the roundest I had ever seen, with a little round head balanced on top, with seemingly no neck in between. He smiled at us, his lips another curve on a figure made up of curves. He beckoned us to follow him; I expected him to roll when he moved, but he glided as if he were on ice. He led us into a side room and closed the door, the noise thankfully diminished. He was still smiling and when he spoke, it was with a breathy, falsetto voice.

'Welcome, welcome to my musical menagerie! I am Father Guiseppe, and who have I the pleasure of meeting?'

I shook his hand and introduced myself and then the boys; Fabio pulled nervously at his trouser leg and Roberto bit his lip; they both looked anxious.

'Well, Roberto and Fabio, you are most welcome. I expect you are thinking to yourself, "what is this awful place I have been brought to? I thought I was here to learn to sing not to make a dreadful noise. Please, signor Agostini, please take us home immediately!"' He threw his head back and laughed a high-pitched laugh that was so contagious we all joined in. 'Do not fear, my little ones. If you have the will to learn I have the expertise to teach you. Believe it, or believe it not, each boy out there is producing

63

the most beautiful music. They are trained to hear just themselves and to block out every other sound. It is a very useful skill. When you came in I was listening to just one boy who was over the other side of the room and was singing about the coming of spring. I was imaging myself with my feet in a cool stream, sitting under a tree dressed in blossom. Ah! *Splendido*! God has given us a truly wonderful gift in music.' He suddenly grew serious. 'Now then, I need to hear you two sing. Do not look so worried. Is there something that you both know that you will be happy to sing to me?'

The boys looked blankly at him, then at each other. I prompted them. 'How about the one you sang me the other evening in the wood. What was it called? Fabio? Roberto?'

Roberto found his voice. 'We know it as '*My own heart*'. It is just a song we sing at weddings. It's not about God or anything.'

Father Guiseppe clapped his little, round hands. 'Wonderful! Now, Fabio, perhaps you could sing first?'

Fabio looked absolutely petrified and shook his head frantically. Then Roberto took a deep breath and started to sing the now familiar words.

'Oh heart, my own heart, fear not I'll forsake thee,
Let gloomy sorrow o'ershadow thee never;

Within my breast here for shelter betake thee,
For thou, thou only, shalt be mine forever.

I seek for slumber, yet still I am waking,
I think on thee still, each step I am taking.

So, tell me, darling, why linger we longer?
Can love unite us together yet stronger?

When he finished he nudged Fabio and gave him a slight nod as if to say, 'it's alright. Just sing as you normally do, you'll be fine.'

Fabio still looked terrified but after a few false starts that had the sweat forming on my forehead, he sang as sweetly and purely as Roberto had. When he had finished Father Guiseppe just said, 'now together' and he closed his eyes and listened with his mouth slightly open as they sang of a love they were doomed never to know. He kept his eyes shut long after the boys had stopped singing and even I was getting a bit restless, when he suddenly opened his eyes wide and clapped again. '*Bene, molto bene.* Come, I need to take you back to Monsignor and give my report. Follow me.'

We retraced the steps we had recently taken with Father Stephen and were soon standing in front of Monsignor's desk again, at which he was still writing. He kept us waiting as he finished the letter, which he signed with a flourish. He sprinkled the page with sand to remove the excess ink then folded the paper in half and slid it into an envelope, which he sealed with melted wax upon which he pressed his ring. Only then did he look up at Father Guiseppe, ignoring me and the boys completely.

'Well? Can they sing?'

The little round priest tilted his head like a robin then tittered. 'Sing? Can they sing? It was like listening to two nightingales, Monsignor. I have not heard such a sound since, well, since ever. It is truly remarkable that two boys should have voices of such quality at the same time. Are you related?' He looked at the boys, who both nodded. Roberto answered.

'Yes, we are cousins, Father, our mothers are sisters.'

Monsignor Mazzini's mouth smiled; his eyes did not. 'Well the boys might as well start now. Take them away, Father. And you!' He glared at the boys. 'Do exactly as you are told and maybe, just maybe, we might make something of you.'

Father Guiseppe left the room and waited for the boys, who didn't move but looked at me beseechingly. I heard Monsignor take a breath, no doubt to shout at them, so I quickly went closer, bent my knees so I was at their level and tried to reassure them.

'Go with Father Guiseppe, he is a good man and will take care of you. I am staying in Florence for a few days and I will come and see you very soon. Listen carefully to your teachers and do the very best that you can; that is all God asks of you. Take care of each other.' With that I gently pushed them out, shut the door and turned towards the Monsignor, trying to keep my fury at bay.

'Tell me, Monsignor, why it is that you are more than happy to take the money for *i castrati*, but you have working here priests who consider them to be, what was it Father Stephen called them, ah yes, an abomination!'

The Monsignor sighed and gave a small shrug. 'It is true, signore, that the Church does not openly condone castration and Father Stephen is of the opinion that we should not accept boys who have undergone the operation. I, on the other hand, do not consider it to be the boys' fault; they are, after all, still God's children. If a boy comes to our school in order to be taught, then I do not turn him away; I feel it is beholden upon me to protect him.'

I was somewhat surprised at this Christian spirit but nonetheless I still could not find it in me to like the man. 'I don't want Father Stephen anywhere near the boys.' 'He won't be. He teaches Latin so that the boys know what they are singing. But he will not teach your two for many a year. They will need to read and write first, which is perhaps where you come in, signore.'

'Me? What do you mean?'

'I have here a letter to me from Conte De Lorenzo and another addressed to you. I suggest you sit and read yours. Perhaps a small wine as a refreshment?'

I felt a sense of foreboding as I took the envelope sealed with il Conte's impress. I noticed a rather exquisite paper knife lying on top of some papers on his desk. It had a ruby and diamond encrusted hilt and a long, pointed, lethal looking gold blade. 'This is a very ornate object for such a mundane task as cutting pages, Monsignor?'

He tried to sound nonchalant, but the pride was clear in his voice. 'It was given to me in recognition of my contribution to education. Pope Benedict himself handed it to me and spoke a few words of thanks. It is not the monetary worth that I value, but the sentiment in which it was given. I use it almost every day and it is a constant reminder of God's purpose for me in life.'

I sat in the chair he had indicated, sipped at the glass of rather excellent wine that he proffered and read the letter from il Conte.

Villa De Lorenzo
May 25th 1756

Philippe,

If you are reading this you must have arrived safely at the conservatoire along with your charges. I am writing this letter just two days after you have left here in order to ensure that it is waiting for you. I have therefore not read any of your reports that I trust you have sent along the way, but I have confidence that all has gone well.

I have decided to go and stay on the coast for a few months. The Prince of Salzburg has a villa there and has invited us for a visit. Do you remember him? He came to stay with us last year, along with his rather quiet and ineffectual wife. She has produced him an heir so she is not totally inadequate. Eleanora is looking peaky and I think the change will do her good.

I want you to stay in Florence. We should have a residence there and I want you to find a suitable place. It needs to be on the same scale as the Villa De Lorenzo. I have written to signor Rossi at the bank; he is expecting you to go there over the next few weeks to draw whatever money you require. I don't need to remind you not to be extravagant.

This, of course, will not take all your time so I have offered your services to Monsignor Mazzini. You have skills I am sure he will find useful in the conservatoire and you can keep an eye on my investment at the same time. You will stay there, which will save costs for your accommodation. Do whatever Monsignor Mazzini asks of you as if you were doing it for me.

Your humble servant, Conte De Lorenzo

I grimaced; there was nothing humble about il Conte. I reread the last paragraph, hoping against hope that I had misunderstood, but no, il Conte's orders were quite clear. I sighed and looked at Monsignor, who eyed me sympathetically.

'Well, signor Agostini, it seems that your stay here will be longer than you anticipated. As il Conte's secretary I assume you are proficient in reading and writing, in which case it would be useful if you could teach our younger boys the basics at least. Our former teacher, Father Ignatius, sadly passed away a few months ago and I have not been able to replace him. What say you?'

What could I say? I could hardly refuse, although the thought of teaching small boys who doubtless didn't want to be taught did not fill me with joy. 'I don't have a musical bone in my body, and words are the only thing I know, so of course, Monsignor, I am happy to offer my services if that is what il Conte wishes.'

Monsignor's lips twitched. 'That is settled then. I suggest you come here tomorrow morning and I will introduce you to your brother teachers and to your students. You will have Father Ignatius's old room on the top floor. Oh, and your duties will include being responsible for the welfare of the boys in dormitory one.'

'Dormitory one? Could I not have number four? That is where Roberto and Fabio are.'

'No, signore. That would not be sensible. They need to learn to stand on their own two feet as quickly as possible. I try to stamp out any bad behaviour, but the other boys often make fun of *i castrati*; they call them the *non integri*, those who are "not whole". Children can be very cruel, as I am sure you are aware. If you show your two boys any preference you will not be doing them any favours.'

I took my leave, admitting to myself that I was beginning to like Monsignor a bit more. As I walked back to the tavern I re-read the whole letter from il Conte. I did remember the Prince; il Conte had despised him. Why on earth would he want to spend time with him?

Unless it was to keep me and Eleanora apart?

Chapter 9

A reluctant teacher

It had been my tutor, Niccolò Vasco, who had urged me to challenge, rather than to blindly accept the Jesuits' control over education. Niccolò had taught me that the Jesuits personified the 'old' ways, those of superstition, censorship and ecclesiastical authority. He had convinced me that there was a better means of education than that imposed by the Jesuits; one that taught modern as opposed to ancient literature, one that used rationalism and science as opposed to myth and religious dogmatism. Here I was though, despite my antagonism towards their ideology, forced by my own selfish ambition and desires, to become a member of one of their institutions; to become a thread in their spider's web of influence and control.

Before settling down for my first night at the conservatoire I prepared to write a report to il Conte, the puppeteer pulling at my strings. As I was laying out all the necessary equipment I studied the many inky marks and scratches upon the table's surface, some of which I could decipher as being names, dates and oftentimes definitely unreligious thoughts. One entry caught my eye, 'Louis 1523 *etiam verbis pluribus*.' I smiled and imagined a young priest, still perhaps a novice, being set a task of learning long verses from the Bible and still being rebellious enough to carve his opinion that there were 'too many words.' I hoped he had not been caught in his misdemeanour for I imagined that the punishment would have been severe.

I mused on those who had inhabited the room before me. Or rather cell; it took little effort to imagine a long line of priests who had forsaken all worldly goods, feeling satisfied, if such a sentiment were allowed, in the evidence of their asceticism and self-denial. The simple wooden table at which I sat was positioned under the window on the far wall and the only other furniture was the bed and at its foot a plain wooden chest, which now contained my clothes. On either side of the bed the varnish on the wooden floor had been worn by countless knees bent in prayer. It somehow comforted me to know that mine would soon join them. Not so comforting was a large wooden cross on the rough white-washed wall opposite the bed, upon which an unnervingly realistic figure of Christ was in the throes of His agonising death, His tortured face made more ghastly by the flickering flames. A reminder, if one was needed, of our debt to Him.

I suddenly felt very tired, but I wanted to complete my report so I dipped my nib in the ink and proceeded to write.

Conservatorio per i poveri della Beata Vergine
May 30th 1756

Al Conte De Lorenzo

You will see from the address that I am now ensconced at the conservatoire as you ordered. I hope that you have received my earlier reports but in case you have not I will summarise:

The brothers, Rafaele and Michel, decided they preferred to return home. I trust they are safely back with their families and that they have returned the purchase price.

Little Luigi unfortunately did not survive the operation. Il Barbiere disposed of the body before I could send it home. Please assure the family he had a Christian burial, although this is far from the truth. It seems unfair to demand they repay the money.

Il Barbiere suffered a fatal sickness. The cause is unknown but I took the opportunity to leave, the remaining two boys, Roberto and Fabio, being sufficiently recovered. The journey to Florence did them no harm and yesterday I handed them over in good health. A Father Guiseppe listened to them sing and he reported to Monsignor Mazzini that they 'sounded like two nightingales'; he seemed very excited with their ability, which bodes well for your investment.

So, I am now teacher of reading and writing for the younger boys, as well as master of a dormitory. I start my new employment tomorrow. This morning was spent in meeting the other teachers, all Jesuit priests, and having my duties explained to me. I visited signor Rossi in the afternoon and he is going to find me a selection of villas to view over the next week or so.

I hope you don't mind me saying that although I am happy to do your bidding, teaching is not a position I am well suited to and so I hope your visit to the Prince's villa is relaxing and brings colour to la Contessa's cheeks, but also that it is short so that I can revert to my proper role and be of more service to you personally.

Please pass on my regards to your wife and daughter,
I am, as always, your servant
Philippe Agostini

I looked out of the window as I waited for the ink to dry. It was dark but I could imagine the view: the forecourt of the conservatoire; its high, protective wall; the rooftops of the Florentine world beyond. The window was open and I could hear the noises of the city: shouts of carousers on their drunken way home; the clip-clop of horses; church bells ringing. And, only just discernible, what sounded like a choir of angels singing their final praises of the day. I wondered if Roberto and Fabio were amongst them.

I put the letter into an envelope and sealed it with a blob of blood red wax. I used the gold ring my father had given me on my sixteenth birthday to identify the seal as being that of the Agostini family; a simple motif of a heraldic lion under an arch of five stars.

I knelt and said my prayers, asking God's forgiveness for my many unchristian thoughts that day, His guidance in my life and His care for the souls of my family, and that of il Conte, trying not to place any particular emphasis on Eleanora. I added Roberto and Fabio to the list and asked God to bless them and to keep their voices pure that they may praise Him. I then washed, using the bowl and jug of water that had been placed on top of the chest, folded my clothes neatly and slipped under the rough, prickly sheets. Heaven forbid that they should be soft and comfortable.

The next morning, I was woken by loud knocking from a sleep haunted by priests carving their names onto tables, doors, walls, Bible covers, the backs of boys, their own faces. Each cut had released a trick of thick blood upon which I was obliged to imprint my family crest, using a giant ring I could hardly hold. The knocking continued until

I shouted out, '*Entra*!' It was the young novice assigned to show me the ropes.

'Good morning and God bless you, signor Agostini. It is going to be a beautiful day again, as always. I have brought you some water and fresh linen. Do you need me to assist you?'

'Good morning, yourself, Brother Marcus. You have no right to sound so bright and cheerful at this ungodly time in the morning. What hour is it, for goodness' sake?'

He looked unperturbed at my sourness. 'It is five and the sun is already up and about, as you must be, signore. We always have a short service in each dormitory at a quarter past the hour so you must hurry. Don't worry, signore,' he had seen the expression of panic on my face, 'this will be led by Father Guiseppe as he is not master of a particular dormitory. Then the boys dress, wash and go to chapel for Matins, after which we all have breakfast together in the refectory. Don't worry, signore,' he said again, 'I will be at your side to guide you. Now, if you are sure you don't need me I will go and make sure the boys are getting up. Join us as soon as you can. We must start the service on time.'

With this gentle reprimand, he left me to get up and put on some clothes quickly. I decided to leave my ablutions until after the service. As I crossed the corridor to the dormitory I heard a sound and turned to see Father Guiseppe gliding towards me. He greeted me with a broad smile and we entered the room together, at which the noise of forty boys shuffling, sniffing, scratching and whispering suddenly ceased. They all stood in their night clothes at the foot of their beds, all eyes fixed on Father Guiseppe. There was total silence, it was as if the building itself was holding its breath. I had a sudden urge to cough and then to laugh but managed to hold it in. I too looked at the priest, who stood perfectly still, his eyes closed, his expression serious, no hint of a smile. Then he opened his eyes and raised a hand; this was evidently a sign, for as one, they all started to chant quietly. I didn't know all the words but recognised some, such as *lavabis* and *asperges*, and supposed them to be asking God to cleanse them of their sins in readiness for a new day. I knew the last verse, as did all Catholics, and joined in.

Gloria Patri, et Filio,
Et Spiritui Sancto.
Sicut erat in principio,
Et nunc, et semper,
Et in saecula saeculorum.
Amen

As soon as they had sung the 'Amen' the boys began to move but didn't stop their chanting. They repeated the words over and over as they all exchanged their night for day wear and then lined up and followed Father Guiseppe out of the dormitory and down the corridor. The sight reminded me of a folk tale I had read when I was much younger, of a strange piper whose music enticed the village children away, never to be seen again. Brother Marcus touched my arm and broke the spell.

'Come, we need to go with the boys to the washhouse, and then on to church.'

As I followed him, the other dormitory doors opened and the boys came out, all chanting, all following a priest. We waited at the top of the stairs to let them go past before we descended. When the boys from dormitory IV came by I kept my eyes open for Roberto and Fabio. They were near the back with the other castrati. They didn't yet have their look, but their difference was obviously known by the *non integri*, who had no wish to associate themselves with my two boys. Their dark eyes looked huge in their small, pale faces, the only colour being the purple smudges that signalled lack of sleep. Roberto came first, followed closely by Fabio. Their mouths opened and closed but as they passed I heard no sound. I tried to catch their eye but their gaze was fixed on the back of the head in front of them. They showed no sign that they were even aware that I was there. They looked so pathetic. I was tempted to pull them out of the line there and then and take them home. As if reading my mind, the ever watchful Brother Marcus held my sleeve and gently shook his head.

By the time we reached the washhouse all the boys were in the process of washing themselves in a long trough that had water running along it, all the while intoning the same chant. I assumed the water came from, and returned to, the river Arno. I stood at the end nearest where it poured from a hole in the wall so that I could wash in clean water. I remembered the lavender scented soap that Eleanora had given me but decided I would be a laughing stock if I used it here. I saw some boys leaving the washhouse to return a few minutes later, and guessed they were going to the jakes, of which I took advantage before following the boys to the church.

La chiesa di santa Caterina was built inside the grounds of the conservatoire, obviously designed by the same architect, it being another plain box. Inside was a different matter; no expense had been spared on the interior. The floor and pillars were of white marble; the pews of highly polished carved mahogany; the candlesticks of gold. I breathed in the pungent smell of melting wax mixed with that of incense; it was almost intoxicating. The most gorgeous thing, however, was the figure of Monsignor Mazzini. He was dressed in a robe the colour of crushed sloes, topped with a cloak of pure white, intricately embroidered with golden thread that glistened in the candlelight. He stood at the front on a raised floor so that, even though he was of a small stature, we all had to look up at him.

At the flick of his wrist the chanting stopped and there followed the familiar service of Matins. I looked around; all I saw were the faces of tired, unenthusiastic boys, albeit who sang their responses beautifully. My stomach rumbled and I suspected that I was not alone in thinking more about food than about God.

We ate breakfast in a large refectory on the ground floor of the conservatoire. The boys sat on benches at long tables, with the adults sitting together on a raised platform at one end. The food was brought in on large trays by some of the slightly older boys, who walked up and down the aisles doling out the bread and cheese to those sitting. No-one started eating until all had been served and the servers themselves were seated. Then a priest stood, said a benediction, after which mouths were instantly stuffed with the still-warm bread.

I noticed Monsignor was not part of our happy throng.

The boys were allowed to talk quietly to their neighbours, but I noticed boys, perhaps the same ones who

78

had served the food, walking up and down, tapping the shoulders of anyone who raised their voices or became too high-spirited. Breakfast was over too quickly for my liking. I would have preferred to sit for a while, perhaps read a few pages of my book and then prepare for the day. But no sooner had I swallowed the last piece of cheese than a bell rang in the distance and the boys all stood and row by row left the room and went off to their lessons. It was then that I saw Roberto and Fabio. I had scoured the faces as I ate but had not found them. I could see them clearly now though, as they stood uncertainly, presumably not knowing where to go. My heart went out to them. I was wondering whether to go to them when I saw a tall boy, one of the *castrati*, bend down to talk to them. They both nodded and then followed him out. I saw they were holding hands.

Brother Marcus was standing by my side, waiting to escort me to my first lesson. 'It seems as if Vincent has befriended your two boys. That is good; he will look after them as best he can. They are probably going to the class you will be teaching; it is for those who cannot read or write. Come, I'll take you there.'

There were ten of them around a circular table, slate and chalk ready in front of them. Roberto and Fabio were indeed there, sitting closely next to each other. As we entered they all turned to look at me. None of them could have been more than about nine; all of them from poor families and inferior to me in every sense. Nonetheless I was suddenly overcome with nerves. What on earth was I doing here? Who was I to teach these boys anything? I silently cursed il Conte, took a deep breath and stepped into the room.

Chapter 10

Villainy!

My sweet Eleanora,

My God, how I miss you! The memory of you is the only good thing in my life. It has been nearly ten weeks since I started working at the conservatoire, and not a minute goes by when you are not in my thoughts. You will not be able to imagine this life of rules, routine and rigour that I have to endure. Each minute of every hour, of every day, is accounted for; each day is the same as every other day, except for Sundays, when my piety is stretched to its limit.

Oh, sweet, sweet Eleanora! When are you coming to Florence so that I can leave this dismal life and return to my rightful place - near to you? Do you think of me, as I do of you, every waking moment? Even as I try and teach the youngsters to form their letters, I imagine you sitting in the corner of the room, your long, beautiful fingers busy with your embroidery, a smile on your lips as you look coyly at me. There is a promise in your glance and sometimes I have to leave the room, such is the affect this vision has on me.

I find life here very dull but I have become quite fond of the boys I teach. They are all just eight or nine years old and quite new here, but only my two boys, Roberto and Fabio, are castrati. Monsignor Mazzini, whom I have learned to respect more and more since our first meeting, warned me that the non integri boys are not accepted by the other 'normal' boys. Even though i castrati keep together in order to protect themselves, I still see evidence every day of bullying, in the bruises caused by pinches and punches.

I feel so sorry for my boys; what sort of life have we forced them into?

I have written to your husband, telling him that I have managed to rent a villa. It is called the Villa Bouganville, for obvious reasons. It has been redecorated and is ready for occupancy. I hope you are satisfied with my choice - I picked it with you in mind. It is on the banks of the river Arno, where all the best villas are located. There is a lawn that slopes gently down to the water and moorings for boats. I often dream of rowing you to a secluded place where we can be alone, where we can make love without fear of being disturbed. There is a beautiful walled rose garden just like in the Villa De Lorenzo, which I know you will love. I walked around it one evening, imaging you by my side enjoying the fragrance that filled the air, your hands warm and soft in mine. Oh, my Eleanora, how I wish....

'You are doing a lot of sighing, Philippe, and your soup will be cold by now.' Father Guiseppe prodded me good-naturedly out of my reverie. He smiled knowingly at me, 'Dreaming of being elsewhere?'

'Forgive me. You are right, I was daydreaming.'

I continued to eat my soup, which was indeed cold, when suddenly the refectory door was thrown open and Monsignor Mazzini, who had hitherto never honoured us with his presence, came storming down the room. He walked with a stick, his passage marked with a loud crack each time it hit the tiled floor. His face was red with anger or exertion, or both. Even from a distance I could see that his nostrils were flared and his mouth just a dark line of fury. He climbed onto the platform on which our table stood and banged his stick three times, demanding, and getting, total silence.

'Villainy!' he bellowed, 'we are harbouring a thief!'

There were murmurs from boys and adults alike. I suspected that they were not so much surprised at his accusation, but more that he should be so shocked. In such an environment as we lived in, acts of petty larceny were almost inevitable. None of us were under the allusion that the boys were saints, nor that any teachings from the priests led to them becoming respecters of other people's possessions. Monsignor banged his stick again. The sound bounced off the walls and the echo reverberated long after the whisperings had ceased. 'Someone has stolen my paper knife!' Not so much a bellow of an angry bull, as the growl of a furious mountain lion.

Another round of murmuring and shuffling of bottoms on seats as we all turned to our neighbours. We all now understood his fury. I knew, as did everyone at the conservatoire, that the paper knife was Monsignor's prized possession. Although he had claimed to me that its monetary value was of no significance, it obviously was to someone else.

Monsignor took a deep breath. 'Tomorrow morning, when I enter my office, I expect to see the paper knife on my desk in its usual place. Nothing more will be said; the boy's own conscience will punish him enough.' His anger dissipated and his shoulders drooped. 'Don't let me down, boys.' With this, he retraced his steps across the refectory, his stick tapping, rather than hammering the tiles, as he walked slowly past the rows of solemn little faces. As the door closed behind him, everyone let out their breath in one universal sigh. Before the chattering could start, Father Guiseppe lifted his rotund body from his chair, clapped his hands and raised his high-pitched voice so that everyone could hear. 'Silence! We all need to speak with God, not each other. Let us pray.' He waited until the boys had put their hands together and hung their heads. 'Dear Father, we pray to you this evening that you help each and every one of us to search our own hearts and to put right any wrongs we have done. Forgive us our sins, Lord, for we are weak and need your love and guidance today and every day. Amen.'

I watched the boys as they filed silently out, trying to see if anyone looked the slightest bit guilty, but all I saw were expressions of curiosity and excitement. After supper and before Compline, the boys had an hour of relatively free time, as long as they stayed within the grounds of the conservatoire, spoke only to boys from their own dormitories and of their own age group. The exception were *i castrati*, who were allowed to keep all together, regardless of dormitory or age, there being safety in numbers. I imagined there would only be one subject of discussion this night.

It was usually during this recreational period that I tried to catch some time with Roberto and Fabio. In my reports to il Conte, I told him they were both doing well, but I was not being totally honest. They were learning their letters well enough and Father Guiseppe was still very excited at their singing potential, but I was especially worried about Roberto. He seemed to have lost his spirit and I didn't understand why.

It was a warm evening and I went directly to the corner of the forecourt where *i castrati* usually gathered. They were indeed there, all chattering away about the theft, but Roberto and Fabio were not of their number. I knew and liked one of the older ones, Vincent, who had shown great kindness to my boys. I asked if he knew where they were but he shook his head and suggested that I look in the washhouse. I wandered in that direction and seeing it to be empty was just about to return to the conservatoire when I heard laughing and jeering from the direction of the latrines. Then the sound of a slap, and then another. I ran round the corner, shouting, 'Stop, stop this instant,' without even knowing who I was shouting at or what I was telling them to stop doing.

There were four of the older boys frozen with their arms raised in the act of attack, towering over two others crouched down, their own arms raised in the act of defence. As one, the bullies lowered their arms and raced away, a boy managing to kick one of the huddled shapes before he scarpered. I ran over to the two boys, knowing them to be Roberto and Fabio, even before they raised their tear-streaked faces.

'It's alright, boys. It's alright. They've gone. Why are you here alone? Why aren't you with the others?'

'With the other freaks, you mean?' Roberto almost snarled.

Oh, my poor boys.

'We have to piss, signore.'

'Let me look at you both. Are you badly hurt?'

Fabio stood and helped Roberto up, who seemed to struggle to stand upright. 'No, signore. They had only just started.'

'Come over here and sit awhile.' I led them to a seat positioned against the wall. I noticed that Roberto had difficulty walking, as if every step was painful.

'Where are you hurt, Roberto?'

The boys shared a glance, then Roberto gave a tight smile. 'It is just my wound, signore. That kick just made it ache a little, that is all.'

We sat in silence for a while, a silence broken by the evening birdsong. Then suddenly the notes were so close, I thought a bird had alighted on my shoulder. I looked around but there was nothing there. Fabio saw my puzzled expression and laughed.

'Father Guiseppe has told us to listen to the birds and to try and sing like them. Did I succeed, signore?'

'You certainly did, Fabio. I remember when you first sang to Father Guiseppe and he said you sounded like nightingales. Perhaps he wants you to sound like a whole forest of birds! What else has he told you to do? Have you actually sung a real song yet?'

Roberto sighed. 'No, signore. We still have to practise our scales, up and down, down and up, time and time again. We have to stand in front of a mirror and watch ourselves to make sure we open our mouths wide, hold our heads up, push our shoulders back. Like so.' He opened his mouth into a huge O, pulled back his shoulders as far as they would go so that his tiny chest was thrust out, and lifted his head so high he was looking at the sky. 'Now, do I look like a proper singer, signore?'

I joined in their laughter. 'Everyone must learn the basics, boys. Father Guiseppe is a good teacher. He says you are doing very well, so just keep on doing what he says, he knows best. How are your lessons with Brother Marcus? He is teaching you the Bible, isn't he?'

Fabio took over. 'He is very friendly, we both like him a lot. He reads us stories and then explains what they mean. Today he told us the one about the Good Sama, Sama, Sama-something.'

'Samaritan,' Roberto chipped in.

'Yes, that's it, the Good Samaritan. I enjoyed that story. He said that soon he will teach us the words of some hymns for when they at last let us sing.'

'And are you both getting enough to eat?'

'No, signore!' they both chorused.

I took out some bread that I had pilfered from the supper table and shared it out between them. I watched as they tore at it. Although Roberto was obviously taking great pleasure in this treat, there was a dullness in his eyes that I could not fathom and which worried me.

'Are you alright, Roberto? Is anything bothering you? Is it the other boys?'

Roberto stopped chewing and looked over my shoulder at the wall behind. 'Of course, signore Philippe. I, we, are perfectly well, aren't we, Fabio? We are both very grateful to il Conte for this opportunity, aren't we, Fabio?'

Fabio nodded twice at this rehearsed response, his mouth being full.

=================

I had got into the habit of rising before dawn and going to the washhouse so that I could cleanse myself in privacy.

That night I could not sleep. I was hot and my tossing and turning just made me hotter and more uncomfortable. I got out of my sweat-soaked bed and decided to go to the washhouse to cool myself, even earlier than usual. I took the soap that Eleanora had given me; there would be no-one there to mock this sign of effeminacy. I stopped outside dormitory one and put my ear to the door. Not a sound. I was in my bare feet and they made a slight slapping sound as I walked down the dimly-lit corridor, but the noise was not enough to wake anyone.

I almost missed it.

I had walked a few steps further on before I realised that I had heard something out of the ordinary. I stopped and listened. There it was again. It was the sound of sobbing, not from one of the dormitories, but from one of the priest's rooms just behind me. I took a few steps back and listened again. Yes, it was definitely the sound of crying and now the murmur of someone trying to soothe. I knew it to be the room of Father Stephen. I tried to avoid him as much as possible as, even after ten weeks, I had not learned to like him one iota more. There was obviously something wrong, but was it really any of my business? I remembered Fabio telling me about the story of the Good Samaritan, but even so I had almost made up my mind to be one of those who walked on by, when I heard the murmur turn into an angry whisper and then the sound of a hard slap.

That decided it. I turned and opened the door onto a scene that both appalled and sickened me.

Father Stephen was kneeling on his bed, his cassock lifted up, revealing his engorged penis. He was astride a naked boy, who was lying face down, sobbing into the pillow. There was an angry red mark of a handprint on his buttock. Father Stephen stared at me in horror and I could not help but notice that his ardour had drooped in an instant. The boy kept his head turned away.

Chapter 11

The bejewelled knife

Father Stephen started stuttering but I didn't listen to him. I was so overwhelmed with revulsion that I strode over to him, yanked him off the bed and threw him onto the floor. I heard with pleasure his shriek of pain and I hoped he had broken a bone or two.

I sat on the side of the bed, still warm from the priest's presence, and put my hand gently on the boy's shoulder. He recoiled at my touch, who could blame him?

'It's alright. It's over now. This won't happen again, I promise.'

'Signor Agostini?' The boy lifted his head slowly and turned towards me, his face wet with tears.

'Oh, signor Agostini! He made me do it. He made me ,' he started to cry again.

I lifted him up and held him tightly. 'Oh, Roberto, my poor, poor boy. I am so sorry this has happened. Why didn't you tell me? Oh, never mind now. Come, here are your clothes. Get dressed and we will go down to the washhouse and you can cleanse away his filth.'

When he tentatively stood up, I noticed a trickle of blood from his anus and I recalled how he had struggled to walk earlier. I couldn't bear to see him in such pain, so when he was dressed I lifted him in my arms. I remembered when I had carried him in the same way at Il Barbiere's for the operation, just three months ago. He seemed to be much lighter now. As I was about to go I heard Father Stephen whimper. I was filled with such righteous indignation that

89

I went back in and kicked him hard in the groin, not once but twice, just to give him something to whimper about.

I carried Roberto all the way to the washhouse and sat him in the trough to let the running water wash away the blood and semen, if not the pain. I gave him the soap and some linen and told him how to use it. He sniffed at it suspiciously but was soon lathering himself all over. He rubbed quite gently at first, but then he got harder and harder, at the same time making a keening sound that sent shivers down my spine. I thought it might do him good to let his distress out, but when his arm started to bleed, so vigorous was his rubbing, I stopped his hand.

'Enough, Roberto. You are clean.'

'I will never be clean. Never!'

I gave him another linen to dry himself and once he was dressed we went outside to sit on the same bench that we had sat on earlier that evening.

'I will make sure he is punished, Roberto, I promise you. How long has it been going on?'

He hung his head and mumbled an answer. I took his chin and lifted it, forcing him to look at me.

'You have done nothing wrong, Roberto. There is nothing to be ashamed of. It is Father Stephen who will suffer, in this life and the next. You are innocent, God knows that.'

Roberto looked at me searchingly, and seemed to be reassured. 'It started a few weeks after we came. He is our dormitory master so he comes in every night to make sure everyone is in their bed and wearing their night clothes.' He gave a twisted smile. 'You know the rule that no-one must sleep naked. The first time he came to my bed, he tapped me on the shoulder and told me to follow him. I wasn't asleep anyway and I couldn't refuse him, could I, signore?'

I patted his hand. 'No, of course not.'

'So, I went with him then and every other night he came to my bed. It wasn't every night. Some nights he took his pleasure elsewhere, but I could never sleep properly, always worrying that he would come. He made me do things to him and he hurt me.'

His whole body shuddered. 'I hate him, signore! Will God be angry with me for hating him so much? So, much, that I wish he were dead?'

'No, Roberto. To hurt a child is to hurt God himself. But do not let your anger devour you. Ask God to help heal your body and your spirit. There are still a few hours of darkness. You go back to the dormitory and try and get some sleep. I will go and see Monsignor first thing in the morning.'

He still walked awkwardly; I guessed the soreness would last a few days. We separated at the foot of the stairs in the entrance hall, he to go upstairs, me to return to the washhouse where I took my time to cleanse myself and to await the first streaks of dawn. I wasn't sure what Monsignor's daily routine was, but as I had to pass his office before reaching his bedroom, I tapped on that door first and immediately got a response. '*Entra*!'

Monsignor looked at me hopefully.

'*Buongiorno*, Philippe. Have you found my paper knife? I came early to see if anyone had left it but it is still not here.' He scanned the desk top again as if to make sure it hadn't miraculously appeared in the last few seconds.

'I'm sorry, Monsignor, but I have more distressing things to discuss with you. It is about Father Stephen.' I explained what I had discovered only a few hours earlier. 'I have no doubt at all that I speak with Conte De Lorenzo's authority when I say that he must go. It is no idle threat to say that I will not hesitate to take Roberto and Fabio out and send them to another conservatoire. I know il Conte will fully support me.'

Monsignor tapped his lips with his stubby fingers. 'I will have a word with him. The life of a priest is not an easy one. He ...'

'No, Monsignor, do not defend him. "A word" is not enough. He is no more a priest than I am; he is a hypocrite. He had the audacity to call my boys an abomination to God, but it is *he* who is the abomination. He is sin incarnate and he must go. Make sure he does, or I will!' I turned and left before he could make any more excuses for his so-called brother.

By the time I went to the first lesson I had my anger under control. We had progressed from learning the letters of the alphabet to reading and writing simple words. I tried to make the classes as enjoyable as possible and, with Monsignor's permission, I had purchased some paper, quills and coloured inks so that they could write any new letter or word on a sheet. I allowed them to add some decoration and then I pinned them to the wall. At the start of each lesson I would point to some of the sheets and ask them to tell me what the letter or word said: *Ave, Gesù, bene, cattivo, Patri, Filio.*

I had three classes that morning, one of which Roberto and Fabio attended. Roberto was by far the better scholar;

he was a quick learner and applied his knowledge well. He often helped Fabio, who seemed to find it hard to remember the shapes of letters and words. During their lesson I noticed that they had their heads together as they worked on a new word, *Dio*.

Each lesson was interrupted that morning by some novices, including Brother Marcus, searching the room and the boys for Monsignor's paper knife. When one of the brothers tried to search Roberto he screamed, 'Don't touch me!' He ran to the corner, his face towards the wall and his hands clamped over his ears, as if to shut out everyone and everything. I whispered to Brother Marcus that I would vouch for Roberto and it was anyway obvious that there was no knife hidden under his scanty clothing.

That afternoon I decided to go to the Villa Bouganville to make sure everything was progressing so that it would be ready for when the family came, whenever that would be. It was just past noon when I left; the sun was at its zenith and most people were inside, away from the fierce summer heat. I crossed to the shady side of the street in an unsuccessful attempt to avoid becoming saturated with sweat. I stopped at a tavern for a glass of wine.

The villa was surrounded by a high wall that marked it out as belonging to someone who valued their privacy, whilst still wanting to announce their high status. The building itself was made of white stone, had a colonnade of fluted pillars running all around it, and there were statues of semi-naked gods and goddesses scattered in the grounds. I thought the whole place was preposterous but I knew Eleanora would love it. Even il Conte, who was a soldier at heart and used to living in a tent with the minimum of personal possessions around him, was not adverse to a certain amount of opulence.

When I had first seen the villa, it had looked very sorry for itself, having been neglected for almost a year. I had therefore managed to get it at a reasonable rental and for a relatively small cost the place had been transformed. The gardens had been tidied and re-stocked; the rooms newly white-washed; the furniture and furnishings refreshed; the windows cleaned and the woodwork polished; and the bougainvillea pruned and draped spectacularly over arches and covered ways. All it needed now was a family to live in it.

The stable block was around the back and I knew this would be where I would find Davide. I heard him before I saw him. By the sound I knew he was brushing a horse and talking to it gently as he did so. I had got to know and like Davide since coming to Florence. He had far more time for his horses than he did for most people, but he seemed to tolerate me. He heard my approach, waved and smiled at me. He continued to brush the horse's rump, long strong strokes from top to bottom, over and over again until the coat shone like burnished copper.

I sat on an overturned bucket and watched him with pleasure. I didn't really need to be at the villa, I just needed to be away from the conservatoire, away from the proximity of Father Stephen.

Davide seemed to sense my mood. 'Everything alright with you, Philippe?' We had long done away with formalities. 'You seem a bit distracted.'

'All is well with me personally thank you, Davide. All the better for seeing you hard at work and me not.'

He grinned at me, his sun scorched face crinkling around his eyes. 'This is not work, this is sheer pleasure. If it is not you with a problem, who?'

So, I told him.

When I finished he threw the brush onto the floor, startling both me and the horse, which flicked back his ears and stamped his hooves.

'*Bastardo*! Do you want me to kill him for you? I could, you know. Roberto is one of our own.'

'Thank you for the offer, my friend. I have told Monsignor to get rid of the priest, otherwise I will take the boys elsewhere. Father Guiseppe says the boys have great potential which, of course, will reflect on the conservatoire. Monsignor will not want to lose them.'

Davide picked up the discarded brush, slapped the horse on its rump to make it walk back into its stall, swept the floor then said, 'Drink?' To which I willingly agreed.

The next morning I woke at my normal early hour to go to the washhouse. It was still pitch black and the shadow cast by the candle flame danced on the walls, like a possessed goblin. When I got to Father Stephen's door I stopped and listened. I didn't expect to hear anything, for all I knew he had already gone. There was no sound but I did notice that the door was ajar, perhaps he didn't close it when he left? I pushed it open to check that he had indeed gone and stood in the entrance, my candle raised to shed light on the room. He had not left. Father Stephen was in bed, on his back. He lay on top of the sheets, completely naked. He could have just been asleep, if it had not been for the knife protruding out of his heart, its bejewelled handle glinting in the soft candlelight.

Chapter 12

Disappointments

Could he still be alive? I didn't want to go any nearer, so I stood in the doorway and watched his chest for a good minute but saw no movement. God forgive me but I felt nothing but relief.

I closed the door and stood in the corridor, uncertain what to do. There was no sound other than my own laboured breathing and my heart beating as if I had run up the side of a mountain. I needed to do something; I couldn't let anyone else find him. Before long everyone would be rising. I had to fetch Monsignor but I didn't want to leave the room unattended. I decided to wake Brother Marcus, who slept a couple of rooms further down the corridor. I knocked quietly; there was an immediate response, '*Si? chi è la?*'

'It's signor Agostini. I need to speak to you urgently.'

He opened the door before I had finished speaking. He was dressed and alert with dusty patches on his knees. He beckoned me in.

'I'm sorry to disturb your prayers, Brother Marcus. They will soon be needed. It is Father Stephen, he is ... dead. I need you to go and fetch Monsignor Mazzini, whilst I stop anyone else going into the room. Will you do that?'

Brother Marcus was a good and quick-witted man. He asked no questions, just nodded and slipped quietly out of his room, still in his bare feet.

I went back to Father Stephen's. I didn't want to look obvious by standing outside so, with my heart in my mouth,

96

I went inside, shut the door and pressed myself against it, trying to keep as far away from the body as was physically possible. Although Father Stephen was the master of dormitory four, he, like me, left the execution of the early morning service to a novice and met up with them either at the church or often just for breakfast. No one would notice our absence for a while yet. I didn't want to look at him, so I closed my eyes but my imagination painted an even more gruesome picture, so I stared instead at the whitewashed wall opposite. After a few minutes I was roused from my reverie by two short raps.

'*Chi è?*' I whispered.

'It's Brother Marcus with Monsignor.'

I opened the door and ushered them both inside. Monsignor surveyed the scene then turned to Brother Marcus, who looked as if he was going to be sick, and told him to go. 'Say nothing yet. Just go about your business as normal.'

Monsignor then walked to the side of the bed and studied the corpse from top to toe. His lip curled; I could not tell whether it was at the sight of death, the blood that had drenched the sheet and pooled onto the floor, or Father Stephen's nakedness. He looked up at me. 'Look where his hands are.'

I hadn't noticed before, but both his hands were cupped around his flaccid penis, as if protecting it. Or hiding it.

Monsignor walked around the bed, bending to look under it. He went to the table and lifted each book and flipped through them searching for something. 'I was hoping to find a note,' he explained. 'It is obvious to me that he felt such guilt at his, er, his unfortunate predilection, that he chose to kill himself. Do you agree?'

I considered his theory and was far from convinced. 'But why would he choose to kill himself with your paper knife? It was taken before I found out about what you call his "unfortunate predilection." Are you saying that he was the thief as well?'

Monsignor shook his head. 'No, maybe he found it and forgot to give it me. I spoke to him yesterday morning and told him he had to leave today. He was understandably upset. Perhaps the thought of the disgrace was too much for him to face and he just used whatever was at hand.'

'But isn't suicide an even greater sin? Isn't he now damned for all eternity?'

Monsignor seemed irritated at my questions. 'Who knows what was going on in his mind? It is clear to me what happened. He found the knife but didn't return it to me, and after being told he was to be dismissed in disgrace, he used it to end his life.'

I considered again, but was no more convinced. 'So, he would either have had to fall onto the knife and then turn over before dying, or he stabbed himself whilst on his back.' I studied the body and the bedding on which it lay. 'The sheet is still quite smooth; it would be far more rumpled if he had turned onto his back having first stabbed himself, and the blood would be more spread over his torso. No, he must have always been on his back.' I imagined myself lying in my own bed, and made a stabbing motion to my heart. 'It cannot be easy to stab yourself whilst on your back, and how, and why, has he positioned his hands so?'

I now thought of Monsignor as a friend but the look he gave me was anything but amicable. 'You are suggesting, then, that Father Stephen did not kill himself? Think very carefully before you answer, Philippe. Think of the implications and the consequences of this being anything but suicide.'

I did as he suggested and thought very carefully. If Father Stephen hadn't killed himself, then someone else had done it for him. At night the conservatoire was as impenetrable as a solid block of marble, so it was just not possible for an outsider to have entered the building. It must, therefore, have been someone from within. I knew that Father Stephen had not been greatly liked by either the priests or the boys, but it was a huge step from disliking someone to murdering him. There was only one person I could think of who had any reason to kill him at this particular time, but I dismissed the thought immediately. Roberto was only eight, maybe nine by now; he just wouldn't have had the strength or the knowledge to plunge the knife into just the right place to cause almost instant death. Would he?

'You are right, Monsignor. Father Stephen obviously took advantage of the knife being to hand and his despair at the prospect of life-long disgrace gave him the strength to stab himself. The position of his hands are his suicide note. There is one good thing that has come out of his death.' Monsignor raised his eyebrows quizzically. 'At least you have got your knife back.'

Life quickly returned to relative normality. Brother Marcus was sworn to secrecy and everyone was merely told that Father Stephen had died in his sleep. Monsignor explained the lack of a service at *la chiesa di santa Caterina* by saying that he was taking the body back to Father Stephen's home town, where there would be due ceremony. In fact, he accompanied the body out to the countryside and had it buried in unhallowed ground.

I watched Roberto carefully over the next few days and he soon regained his former spirit and his jaunty walk. There was nothing, as I knew there would not be, to indicate that he had taken vengeance into his own hands. About a month after Brother Stephen's unmourned demise, I received a letter from il Conte. It was short and to the point.

Villa De Lorenzo
September 1756

Philippe,

As you will see, we are returned home. La Contessa is still slightly under the weather and prefers to be here for a few weeks before our move to Florence. I need you here. Make your apologies to Monsignor Mazzini and come back as quickly as possible. Bring the boys.

Your servant,
Conte De Lorenzo

My poor Eleanora! How I wish I was with her. I would soon put some colour into her cheeks.

When I told Monsignor that I had been told to return, he tutted.

'That is a shame. You have turned out to be a fine teacher. I had hoped you could stay longer.'

'Il Conte would like me to take the boys. I expect he wants to see how their singing has improved.'

Monsignor shook his head vehemently. 'No, absolutely not! The ties with their families have been irrevocably torn, but the wounds are still raw. It would be cruel to all concerned. I never let any boy return home for a visit after only a few months, and after that they have no desire to. I will write to il Conte and explain.'

That evening I told the boys that I was going away for a few weeks. I didn't tell them I may never return. They naturally asked me where I was going and without thinking I said, 'Home.'

Fabio's eyes lit up. 'Home? Oh, signore, you are taking us with you aren't you?'

Roberto too was nodding enthusiastically. 'Si, signore. We long to see our families.' He noticed my expression. 'Signore? You cannot mean to go home and not take us?'

'I'm sorry, boys, but I cannot take you with me.' I wanted them to blame someone other than myself. 'Monsignor forbids it. You are at an important time in your training. It would do a lot of harm if you were to leave the conservatoire at this time. I will take you home as soon as Monsignor says it is alright to do so. I promise I will go and see your families myself and tell them how well you are doing. Would you like me to help you write a letter to your Mama and Papa?'

'There is no point, signore. They cannot read.'

I kicked myself for my tactlessness and for raising their hopes, only to immediately dash them.

We separated then for the night and I left early the next morning, Davide bringing my horse at first light. I took with me an image of their doleful faces, Fabio's eyes brimming with unshed tears, Roberto's teeth clenched.

We rode hard and fast, being unencumbered by a carriage or two convalescent boys. We arrived at dusk on the third day, saddle sore and dusty, but both pleased to be there, though for very different reasons. Whilst Davide took the horses to the stables I went directly to il Conte's study, keeping alert en-route for any sight of Eleanora. I was disappointed.

Il Conte greeted me with a firm hand-shake and a tight smile at my dishabille.

'It is good to see you, Philippe, though I would gladly have waited a few minutes more for you to rinse the dirt from your face and to change your attire.'

'Apologies, *mio signore*, I wanted to let you know as soon as I was back. I have sorely missed being at your side. And la Contessa? How is she faring?'

'She is as well as can be expected. Where are the boys? Did you leave them with their families?'

'Ah. I have a letter here from Monsignor Mazzini explaining why he would not allow me to bring them.'

Il Conte held out his hand and pursed his lips. 'So, Philippe, you take orders from a Jesuit priest rather than me, do you?' He opened the envelope and quickly read through the letter. '*Capisco*. He confirms what you say in your reports, that they are learning well and he is pleased with their progress. He thinks to take them out of the conservatoire now would be detrimental to their development. He suggests we listen to them when we are in Florence; he says they will be part of a choir singing in the cathedral in a month or so. *Bene*.'

He looked me up and down. 'Go and get tidied up before supper. We have a lot of work to do over the next few weeks. I want to make sure that this place continues to run smoothly and profitably whilst we are in Florence.'

I took special care to scrub myself clean and to dress well for dinner, all for the sake of Eleanora. I was, however, disappointed again.

For the next two days il Conte and I were either locked in his study poring over accounts and legal documents, or riding around the estate, visiting all the vineyards and checking up on their managers. As we rode through Montalcino on the second day, I remembered my promise to the boys to visit their families, a promise I kept later that evening.

I walked down from the Villa De Lorenzo, it being only a thirty minute stroll, and I entered the outskirts of the village as the men returned from their day's work. I made my way to the house I had gone to all those months ago. I felt the cold stares of the villagers and heard the sound of whispered curses and of gobs of phlegm hitting the dust.

The boys' families lived next to each other in rough, stone buildings of indeterminate shape; it was difficult to see where one stopped and the other started. There were some new looking buildings that, by the smell emanating from them, housed goats. I assumed that these had been built with the gold I had handed over to them in exchange for their sons. I aimed for the doorway of the nearest building, trying to avoid stepping on the dusty, scrawny chickens that seemed to consider my boots as a source of food. I stood in the doorway looking into the room, waiting for my eyes to adjust to the gloom. There was a hubbub of noise as children raced round the rooms, shouting at the top of their voices; two women chattered together as they prepared the evening meal; two men groaned as they relaxed in their chairs after a hard day's labour. Gradually the noise diminished as they all stopped what they were doing and stared at me, even the baby who had been crying for attention. The silence was just becoming awkward when one of the women came towards me, still wielding the knife she had been using to slice the vegetables.

'Signore? Can we help you?'

'*Buonasera signora*. I am Philippe Agostini. I ...' Before I could say anything more, one of the men lurched to his feet and strode over to me. He was still wearing his smock that was stained red with the juices of the grapes. It looked like blood.

'You! You are the one who took our boys!' I recognised him as being the spokesperson on my previous visit.

'*Buonasera*. I did not take your boys without your consent, signore. You agreed to sell them to il Conte and yes, it is I who accompanied them to Florence. They are doing well, if you are interested?'

The woman with the knife was joined by the other, her sister surely, so similar were their looks. They both spoke at the same time. 'Oh, signor Agostini, are they really alright? Are they eating properly? Are they being well looked after? Can they still sing? Can we see them?'

I held up my hand to stop the barrage of questions. 'One at a time, please. I will tell you everything if I may be allowed to sit down?'

The man who had approached me, either Roberto's or Fabio's father, continued to look at me suspiciously whilst the woman with the knife frowned at him, pushed him aside and led me to the chair he had just recently vacated.

Everyone, men, women, children, gathered around me as I told of the boys' journey and their life in Florence, avoiding mention of the details of their operation, the deaths of Luigi and Il Barbiere, and especially of Roberto's abuse by Father Stephen. I finished by saying that I had not been able to bring the boys home but that they sent their fondest love to their mothers and their respect to their fathers, at which the two mothers openly wept and the two fathers glowered and cleared their throats.

I left soon after, having promised to give their love to the boys and to bring them home for a visit very soon, the latter I suspected I would not be able to keep.

It was a lovely evening, still light and warm enough to remain outside for a few hours more. I didn't want to return to the Villa; I still hadn't seen Eleanora and I didn't think this evening would be an exception. I decided to go for a walk and took the first path out of the village and up the side of the hill. The track went alongside a small stream that chuckled at my ungainly movements as it nimbly leapt from stone to stone on its way down to the sea. After half an hour I was sweating with the effort of climbing what was now a steep, rocky path. There was a large copse on the other side of the stream that looked cool and inviting. I looked in vain for a bridge to cross. The rivulet was not very wide - perhaps the length of one man - and the water didn't even reach to my knees, so I took off my boots and started to wade across. I was only half way when my feet slipped from under me on the mossy stones. I lost my balance and fell heavily, dropping my boots into the water and hurting my backside as well as my masculine pride.

By the time I had pulled myself onto the opposite bank I was soaked from head to toe. At least there was no-one to witness my embarrassment. Taking advantage of my isolation, I stripped naked, rung out my britches and shirt and lay them out on the grass, hoping to dry them at least partially in the heat of the dying sun. I was facing the wood and standing with my arms open wide, letting the evening breeze waft over my damp skin, when I heard the rustle of leaves and the snapping of twigs.

I had almost convinced myself that it was just a goat or a deer when I caught a glimpse of red moving away from me, further into the wood. No animal that I knew of had red hind quarters. I suddenly felt very exposed, vulnerable and embarrassed. I quickly pulled on my still damp clothes, put on my wet boots and ran into the trees, determined to catch up with the voyeur to give him a piece of my mind. I kept my focus on a tree near where I had last seen the patch of cloth. There was no path, however, and I had to make my way round thickets of brambles and trunks too close together to squeeze between. After about ten minutes I acknowledged to myself that one tree looked very much like any other and I was no longer sure whether I was even going in the right direction.

I lost my desire to chastise and turned to go back but realised I didn't know where back was. I cursed my stupidity at racing into an unknown wood without marking my route. I tried to peer through the trees but could see no lightness that would signify their boundary. During my pointless chase dusk had fallen and I could not even see well enough to identify a broken twig to indicate the direction I had come from. I felt a wave of panic. I am not a coward but the thought of spending the night alone in a wood filled me with dread. I suddenly became the little boy who had scared himself half to death having read a tale of the *lupo mannaro*, the half man, half wolf who came out at night and devoured naughty boys.

The silence was broken by a long howl.

Chapter 13

Revelation

My inclination was to run away from the sound but suddenly there came a muffled voice from behind me, '*Silenzio*, Pepe!' a command that was immediately obeyed. I turned and peered through the darkness, trying to see who had spoken. I called out hopefully, '*Ciao*, is anyone there?'

There was no verbal response but a rectangle of brightness suddenly appeared just a short distance away. I walked towards it, hardly noticing the thorns that tore at my clothes and skin. As I neared, I realised that a door had been opened and someone was standing on the threshold but all I could see was a black silhouette. I was overcome with relief, not sparing a thought for what sort of person might live in such an isolated location.

'I am so glad I have found you, signore, and I apologise if I have disturbed you, but I'm afraid I find myself lost in this wood. I would be most grateful if you could point me in the right direction to get back to Montalcino.'

The shadow spoke and I was startled to hear the voice of a female. 'You are a fool to be out in the woods once the sun has gone down. I suppose you had better come in.'

She shut and barred the door firmly behind me then stood facing me. She was the same height as me, tall for a woman, and her eyes glared directly into mine. She was past her prime and her tanned skin had the beginning of lines around her eyes and mouth. Her expression was one of scorn with no glimmer of warmth and I felt awkward and unwelcome. Nonetheless, I was determined to maintain the social niceties, so I gave her a short bow. 'Philippe Agostini at your service, signora, secretary to Count De Lorenzo.' I waited for her to introduce herself.

She continued to glower at me, then shrugged dismissively. 'I know who you are. And it is signorina.' Her voice was deep but though her accent was uncultured it had the pleasing lilting quality of the hill people. She brushed passed me and took a seat by the fire. A little tan and white terrier followed at her heels and eyed me suspiciously.

'And you must be Pepe, you have a very loud howl for such a small dog.' I bent to stroke him but withdrew my hand immediately as he faced me, his hackles raised and teeth bared, a low growl emanating from his throat. The woman spoke a few quiet words; the dog looked balefully at me for a few seconds more and then curled up at her feet.

'Don't just stand there, sit down. He won't bite, not unless he thinks you are going to hurt me.'

I walked tentatively to a chair on the other side of the fire and sat down, my eyes never leaving those of the terrier. 'Why on earth would I wish to harm you, signorina?'

'Men are violent by nature.'

'Not all men, signorina. Why did you invite me into your home if you feared me?'

She scowled at me. 'I didn't say I am frightened of you. I merely said that Pepe is very protective and will attack if he thinks anyone is going to hurt me.'

I did not feel the conversation was going well. 'Please, signorina, I assure you that I am most grateful for your hospitality and it is I who am at your mercy.' It was warm by the fire and I noticed steam rising from my still damp clothes. The woman took a shawl from around her shoulders and put it on the back of her chair. It was red.

'It was you spying on me by the river! You are the reason I ran into the wood and got lost.'

She gave a throaty laugh. 'How typical that you think you were the reason for my being there. These woods are my home and I come and go as I please. I wanted to gather some watercress from the river but your presence there prevented me. I recognised you from la Contessa's description of you.'

I felt my cheeks redden when I realised that she had seen me naked. I shook my head in confusion. 'La Contessa? Why would she describe me to you? I don't understand.'

'No, signore, there is a lot you do not understand. Are you hungry?'

I was confounded by the sudden change of subject, but I realised that my stomach was indeed complaining at the lack of food. I nodded but asked again, 'Why has la Contessa been discussing me with you?'

She ignored my question and went over to a large table that stood in the centre of the room. There was hardly space for her to work, so cluttered was it with pans, piles of herbs and roots, different sized bowls and jars, and countless empty bottles. The glass reflected the fire and candlelight and something stirred in my memory, but I couldn't quite take hold of it. I studied the woman as she poured out two mugs of wine and broke off chunks of bread. She wore a plain green dress that didn't quite reach the floor, revealing bared, dirty feet. The hem and the seams were frayed and the skirt was threadbare in places. Her copper-coloured hair was left loose and hung in a tangle of unkempt waves almost down to her waist. When she handed me the victuals I noticed her hands were rough and engrained with dirt. She then took the lid off a large pot that hung over the fire. A most delicious smell wafted out and my stomach growled in anticipation.

All the while she maintained a stony silence that I was loathe to break, so we ate with only food passing our lips. I took the opportunity to study my surroundings. It was a large square room with one corner curtained off, where, I assumed, she slept. There were baskets full of roots, vegetables and flowers on the earthen floor and herbs drying from every rafter. The only other piece of furniture was a dresser bearing a few non-matching bowls and plates. Every wall was lined with shelves that were laden with green, blue, brown and clear bottles of every size and shape. Each had a label marked with a symbol, whose meaning I was not able to determine and each contained a liquid that shimmered, making it look as if the stars had come inside for the night. I suddenly remembered Roberto's and Fabio's account of such a room.

'You're *La Strega*! The boys told me about you.'

She looked at me, her black eyes full of anger and she almost spat her words at me. 'No! My name is Sofia. The inquisition may be a thing of the past, signore, but there are still ignorant people who fear what they do not understand and resort to mockery and abuse. I live alone, as my mother did, and her mother before her, and I make use of God's gifts to heal. I do not read the stars; I do not speak in a secret language; I do not get rid of evil spirits by sorcery; I do not make magic potions that will make someone fall in love, grow a beard or drop down dead and Pepe is not my familiar. Those who take the time to know me realise that I am merely a simple woman who can help ease the pains caused by hard work, poor diet and child-bearing.'

'I apologise, er, Sofia. The boys did say you made them very welcome and gave them refreshments.' I remembered the little glass bottle that had prompted the boys telling me of their visit. 'If Fabio were here, he would make you an abject apology.'

Sofia raised her eye-brows.

'Fabio loves shiny things and he told me that one of the little bottles was glittering in the sunlight and before he knew what he was doing, he took it for his collection.' Her expression became even grimmer. The loss of a bottle was obviously of far more consequence than I had supposed. I tried to reassure her. 'It was only a small bottle, signorina, and it was empty. Please accept my apology on his behalf, he is not a bad boy and meant no harm. I will willingly pay for it.'

'Phht! I don't need your coin, signore. Did he say where he took it from?'

I tried to recall what he had said but it had been many months ago and much had happened since. 'No, I don't remember but he showed me the bottle.'

'Describe it exactly.'

'It fitted in the palm of my hand and it had a glass stopper that fitted very tightly and was shaped like a teardrop. The glass was clear, and it was empty. That is all I can remember.'

'Are you sure it was empty? Did it have a label?'

I closed my eyes, trying to visualise the scene. 'I am sure there was nothing in it, but I don't think there was a label on it. Maybe it fell off.'

Sofia bit at her lip and then shrugged. '*Non importa*. And the boys, are you happy with your role in the ruination of their lives?'

I felt angry at the accusation. 'Il Conte did not force the parents to give up their sons. He offered them money and they accepted. They could quite easily have refused.'

'You think so? Have you seen how these people live? Do you really think they would not have grabbed at the chance for a better life for themselves and for their sons? Did you explain to them what exactly would be done to the boys, how their lives would never be the same again, how they would be expected to perform at the whim of others, how it is not God who demands this sacrifice but a rich fool who wants to impress other rich fools? Was this explained to them? Was it?'

She was shouting at the end and I shouted back. 'No! It was il Conte who promised them all a life of fame and riches, not me! I am merely his secretary and do as I am told. I looked after them as best as I could.'

Her lips curled in contempt. 'Try telling that to Luigi's family. And will you be there when the reality of what has been done to them hits Roberto and Fabio? When they realise that they can never have a normal life, get married, have children? What will you be able to do for them then?'

I opened my mouth but closed it again. She was right and was only saying what I felt. I said nothing, though; I wasn't going to admit anything to her. 'I have seen how the families have made good use of the money. In fact that is where I was before I took a walk up the hill.'

Sofia shook her head sadly, 'But at what cost to the boys? There is not enough gold in the world to compensate for what they have lost.' She topped up her own and my wine. 'Eleanora told me about how it was her story that started this whole sorry state of affairs. She should learn to control her prattling tongue.'

I was angry at her criticism of my beloved. 'Take care, signorina, how you speak of your betters.'

Her lips twisted in a sardonic smile. 'We doubtless have very different opinions as to who my betters are.'

I had no desire to argue with this woman, especially one whose dog didn't take his malevolent eyes off me. 'How is it that you have la Contessa's ear?'

'She has been coming here since she became a young bride. She was but sixteen when she married the Count, who, as you know, was almost twice her age.'

'Yes, I was working for il Conte when his first wife, Regina, died giving birth to Isabella, and when he married Eleanora just a year later. She was very young and frightened and she turned to me for advice and friendship. So, why did she need to come here?'

Sofia's mouth twitched. 'There are some things no man can give advice on. My mother was recommended to her by one of the servants and she came at first for medicines to ease her monthly pains, then to make her more fertile and then to try and prevent the miscarriages that she had suffered.'

'She didn't tell me about any miscarriages.'

'No, well, I think you will find there are quite a few things she hasn't told you. Anyway, over time she looked on my mother as if she were her own. When Mama died, Eleanora continued to visit and we have become like sisters.'

I found it hard to imagine the elegant Eleanora sitting in these squalid conditions and sharing all her intimate concerns with this unrefined, uneducated woman.

Sofia seemed to read my thoughts. 'I may not have any skills that so-called society recognises, but Eleanora knows she can trust me and I will always be honest with her. She values my opinion, apart from when I disagree with her, of course.' She paused for a moment. 'One of the things we don't agree on is you.'

'Me? What do you mean? What has she said about me?'

She looked at me reflectively as if wondering whether to tell me. 'She *says* that she loves you.'

'I know she does, and I love her. What started out as friendship soon turned to love. Il Conte is a soldier and does not know how to handle a woman such as Eleanora.'

'And you do?'

'Yes, we discuss books, paintings, nature and love. Il Conte talks only of horses, war and money. She deserves more and I know I can give her the life she yearns for. We are going to go away once I have saved enough money for a fresh start. I just need a bit more time.'

'Ah, signor Agostini, time is something you no longer have.'

'What do you mean?'

'She has not told you?'

115

'Told me what? For goodness sake, what are you talking about?'

'Eleanora is with child. She seems to be managing to hold onto this one.'

I felt as if I had been kicked in the stomach by the hind leg of a horse. I felt the blood flood to my face and then drain away again, leaving me feeling quite faint. Sofia handed me my wine which I gulped down in one, whilst I tried to put my thoughts together. Eleanora had promised me that she was no longer having relations with her husband so the baby must be mine. This is not how we had planned it, but it need not change anything; we would just take the child with us. My child. I felt myself smiling and repeated the words out loud, 'My child.'

'It may indeed be your child, signore, but then again it may not.' She waited for a few seconds for this seed of doubt to be planted. 'Can you give it as good a life as the Count can?'

'I know I will never have as much money as il Conte, but I have a skill that many men will pay good wages for. So, I will be able to give them both a good life and I will take great care of them.' I averted my gaze and stared into the fire, unable to look her in the eye. 'You say it might be the Count's child? How can that be? I thought ....'

'Ah, again Eleanora's version of the truth is not always the same as the reality. The Count did not force himself on her; he is her husband and has his rights that she is quite happy to provide. She did not want to upset you by telling you that they were still sleeping together. She says the child is yours, but she probably says the same to her husband.' Sofia paused as if to allow her words to sink in. 'Eleanora

116

enjoys being a countess and the many privileges it brings. How sure are you that she really will give all that up to live with you? It doesn't matter where you run away to, you will never be able to climb far up the social ladder. You will be living a lie, quietly and soberly; that is not Eleanora's style.'

If Sofia had been a man I would have hit him for being so disrespectful but all I could do was clench my fists and grind my teeth. 'You don't know Eleanora at all! She knows how we will live and she is willing to give up all the fripperies for her love of me.'

'You are fools, both of you. Eleanora is dishonest and fickle, whilst you are idealistic and naive.'

I stood up angrily. 'You go too far!' She continued to sit, the dog bared his teeth, growling menacingly and I, feeling foolish in my anger at this woman, sat back down again. 'You think she should stay with il Conte, although she doesn't love him?'

'There are many sorts of love, signore. She may not love him in a romantic way but she loves the life he can offer her. This baby is the chance for them to be a proper family. You should allow them that chance.'

'What about my chance to have a proper family?'

'You should choose a woman who is not already married, signore. Now, I will show you the way out of the wood to a path that will take you to the village.' She stood up and put the shawl around her shoulders. She thrust a lighted lamp into my hand and strode across the room to the door, unbarred it and walked out into the night, whilst I was still struggling up from my seat.

I had to run after her in order to catch her up. She didn't acknowledge my presence and walked purposefully onwards with no hesitation in her step, the little dog bounding at her heels. It took but a few minutes to reach the edge of the wood and for her to show me the path that the bright moonlight revealed as a pale meandering line drawn on the dark hillside.

She took the lamp from my hands and without a word of farewell disappeared back into the wood; the only indication of her existence being the disappearing glow and the rustle of leaves that could well have just been the wind - and the seed of doubt she had sown in my heart.

Chapter 14

Gloria a Dio

I finally saw Eleanora the next day. I was just returning from the stables having given il Conte's instructions to Davide and I caught a glimpse of her as she disappeared through a gate. I looked around to make sure that no-one was watching but everyone was going about their normal business and none seemed to be interested in me. I sauntered over the lawn and, with one final check that there were no inquisitive watchers, slipped into the sanctuary of the walled rose garden. She was strolling along one of the pebbled paths, bending every now and then to smell the blooms. She was dressed all in white and protected herself with a lace parasol. She seemed to shine in the bright sunlight and I would not have been surprised to see wings sprouting from her back, so angelic did she look. She turned slightly and I saw the evidence of her pregnancy. Her stomach was beautifully curved, mirrored by the roundedness of her full breasts. I felt a wave of adoration wash over me, so intense that I gasped.

She must have heard me for she turned and, seeing who it was, gave a beatific smile that made my toes curl and my organ harden. Without having to say anything we both walked towards a bower that was a favourite trysting place of ours. She was seated when I arrived. I knelt before her, took her hands in mine and kissed them over and over again; my heart wanting to burst out of the constraints of my body, so great was my joy at seeing her after such a long absence.

119

'Oh, Philippe. Get up off the ground; you will dirty your britches.'

I laughed at her pragmatism and sat down beside her, still holding her hands tightly in mine. Now that I was close to her I could see dark smudges under her eyes, and her skin, always pale, was almost translucent. 'My poor, Eleanora, you are not bearing our child with ease.'

She looked at me, searching my face for an answer to an unasked question.

'I got lost in the woods yesterday evening and happened upon Sofia's little hideaway. She told me. She made it quite clear what she thinks of me, and what she thinks you should do.' I took her chin and turned her face to mine. 'She said you cannot be sure if the baby is mine.'

A tinge of pink touched her cheeks but was gone in an instant. 'Oh, Philippe, I know it is yours. But Carlos is my husband and if our love was to remain a secret I had to keep up the appearances of being a wife, you do see that, don't you? I told you a white lie by saying that we were not having relations. I don't love him, Philippe; it is you I love, and it is our love that has created this child. You do believe me, don't you, my darling?' She placed my hand onto her stomach; all I felt was the tightness of her rounded belly.

The bile rose in my gorge at the thought of il Conte taking his pleasure with my fragile, beautiful Eleanora. I answered her by kissing those sweet lips and wiping a tear that was slowly trickling down her hollow cheek.

'He keeps his distance now, of course, so I no longer have to suffer his advances. But he is being very attentive and seems to be looking forward to having another child.'

'But he won't be having another child, will he? If we can't go before the birth then we will be gone soon after, won't we, Eleanora?'

She gave a little sigh. 'Yes, of course, my darling. As soon as I am recovered and the baby is robust enough, we will leave. I need to go back to the villa now; I am tired. I am always tired.'

I stroked Eleanora's belly. 'You need to take care of yourself, and Eduardo.'

Her laugh was like a wind chime swaying in a gentle breeze. 'So, you have already decided it is going to be a boy? What if it is a girl, what then?'

'I will still love her, of course I will. I have always liked the name Francesca. Eduardo or Francesca, do the names please you?

'Sofia says that we need to wait until the baby is born; we will only know its name when we have seen its face.'

'Sofia this and Sofia that. I don't like that woman. At least in Florence she will not be able to impart her unwanted words of wisdom. You go back to the villa; I will follow in a few minutes.' I watched as she swayed down the path and my stomach clenched in love and fear in equal measure.

I saw Eleanora only a few more times over the next few days, and always in the presence of il Conte. On the day I was to return to Florence in order to make sure that the new villa was ready for the family's arrival, I managed to catch her alone in the library. Il Conte had gone to his study to fetch some papers for me to take and we knew we only had a few minutes before he came back. We clung to each other as if it were the last time we would ever see each other. I stroked her back as she tried not to cry but I released my hold on her in amazement as something prodded me in my stomach. 'What the ...?'

She laughed at my confusion. 'He is saying goodbye to you in his own way.' She looked towards the door and took my hand quickly and moved it over her belly, following the little foot that was moving about inside.

'It is indeed a miracle, is it not, Philippe?' We both jumped at il Conte's voice, neither of us having heard his entry back into the library, so engrossed were we. 'Miracle or not, remove your hand, Philippe.' I hastily pulled away apologising for my temerity in touching his wife in such a personal manner. I thought I saw a flash of anger in his eyes. He handed me the papers. 'We will see you in a couple of week's time. I am thinking of throwing a party a few weeks after we have settled into the new villa. I want the boys to sing. Tell Monsignor I will not take "no" for an answer.'

They walked with me to my horse and waited as I rode away. I turned for one last look. The sight of him with his arms protectively around her shoulders and her leaning into him made me want to go back, tear her away from his arms, throw her onto the back of my horse and take her away for ever. Instead, I waved and walked on, my jaw clenched and my hands grasping the reins too tightly.

Once they were out of sight, however, I managed to push my jealousy to the back of my mind. I relaxed and started to enjoy the journey back to Florence, which was leisurely and uneventful. On the third day I passed through a village fair and spent an enjoyable hour walking around the stalls, savouring the sights, sounds and smells. I bought some cooked chicken, and a loaf of bread to eat later that night. Whilst pushing my way through a crowd I instinctively took a piece of paper that was thrust under my nose by an unseen person. It was an inexpertly printed pamphlet; I glanced at the title and slipped it into my pocket for later scrutiny.

That evening I reached the deserted village we had stopped at on the initial journey and I decided to spend the night there again. The autumn evenings were getting chilly, so I lit a fire and, once I had satisfied my hunger, I took out the pamphlet. I was intrigued by the title 'Enquiry not superstition: why the Jesuits must be stopped,' and I wanted to see whether I agreed with the anonymous writer's opinions on the subject. It was not a well presented thesis and the printing was of such poor quality that some words were illegible. Even so, I found myself nodding as I read through his arguments. It appeared that the writer had read the same books that my tutor, Niccolò Vasco, had encouraged me to read. The pamphleteer also questioned the Jesuits' excessive wealth, political influence, if not interference, and their unconditional support of the Pope, to such an extent that they were referred to as the 'Pope's sword arm.' I agreed with the conclusion that they belonged to the traditional past and that their ideology was inhibiting free intellectual enquiry and the growing demand for secular authority, as opposed to one imposed by the Papacy.

Many of the pages were taken up with an all-inclusive attack on the looseness of the Jesuits' morals and their lack of self-discipline, as well as their unaccountable wealth, which he wanted distributed to the poor forthwith. My only real experience with the Jesuits was my time working at the conservatoire. It was not my choice to take on the role of teacher; over time, however, my antagonism towards everyone and everything Jesuit-related had mellowed into an understanding and tolerance of the individuals I had grown to admire. Father Guiseppe and Brother Marcus, in particular, were two of the most gentle, kind and spiritual men I had ever met. I counted them, as well as Monsignor Mazzini, as some of my closest friends.

Father Stephen had been the exception and, despite what the pamphleteer inferred, I was certain that such men were not confined to the Church. The pamphlet ended with a description of a new school in Florence, to be run by secular scholars from all around Europe, who would teach all branches of knowledge in an unbiased and rational methodology. He wrote in large letters that Maria Theresa herself, the Grand Duchess of Tuscany, had contributed towards the setting up of the school. I wondered whether music would be taught at this new school, and whether boys like Fabio and Roberto would be welcomed.

I arrived at the Villa Bouganville early the next morning and spent the next few hours chivvying the servants into action. There was little left to do until the trunks arrived in a few days' time, followed soon after by the De Lorenzo family itself. Late that afternoon, once the sun had lost its fierce heat, I went into the city to do some business with the banker, signor Rossi, who was used by both il Conte and Monsignor Mazzini. Once we had finished, I agreed to his suggestion to share a meal at a new tavern that had just opened nearby. He was a short, rotund man in his fifties, who insisted on wearing a jacket far too tight for him, and a bright red cravat around his neck that he used almost continuously to wipe the sweat from his brow. He wore a pair of glasses that were prevented from slipping off his button nose by matching red ribbon tied round his ears.

The tavern was called '*All'ombra della Duomo*' and it was indeed in the cathedral's shadow, making it a cool and inviting place to sit outside and watch the Florentines go by. We chatted amicably whilst we waited for our food and drink to be served. It was during the silence enforced by our eating that I heard a sound that made the hairs on the back of my neck stand on end. It was singing, but of such purity and clarity that the notes seemed to cut through the air like a sharp knife through paper. I had heard beautiful singing at the conservatoire, of course, but somehow hearing it on the streets of Florence whilst eating mutton stew seemed incongruous and uncanny.

My companion saw my interest. 'That will be one of the boys from the conservatoire. They often sing outside of the cathedral whilst younger boys beg for money.'

I was shocked. 'The boys beg? That is not right, surely? I know il Conte pays handsomely for the two boys he is sponsoring.'

'Not all the boys at the conservatoire are lucky enough to have generous benefactors and anyway, sponsorship is not enough to keep the school running. The boys have to hand over everything they earn, whether it is from an official engagement or not. Monsignor Mazzini is constantly bemoaning the lack of funds.'

The singing continued whilst we ate and after we parted I decided to go and see who it was; it wouldn't be Roberto or Fabio as I knew that they wouldn't be allowed to sing in public until they had been at the conservatoire for at least a year. I recognised the singer immediately; it was Vincent, who had befriended the boys and taken them under his wing. He was standing on the steps, his eyes closed and seemingly effortlessly producing the sound of an angel. I stood with the small crowd who stood enraptured and joined in their loud 'Amen,' after Vincent had ended his song of praise on an impossibly high note. In an obviously well rehearsed routine, before the crowd could disperse, a number of small boys darted amongst us, begging bowls thrust out, heads bowed, repeating the same words, over and over again, '*Gloria a Dio, Gloria a Dio.*'

I didn't condone the begging but everyone else seemed to be contributing and I didn't want to look churlish. It was only once I had put a handful of coins into the bowl and had received a whispered, '*Grazie, signore,*' that I looked at the boy.

'Fabio?'

Chapter 15

The plan

Everyone turned at my raised voice. I grabbed his arm and pulled him to the side. 'What are you doing here? Is Roberto here as well?' Fabio nodded. Before I could call out his name, I felt a warm little hand clutch mine.

'Oh, signor Agostini, you are back! We did not see you at the conservatoire. Did you visit Mama and Papa? Are they alright? Did you tell them all about how we are doing? How Father Guiseppe says our voices are the best he has ever heard? '

I could not help laughing at the barrage of questions. I sat on the cathedral steps, released my grip on Fabio's arm and patted the warm stone. They sat on either side, Roberto still holding my hand.

'I only got back this morning. I am staying at the villa at least until the family move in. Yes, I saw both your parents, *and* brothers and sisters *and* aunts and uncles; all are quite well. I told them about your life at the conservatoire and how Father Guiseppe thinks you both sing like nightingales.' I felt Roberto stiffen. I squeezed his hand. 'I told them all the good things, none of the bad. They miss you, of course, but I think I reassured them that you are happy here and doing well. They are all very proud of you and grateful.'

'Grateful?' they both asked in unison.

'Yes, grateful. They have used the money il Conte gave them to build new shelters for the animals, to buy more animals, to enlarge the houses to give everyone more room.'

We sat in our own bubble of silence, broken only by the occasional sniff. We sat whilst the crowd finally dispersed and the other boys, having glanced curiously at us, had returned to the conservatoire.

'Right, come on, you two. I'll walk back with you. I want a few words with Monsignor.'

'Are you cross with us, signore?' Roberto looked up at me, his brow furrowed with worry. 'We were just doing as we were told. All the younger boys have to go out and collect money, until they are old enough to sing themselves. There is no harm, surely? The people like the singing and are happy to pay.'

I kept my thoughts to myself until I had returned them to the conservatoire and I had found Monsignor to be in his room. 'You waited until I had gone before throwing my boys out onto the streets to beg? To beg? Does il Conte not pay you enough?'

Monsignor ignored my outburst. 'Welcome back, Philippe. Take a seat. Would you like a glass of wine? I have just had a new case delivered, it is very good.'

'Paid for from the proceeds of begging? No thank you!'

Monsignor sighed. 'The case was a gift from the Grand Duchess herself. She is a great supporter of education, if not of the Jesuits.'

I remembered the pamphlet I had read the previous evening. 'I have heard there is to be a new school here in Florence, one run by secular staff. Does this worry you? Perhaps she will transfer her support to them?'

Monsignor sighed again, a sigh that seemed full of disappointment. 'I am a religious man, not a political one. I don't understand what has changed, but I hear more and more that we Jesuits are now being held up in contempt rather than respect. Only the other day, Prince Ferdinand, one of the Grand Duchess's little lap dogs, told me to my face that we were too independent of the rule of those we are meant to serve. I had to bite my tongue; but I longed to tell him that I serve only God and His representative on earth, the Holy Father.' He shook his head sadly. 'We seem to be blamed for all the ills of the world but all I want is to continue with my calling, which is to educate these poor boys and prepare them to use their God-given voices to praise Him. So, until told otherwise by our Holy Father, I will stay here and do just that.' He twirled the wine in his glass, drank it in one and then slammed it onto the table. 'Unfortunately, all this,' he waved both arms in a wide circle, 'all this costs money, which I am finding harder and harder to find each month, hence the need to send the boys out onto the streets.' He gave me a wry smile. 'But I won't send Roberto and Fabio out again, if that is your wish.'

I felt torn and confused. On the one hand, I believed that the Jesuits in general did have too much power, too much wealth and were well over-due for a good shake up. On the other hand, I had nothing but admiration for the man sitting opposite me, and for all the other priests who gave up their lives so that others may have better ones. 'Maybe we can agree on a compromise? I would prefer that they earned money rather than begged for it. I know that normally they would not be allowed to sing in public for another year or so, but as Father Guiseppe is constantly telling me how good they are, perhaps they could be an exception to the rule?'

Monsignor looked unblinkingly at me for a full minute, but I could tell he wasn't seeing me. 'They are very young and inexperienced, but we can see how they handle themselves at the next opportunity - something small and one where any mistakes will not be noticed. Perhaps you could be there to give them some support?'

'I would be happy to, just give me some notice. Il Conte has also requested that they sing at a soiree he will be giving a few weeks' after they have settled into their new home. He won't pay, of course, but it will be good practise for them.'

Our conversation drifted onto general topics and we parted as good friends once again, both mellowed by a few glasses of the excellent wine. As we shook hands, Monsignor asked whether I would be able to return to my teaching post, even if only occasionally. I was surprised to realise that I rather hoped il Conte would allow me to.

It was the hour in the evening when the boys could relax so I went in search of Roberto and Fabio before leaving to return to the villa. I found them seated on the ground, along with the other *castrati*. I sat with them for a while, their strangeness never ceasing to surprise and intrigue me. Even sitting down, the difference in the older boys' appearance was marked. Although an observer could not easily see that they were a good head taller than their contemporaries, their unusually long necks, free of an Adam's apple, and the plumpness of their thighs and upper arms could not be missed. Some, including Vincent, had what can only be described as breasts adorning their rounded chests. None of them had any facial hair; whilst their peers were beginning to compare the immature growth on their upper lips, these boys' faces were completely nude. I knew it would be just a few years more before I would see these changes in Roberto and Fabio's bodies.

The most obvious difference, of course, was their voices. Not for these boys the embarrassment of their voices breaking at inopportune moments. No, for them their voices would remain, and ever would remain, like that of a child.

I liked these boys and knew that most of them had at least a chance of a better life here; if they had stayed with their families they would never have had anything to look forward to other than hard labour and never-ending poverty. Maybe, because I was of their number, they were not taunted or disturbed in any way by the *integri* and they chatted contentedly together for the remainder of the recreational period. When I left I had to smile at the sight of Vincent with an arm around my two boys, all of them giggling. I wished Sofia could have seen them.

I had been back in Florence for a week when the bulk of the family's baggage arrived, followed a week later by the family itself. It took another week for them to be fully settled: il Conte to ensconce himself in a study whose furniture had to be rearranged a number of times until he was satisfied with the view from every perceivable angle; the books to have been placed on the library shelves in the correct sequence according to my own indexing system; the pictures to have been hung on the right walls; the gardeners to have reorganised the tools; Eleanora and I to have discovered a few places where we could be together in

131

private. I had dreamed of rowing her down the river to find somewhere totally secluded where we could make love, but that was out of the question now.

I saw her only infrequently; each time I was concerned at her pallor and air of total exhaustion. She tried to reassure me that it was just the result of the move and that she would be well soon. We spent what little time we had together holding hands, kissing, marvelling at the life she bore within her and dreaming of our future together. She was due to give birth, according to the witch Sofia, in early January, about three months away and Eleanora said she would probably be ready to run away with me three months later. Eleanora never ceased to thrill at hearing me explain the plan and always wanted me to repeat the details.

'We will wait for your husband to go away to Rome on his annual visit. Every year I have worked for him he has gone in April, which suits our plans perfectly. I will pretend to be sick and suggest I join him in a few days time, when I am feeling better. He won't want to delay his departure so he is bound to agree. A couple of days later, you will say that you have decided to join your husband and take the opportunity to visit your parents and show off Eduardo.'

'Or Francesca,' Eleanora interrupted.

'Indeed, or Francesca. I will have miraculously recovered from my mysterious illness by then and offer to escort you. So, everyone will think we are on our way to Rome, but in fact we will make our way to Livorno, where we will be able to book a passage to Corsica. You are certain that your family there will welcome us?'

'Oh yes, Philippe. As you know, cousin Tommaso often writes to me care of another member of the family. This time, knowing I am now living in Florence, he wrote to cousin Carolina, who came to visit this morning and brought the letter with her. I have it here.' She handed me a single sheet of paper, covered on both sides with a flamboyant hand. I skimmed over the family news and focussed on the bit that was pertinent.

As to you staying in a tavern until you find somewhere to live, we won't hear of it! Maria and I will be more than happy to accommodate you and Philippe here for as long as necessary. As I said in my previous letter, we have just managed to get rid of the Genoese, and we now have a ruler called Pascquale Paola. He is an incredibly patriotic and intelligent man and already he has made some significant reforms, all for the better for the Corsicans. These are exciting times and I am sure there will be a job for Philippe in the new administration. I look forward to meeting you and your husband. Let me know when you think you will be arriving in Corsica.

'What a very amenable man he sounds. Why does he say he is looking forward to meeting your husband? It sounds as if he thinks we are married. You have told him about Carlos, haven't you?'

Eleanora looked sheepish. 'I told him Carlos was an ogre and died in a duel, leaving me penniless, and that you married me out of love. I wanted him to feel sorry for me and to agree to help us. It is easier if they think we are married, especially as we will have a child.'

I remembered Sofia's barbed comment about us having to live a lie and I felt the seed of doubt she had planted beginning to take root. But talking of the future had brought a sparkle to Eleanora's eyes and a slight colour to her cheeks and I didn't want to be the one to disenchant her. She soon paled again, however, at the sound of her husband's voice.

'Eleanora, where the devil are you? Eleanora?'

We both sat as still as one of the marble statues that adorned the gardens, then Eleanora fluttered her hands and began to stand up. She would have to answer him within just a few seconds and I could not be there when he joined her. We had been sitting under an old, gnarled olive tree whose outstretched branches gave us shelter but also over hung the wall that divided this bit of the garden and the river. Without giving it a further thought I clambered up the tree, along one of its branches and dropped down over the wall and out of sight. The landing was soft and noiseless, save for the squelching noise as the sticky earth sucked me in up to my ankles. I dared not move and had to stand listening to il Conte gently chastising his wife for not telling him where she was and for being outside without a parasol. Meanwhile, the mud seeped into my boots and I sank deeper and deeper into the mire.

A man passed me by, rowing a boat full of grapes just harvested. He gave me a toothless grin and winked but did not offer to help me out of my predicament.

Chapter 16

Every picture tells a story

It was il Conte himself who enabled Eleanora and I to see each other openly and with reason. The morning after my encounter with the muddy banks of the Arno, he called me into his study. 'Philippe, as I mentioned before, I want to throw a dinner for a few select people in about four weeks' time. If I am to succeed here in Florence then I have to make my face and name known to those who have the right sort of influence. I want you to send out invitations. Here, I've made a list.'

He handed me a sheet of paper. I scanned the fifteen or so names, recognising some: the Grand Duchess; Prince Ferdinand, her sycophant; the Prince of Saltzburg, whose villa the De Lorenzo's had recently stayed in. A few of the others I had heard mentioned by the gossip-mongers as I was walking about the city. It is an unfortunate fact that the more influence a person has, the more liable they are of having their private lives secretly dissected and mocked by the people they have influence over.

'You will need to find out the names of their spouses, if they have one, otherwise their *innamorata*.'

'What if they don't have either?'

Il Conte gave a humourless smile. 'They will all have someone they can bring. La Contessa is not strong enough to arrange a dinner of this size and importance. I need you to do most of the work, but you must seek her advice, especially regarding the menu; she is far more skilled at choosing the right combination of foods and wines than

135

either you or I. And Philippe, arrange with Monsignor for the boys to sing. Something serious and impressive, mind you, not some folk song.' As I turned to leave he added, 'I want this to be a success, Philippe. Don't let me down.'

So, it was that the next few days were spent in writing and delivering invitations, making sure the gardeners could provide sufficient blooms to decorate the rooms and table, and booking additional staff to cook and serve. I visited the conservatoire to ask Father Guiseppe to select a group of boys, which had to include Roberto and Fabio of course, who were capable of singing something 'serious and impressive.' Best of all though, I was able to sit for long, glorious hours in the rose garden with my beloved, ostensibly discussing the arrangements for the dinner. Once I had given her an update on the previous day's tasks and added new ones that she dictated to me, we were able to talk of other, more intimate things.

One of the first things Eleanora had told me to do was to arrange for a dressmaker to attend to her, in order to measure her for a new dress, necessitated by her condition and by il Conte's desire for her to outshine the other women. On the day signora Turati arrived, I escorted her to la Contessa's chambers. I was not allowed into the rooms but I decided to stay close by in case I was needed. I took advantage of the time to review the, by now, very long list of tasks. I had managed to cross a few off, but these were an insignificant number compared to those still to be done. As I considered what to do next the door to Eleanora's bedchamber was suddenly flung open and signora Turati rushed out, her eyes wide in terror, shouting, 'Help her, help her!'

Others heard but I was the first to rush in, disregarding protocol. My Eleanora was collapsed on the floor, like a puppet whose strings had been cut, dressed only in her undergarments and a tape measure that lay over her legs like a snake. She looked frighteningly pale. I knelt by her side and shook her by the shoulders in an attempt to rouse her. Her body remained limp and in a panic I slapped her cheek. I heard a gasp behind me. There was a sheen of sweat on her forehead and her breathing was too shallow, the swell of her bosom barely rising over her stays. Although her corset had been adjusted to accommodate her swelling belly, I was certain that it needed to be removed so that she could breathe more freely. I had undone her laces many times before, taking my time and enjoying her moans of pleasure as her body was slowly released. Now, though, my fingers fumbled in my haste and I cursed in frustration. There were more gasps behind me and I turned angrily to the crowd that had gathered. 'Don't just stand there wringing your hands and tutting, someone get this contraption off her, she needs to be able to breathe properly.' I recognised one of Eleanora's maids and pointed at her. 'You, get your mistress some water and smelling salts.' No-one moved for what seemed seconds but then the maid bustled off to do my bidding and signora Turati knelt beside me and deftly loosened the laces.

It was the smelling salts that finally roused her. Eleanora looked around wildly, taking in her surroundings, the people crowded around her and finally her state of undress. It was signora Turati who suddenly realised the impropriety of me still being there and whispered to me, 'You should leave signore. It is not right that you see la

Contessa like this.' I tried to catch Eleanora's eye but she was being helped up by one maid, whilst another covered her near nakedness with a robe.

I felt obliged to tell il Conte. He paled when I told him of his wife's collapse and rose to his feet as if to rush to her side. I assured him that she seemed to be recovered and she was being looked after. Il Conte sat back down, his concern evident in the deep lines that furrowed his brow.

'She is not carrying this baby well, Philippe. She still has three months left; she needs to rest with no exertion whatsoever.'

'Should we cancel the dinner? Perhaps it is too much for her?'

'No! You are managing everything aren't you? Carry on with what you are doing and just make sure you don't make any further demands on her. This dinner is important.'

That afternoon I had arranged to visit the conservatoire to hear the boys who Father Guiseppe had selected to sing at the so-important dinner. I hadn't been there as a teacher for a month but I still felt at home when I stepped through the large wooden door, out of the light and into the shadowy interior. I made my way to the music room; by now I was able to step into the space and immediately isolate and appreciate each sound. I no longer just heard a babble but instead could pick out a boy singing a scale and holding the top note for as long as possible, another trying to emulate the trill of a song bird, yet another repeating a cadenza over and over. Others were copying music onto their slates to practise later on, older boys helping the younger ones.

Then I heard a choir of angels.

There were five boys, all *castrati*, standing in a circle around Father Guiseppe, who was turning round and round, his eyes closed, nodding and smiling as each boy's voice beset his eardrums. They were singing *Ubi Caritas et Amor*, whose first line of every verse starts with, 'Where charity and love are, God is there.' This was a clever choice by Father Guiseppe that il Conte would consider particularly appropriate to himself and whose inference would not be lost on the dinner guests. I was familiar with the words but it was as if I was hearing it for the very first time. Although Roberto and Fabio sang purely and sweetly, the other *castrati*, who were older and whose bodies had therefore changed, produced a sound that had a deeper resonance and quality that made me shiver, despite the warmth of the room.

Roberto stumbled on a word and Father Guiseppe held up his hands to stop them. 'No, no, no! Not only Roberto, but all of you *must* know the words perfectly. Il Conte is a much-valued sponsor of the conservatoire and we are depending on you to give a good impression and show that his charity is not wasted. Now, go away and learn the words until you can say them forwards, backwards and sidewards. We will practise again tomorrow.'

As they left Roberto grinned at me but Fabio looked downcast and embarrassed at his cousin's failure. I winked at him but only received a pursed lip in response. Father Guiseppe shook my hand and his head. 'It is asking too much of them, too soon. My fear is that they will forget everything at the crucial time and revert to being village urchins. They are nightingale fledglings, too young to leave the nest and their wings are not developed enough for them to fly.' He rubbed his hands over his face, as if trying to wipe away his worries. 'Perhaps I should add more boys to the group. That way it won't be so obvious if either Roberto or Fabio forgets the words or simply dries up. Yes, that's what I'll do.' He went off muttering to himself.

I went in search of the boys and found the whole group sitting under an olive tree. The older ones chanted a line at a time, whilst the two younger ones repeated it. They all looked miserable. When they had finished I asked if anyone knew what the words meant. The older boys did but Roberto and Fabio shook their heads.

'It will be easier to remember the words if you know what they mean. I'll translate it for you:
Where charity and love are, God is there.
Love of Christ has gathered us into one.
Let us rejoice in Him and be glad.
Let us fear, and let us love the living God.
And from a sincere heart let us love one.

Where charity and love are, God is there.
At the same time, therefore, are gathered into one:
Lest we be divided in mind, let us beware.
Let evil impulses stop, let controversy cease.
And in the midst of us be Christ our God.

Where charity and love are, God is there.
At the same time we see that with the saints also,
Thy face in glory, O Christ our God:
The joy that is immense and good, Unto the
World without end. Amen.

Roberto, Fabio, come with me. We'll go for a walk and I'll help you learn your words.'

The older boys looked relieved and smiled at me, their round faces nodding in unison. I led my boys out of the conservatoire, along the road and down to the river, where we sat and chatted amicably for a while. I remembered how they had loved to swim, so I suggested they strip off and take advantage of the mild weather. They both shook their heads. I must have looked puzzled for Roberto explained, 'If anyone sees us they will jeer at us and throw stones.'

'But no-one will see you once you are in the water.' They both shook their heads stubbornly so I didn't pursue it but I was saddened to think that this was something else we had taken from them.

'Alright, let's see if I can help you remember these words. Let's take each line and understand what it means. What I do, when I am trying to learn new words, is to paint a picture in my head that tells me what the words mean. A number of pictures tell a story, which is far easier to remember and somehow that seems to help me remember the words as well.' I could see that they didn't understand. 'The first line means that God is there when charity and love is present. Roberto, what comes to your mind when I say these words? See if you can describe the scene in your head.'

Roberto tilted his head and considered. 'I think of the poor soldiers who have lost legs or arms and who beg outside the cathedral. Father Guiseppe always puts money into their caps. That is charity, isn't it?'

'Excellent, Roberto. Now keep that scene in your mind. The second line says how God's love gathers us all

141

together. Fabio, your turn. Can you think of a picture that would show that?' Fabio blushed and looked down, shaking his head.

Roberto bounced up and down. 'I know. Think of us all in church every morning. We are all gathered there to praise God, who loves us.'

'You have the idea, Roberto, well done. Do you see Fabio? We have the beginnings of a story. On the way to church you pass a limbless soldier and Father Guiseppe puts money into his cap because he is being charitable and loving and doing God's work. You then all gather in church because you want to rejoice in Him and be glad, which is actually the third line.'

It took an hour for the more creative Roberto to envision a story that matched the words of the hymn and whose sequence was easy enough for them both to remember. We then went back to the Latin and repeated each sentence whilst imagining the relevant part of the story. I don't know whether it really helped but by the end of our time together both boys could repeat the whole hymn faultlessly. Their pronunciation was far from perfect but after more practise I was convinced they would improve. Most importantly, I had spent time with them which had done my soul good.

Evening was drawing in so I said my farewell to the boys, they to go to the refectory and me to return to the villa. The gate in the outer wall was always locked so I rang the little bell to summon the porter. He was an old man, his back bent as if he were carrying a heavy load. He was completely bald and his skin was burnt almost black, creased and loose over his bones, with no flesh in between.

He always gave me a grin when he saw me, revealing his pink, toothless gums.

When I had asked Monsignor about him he had shrugged. 'We don't know anything about him. He knocked on the gate over thirty years ago. He was wearing a habit and had a tonsure, albeit almost grown over, so we assumed he was once a monk. His clothes were filthy and ripped, as was his whole body. He didn't speak whilst we fed him and bathed his wounds, and afterwards, when we asked him what had happened, he opened his mouth and showed us that his tongue had been ripped out.' Monsignor had paused for effect. 'He apparently couldn't write either so he was not able to tell his tale. We tried asking him questions with a "yes" or "no" answer, so that he could just shake or nod his head, but he became extremely distressed so we stopped, and never started again. The Monsignor at the time made some enquiries but never found any information about him. He was asked if he wanted to go to a monastery but he shook his head and so he stayed here. We called him Pietro. He obviously can't teach but he does odd jobs and makes an excellent porter. The boys love him.'

As Pietro shuffled towards me I noticed he was carrying a piece of paper, starkly white against his black habit. He handed it to me; it was a note from Father Guiseppe.

R and F will be part of a choir attending a funeral tonight. Can you be there to support? Join us now for supper.

G

I put a small coin into the monk's hand and walked back to the conservatoire.

Chapter 17

The vigil

I had always enjoyed the last meal of the day: the prayers chanted wearily by the boys and priests alike, the sense of a day finished and a new one to come, the anticipation of some free time. After supper, I joined Father Guiseppe as he led a group of boys to one of the small rooms that led off from the main entrance hall. He unlocked the door and came out carrying a pile of surplices. Before handing them out he asked for silence.

'Now, this is the first time some of you are going to attend a vigil and funeral, and that includes signor Agostini.' All eyes swivelled to look at me, as if they had to remind themselves who I was. 'At all times you must remember why you are there. Frances, why is that?'

Frances looked startled but then repeated, 'To be as one of God's angels at the side of the departed, to pray for his soul and to praise God in His mercy.'

'Good. Remember that the family is grieving for the loss of a loved one and to them you are not individual boys but rather like the candles, the hymn books and the chalice, you are tools to be used in the service of God. Now, put these on.'

Each boy slipped on the pristine white surplices with a frill around the neck and a deep red sash over the left shoulder. Despite their different heights and colourings they were all transformed into cherubs and I had to look carefully to distinguish Roberto and Fabio. Father Guiseppe then handed the boys a candle each. He lit a taper from one of the large candles that illuminated the hall, and touched the wick of each smaller candle, intoning a blessing as each flame took hold and flickered in the draught.

The priest put each boy in a line according to his height, my boys being at the front, then clapped his hands and waited for them to set their faces into a serious expression. He led them out of the hall, across the courtyard and through the gate, which Pietro had already opened. Once on the street he started a chant that the boys joined in; a quiet mantra thanking God for the day and asking Him to keep them safe through the night.

Darkness had fallen and the candles cast shadows on the boys' faces and dancing sprites on the walls. Father Guiseppe led them slowly down alleyways until he came to a small church. Even before we got there I heard the high pitched keening of the professional mourners and I knew that the deceased came from a wealthy family. The priest headed the line of boys as they continued down the aisle but suddenly the boy at the front stopped, causing everyone behind to stumble into one another. I realised that it was Roberto but before I could go to him to see what the problem was, Father Guiseppe had retraced his steps, patted Roberto's cheek and whispered something into his ear. Roberto looked around for me, then at his feet, then into Father Guiseppe's eyes. He nodded slowly, straightened his back, held his head high and walked forwards, the others following. I kept to the side to avoid interfering with the ritual and when I got nearer to the front I understood what had distressed Roberto.

The body in the open coffin was that of a child; she could only have been about three years old. She was dressed in a white frock, ornately decorated with gauze and lace. She had her plump, pink arms crossed over her chest. Even from where I stood in the shadows I could see that her lips and cheeks had been coloured red to cover the pallor of death. Her black hair was spread out on a white lacy pillow and flowers were sprinkled on the locks. The smell of incense concealed any smell of corruption there may have been.

The mourners stopped their wailing and left, whilst the boys made a circle around the coffin, with Father Guiseppe standing at the head. Their singing changed from one of thanks to one of lamentation as they asked God to take the child's soul and give comfort to her family. I sat in a pew where the boys could see me and I could see if any of the candles needed replenishing or if one of the boys needed to go outside to piss.

Despite the discomfort of the hard, wooden seats I managed to doze and dreamt of Eleanora floating on her back in a river, flowers scattered over her naked body and in her hair, a sweet smile on her lips, her eyes closed. Even though it was my dream I didn't know whether she was sleeping or dead. I woke with a start when Father Guiseppe touched me on my arm.

'The vigil is over, Philippe. The family are here and we must now accompany the body to the burial site. Then we can go back to the conservatoire and have a hearty breakfast.'

The family were grouped to one side, the women weeping loudly, the men trying not to. The boys had

146

stopped singing and the local priest said a prayer whilst just two men lifted the tiny, white coffin, now closed, onto their shoulders and carried it slowly down the aisle. The boys followed, singing once again, their voices hardly heard over the grief-stricken wails of the mother and grand-mothers. I genuflected as the cortege passed, waited until they had all left the church and then followed at a discrete distance. It was still early in the morning and the sun had only just risen. There were not many people about but those that were stopped whatever they were doing, crossed themselves and bowed their heads until the procession had passed.

We walked for about fifteen minutes, climbing gently until we reached a cemetery on the side of the hill that overlooked Florence and the river Arno that glistened as it snaked its way through the city. It was a cool, serene place with the yew trees casting shade over the eternal sleepers. There were gravel paths meandering between the headstones and we followed one that continued to slope up until we reached the summit, on which stood the crypts of the wealthy. I made myself a mental note to suggest to il Conte that he should construct such an edifice if he wanted to be respected by those of influence.

I waited outside as the body of the child was entombed in marble; the boys sang of the hope of resurrection and I mused on my parents. My mother was buried in a simple wooden coffin in the graveyard of the village church, along with her own parents and siblings. My father was not far away but on the other side of the wall in an unmarked grave, although I knew exactly where he lay. I hadn't visited them since I had left to work for il Conte some eight years ago. I felt a yearning to pay my respects to them and I promised myself that I would go at the next opportunity, certainly before Eleanora and I left for Corsica.

Father Guiseppe finally herded the boys out, whilst the family remained; how hard it must be to leave one's daughter alone in such a place. The boys looked exhausted but pleased with themselves. Father Guiseppe reminded them to remain decorous so they maintained their line and walked quietly back to the conservatoire, where they gladly removed their surplices, which had become inexplicably grubby.

We had missed the normal breakfast time but food had been kept for us. The boys sat together and Father Guiseppe and I sat at another table. I asked him how my boys had done.

'Very well, very well. After the initial shock of seeing it was the body of a young girl they carried out their duties very well indeed. I knew it was a child, of course, but I decided not to tell the boys so that they didn't worry about it beforehand. Maybe I should have said something before we entered the church. Poor Roberto nearly fainted, but he recovered himself.'

'Are they allowed to go to bed for a few hours? They must be tired, as you must be, my friend.'

'Ah, no. We do not have special treatment; it is our duty and joy to serve God in such a way. Mind you, the teachers do give them some lassitude and will tolerate the occasional yawn.'

'I thought you would like to know that I have tried to help Roberto and Fabio learn their lines for the party piece.

They could remember them all by the time I left them yesterday evening.'

'Ah, good. They already knew the words we sang last night; they are simple and very repetitive. The ones they have to learn, the party piece as you call it, is far more difficult and I do wonder if it is perhaps a bit too complex.'

'Remember that il Conte wants it to be serious and impressive; I suspect that will only be achieved with something that is complex. Let me know how they are doing; I am more than happy to come again to help if you need me to.'

I took my leave soon after and made my weary way back to the Villa Bouganville in time for a second breakfast with il Conte. I told him where I had been and suggested he might like to consider purchasing a family vault. He gave me a wry look.

'You are not wishing us dead are you, Philippe?'

Only you, I thought.

'Of course not, *mio signore*. I merely thought that it would add to your standing in the community.'

I managed to see Eleanora a few times over the next weeks but only for a few minutes and I asked for no further advice, not wanting her to exert herself in any way. Her condition was more and more evident and she complained about her tiredness, the baby keeping her awake as he explored the dark cave in which he nestled. I tried to reassure her with knowledge I had gleaned from books. There was a library in Florence that had been founded some fifty years ago and had been open to the public for the last decade or so. One of the keepers told me that they housed over six million volumes, including the latest books on pregnancy and childbirth.

'It is good that the baby moves, it shows he will be active. Remember how I said that to begin with he is as small as a pea and he grows steadily over the months? There is nothing to be frightened about, my darling; God made a woman's body to give birth.'

Eleanora's expression was of horror and she looked around to see if anyone had heard me. 'Ssh, Philippe! It is not right that you know so much about the workings of a woman's body. And it is alright for you to say not to be frightened, but I am. Look at the size of me. You say my body is made to give birth, but in God's name, how? It will tear me apart, I know it will. I just can't do this, Philippe.'

I took her hand. 'Oh, my poor Eleanora. I don't know how women do it, but they do, all the time! It is the most natural thing in the world.'

'Isabella's mother died giving birth to her.'

'But that doesn't mean the same will happen to you. In fact, it is most unlikely to happen again just because it *did* happen then.'

I wasn't sure my logic was sound, but it seemed to reassure her a little.

'I wish Sophie could be with me for the birth. I think I will ask Carlos to send for her.'

'The witch? Why on earth do you want her here for? You will have the best Florentine doctors looking after you. They won't tolerate the witch and her meddling.'

'We'll see, Philippe, we'll see.'

Chapter 18

One step up the ladder

I was not invited to the dinner as a guest, naturally, but I was in the background, making sure everything was running smoothly. I had hired a herald to announce each guest as they arrived, his splendid black, red and gold uniform outshining those of many of the princes and dukes.

I stood in the shadows of a recess in the hallway as the guests arrived. I watched as the maids removed their outer clothing and then ushered them to the entrance of the salon, where their names were proclaimed in a loud, ringing tone that rebounded off the walls of the hallway. Il Conte and la Contessa then greeted them and exchanged a few polite words, after which they disappeared from my sight, but from the sound of voices and clinking, I knew that they would be mingling with the other guests and enjoying a glass or two of il Conte's best *vino*.

From my standpoint in the shadows I had a good view of Eleanora. My first sight of her had taken my breath away, so exquisite did she look. She wore an ornate dress with a hooped skirt that hid her condition, as if it were something to be ashamed of. The material was a heavy golden silk, embossed with leaves and embroidered with flowers bedewed with pearl drops. The material fell to the ground in beautiful, deep pleats, from the scooped neckline that accentuated her rounded breasts, to her tiny feet, decked in golden slippers. Around her neck she wore a cluster of rubies hanging from a thick gold chain; a wedding present from her husband. I remembered that Sofia had told me how Eleanora loved the material benefits of being married to a count but I blocked out the memory.

Eleanora's face was even whiter than normal and although the dark smudges under her eyes had been concealed, I knew she was exhausted. Not for the first time I wondered if the baby, our baby, was draining her of her blood, of her vitality. For a moment I wished she wasn't pregnant but then instead I felt a surge of anger towards il Conte for insisting she attend this ridiculous dinner, held purely for his own social advancement. I was distracted for a while by the arrival of Father Guiseppe and the choir of *i castrati*, which he had increased in size to seven. They would not be singing until after the meal, so I took them to the kitchens and asked one of the maids to make sure they were given a decent meal. She was flustered and looked as though she was going to refuse. I slipped a coin into her hand and gave her what I hoped was an encouraging smile and, although she still looked harassed, she consented. I left them tucking into a selection of meats and poultry, vegetables, cheeses and fresh bread.

When I returned to my recess the door was closed; all the guests must have arrived and were now being courted by il Conte. I went back to the kitchen and sat with the boys but I was too tense to eat anything myself. I took great pleasure in watching Roberto and Fabio look around in wonderment as the chefs rushed from stove to stove, tasting the consommé here, prodding a huge joint of pork there and making sure the vegetables were *al dente*, as il Conte liked them to be. The cooks under them raced from pot to table to oven back to pot, carrying out the shouted orders, the sweat pouring down their faces and undoubtedly adding seasoning to the food.

When the boys had finished eating, Father Guiseppe asked if they could go somewhere to practise for one last time, so I led them to the music room. I took them up the back stairs and along candle-lit corridors. As we turned one of the corners I saw a glimpse of the hem of a pink nightdress. I guessed that Isabella had been peeking at the guests and was only now sneaking back to her bedroom. I left Father Guiseppe and the boys to their preparations whilst I returned to Isabella's bed chamber. I tapped on the door but got no response.

'I know you are awake, Isabella. I just saw you running down the corridor. I'm not cross but I thought you might like to come and hear the boys singing. They are only practising but I would like to know what you think of them.'

I heard light footsteps, then the door opened and Isabella stuck her head out.

'You won't tell Papa that I was up?'

'I won't say anything, I promise.'

She put her hand in mine and we made our way to where the boys were singing, their voices muted by the intervening walls and doors. When we entered the music room they stopped and all eyes turned to see who it was. Father Guiseppe smiled when I introduced Isabella and bowed to her.

'Wonderful! Now we have a proper audience. Please be seated, signorina, and we will sing for you.'

We settled ourselves and the priest raised his hand then brought it down as a sign for the boys to start. How can I describe something that was so sublime, so hauntingly beautiful? I closed my eyes and had a vision of a mist of sound coming out of the mouths of each boy and slowly drifting upwards, whereupon each droplet burst, showering those of us below with notes that hovered in the air, in perfect harmony with each other. I was greatly moved and I glanced at Isabella and saw that she had tears in her eyes. She was the same age as my boys but already seemed to appreciate that these *castrati* were special.

When they finished there was a moment's silence then Isabella and I clapped enthusiastically and appreciatively, whilst the boys blushed and grinned, and Father Guiseppe nodded contentedly.

'Are we good enough, Isabella? Do you think your father will be satisfied? Signor Agostini, what say you?'

We could only nod and smile, words seemed inadequate.

I went to congratulate the boys and Isabella followed me. I introduced them all to her and then picked out Roberto and Fabio. 'These two are cousins and are protégés of your father. They used to live in Montalcino but now live in a conservatoire here in Florence.'

The boys were too embarrassed to say anything but Isabella suffered no such inhibitions.

'Oh, I know you! You were singing at the wedding in the village earlier this year. I said to Papa that you sounded like angels, and you still do. You sang beautifully, Papa will be enchanted, I know he will. As will all the guests.'

I was proud of her diplomacy and told her I needed to get her back to her bedroom as the boys soon would have to sing before the guests. Much to the boys' surprise she gave them both a kiss on the cheek and then skipped away, leaving them looking both sheepish and pleased.

I wished them all good luck and then made sure Isabella returned to her bed. Whether the singing had awakened some emotion deep within, I don't know, but I felt a wave of love for her and having tucked her in, I planted a kiss on her forehead. As I turned to go, Isabella called out softly, 'Philippe? Why did the bigger boys look so strange and sing with such high voices, like women but different? Will Roberto and Fabio grow up looking like that?'

'Hush, Isabella. I will explain another day. Go to sleep now.'

Would I ever be able to explain why we had done what we had to the boys? Would she agree that the ends justified the means?

I suddenly felt exhausted and having shown Father Guiseppe where he and the boys should wait until they were called, and wishing them good luck again, I went to my room. I lay on my bed, staring at the white ceiling but seeing Eleanora sitting serenely on a chair in the shade of a tree, whilst I pushed a young child, an Eduardo or a Francesca, on a swing, all of us laughing happily. How I wished I could take Eleanora away right now, but I knew she was too frail to make the journey. No, we must both be patient and wait for the right time. Just five more months.

The next day il Conte called me into his study and shook my hand.

'Well done for arranging the dinner so well, Philippe. It went off magnificently and everyone complimented me on the event, especially the choir after the meal. They were truly magnificent and the Grand Duchess herself praised me for my patronage of the two youngsters. Then Prince Ferdinand asked if I would be interested in joining the court as an adviser. He didn't say an adviser of what but I have a good feeling that this will be my step up the ladder. People are beginning to take notice of me, Philippe, and to take me seriously.'

'I'm glad it has turned out as you wished, *mio signore*. Maybe now is the time for me to ask if you would agree to me working at the conservatoire again? I find that I enjoy teaching and am rather good at it. I can still carry on with my duties to you as your secretary, without detriment to either position.'

Il Conte considered for a moment. 'As long as your service to me always takes priority, then, yes, you may be a teacher of small boys for an hour or two a day. I will, of course, reduce your wages accordingly.'

I bit back a retort. I had no intention of asking for payment from Monsignor, I knew that funds were stretched to the limit. Il Conte had covered the cost before when I was doing his bidding, but now that it was my own initiative he was being unnecessarily niggardly. He knew full well that I would do the same amount of work for him as I had ever done. I needed to save as much money as I could in readiness for starting a new life with Eleanora and our child, but I could hardly admit that to il Conte.

'And how is la Contessa? Not too exhausted after last night, I hope?'

'She is indeed tired. I've ordered her to stay in bed for a few days and rest. I told her she needn't attend the dinner; that it would be too much for her, but she insisted. She said she couldn't let me down. She is a very dutiful wife. You should get yourself one, Philippe. Is there no pretty girl you have your eye on?'

I forced myself to grin at his teasing. 'Not yet, *mio signore*. Perhaps now we are settled in Florence I will find myself a good wife.'

The social niceties being over, we got down to some work for a few hours then I went into Florence to do some business. Whilst there, I took the opportunity to pay Monsignor Mazzini a visit. As was our habit now, we shared a glass of the excellent wine provided by the Grand Duchess.

'I thought I would tell you that il Conte has agreed to release me for a few hours a day so that I can continue to teach the youngsters, if you still want me?'

I waited for him to say how pleased he was, but he seemed embarrassed. I thought I knew the reason why. 'It is alright, my friend. I expect no remuneration. Il Conte will continue to pay me as normal.' How easily the lie came out of my mouth.

He smiled in relief. 'Then that is indeed good news. I am most grateful to il Conte for his continuing generosity. Now tell me, Philippe. Is it the act of teaching you enjoy, or being with Roberto and Fabio?'

'Both I suppose. I have surprised myself by how much I look forward to teaching all the boys their letters and their pleasure when they realise they are beginning to read and write. I admit, I also enjoy spending some time with my boys.'

We agreed that I would spend two hours at the conservatoire each morning. I saw no reason to tell him yet that I would be leaving in March or April the following year.

I soon established a routine. I no longer had the role of dormitory master, which I had been assigned when I first worked at the conservatoire and at which, I am the first to admit, I was not particularly competent. I chose to join them all at the early morning service and then breakfast, after which I took the lessons with the younger boys. It felt good to be back after an absence of a month or so and once I had chastised them all for not continuing with their studies, we soon picked up where we had left off and they remembered the letters and words I had taught them.

Monsignor had been very perceptive. I did enjoy being with my boys and I felt responsible for their welfare. I realised with a pang that I would be sorry to leave them when I went to Corsica. I had grown very fond of them and I hoped they of me. Maybe I was wrong to continue seeing them and I worried that they would not forgive me when I left, but I wasn't strong enough to keep my distance from them and break the bond.

I got into the habit of returning to the conservatoire during the evening recreational period and I sat with *i castrati* as they discussed their day and what the future might hold for them. It pleased me that my boys had settled in so well with this group; they would need them when I left.

It was some three weeks later when il Conte intercepted me early one morning as I was leaving for church. He looked pale and dishevelled, as if he had slept in his clothes, or hadn't slept at all.

'Philippe, thank God I have caught you. I need you to do something for me.'

'Of course, *mio signore*, anything.'

'It's Eleanora. She is getting herself into a nervous state. She says she can't feel the baby. I am certain I felt it move but she won't listen and is becoming hysterical.'

I physically flinched at the thought of his hands on Eleanora's belly, caressing it and feeling *our* baby move inside. Il Conte didn't seem to notice; perhaps he thought I was merely showing my concern.

'She insists a healing woman she befriended back in Montalcino is brought here. She says she trusts her and that this woman will know what to do, which is more than I do, Philippe. She won't let the doctors anywhere near her although I keep telling her that they are the best in Florence, in the whole of Italy. She is making herself ill and I am worried she will harm herself and the baby. Will you go and get this woman, Philippe?'

Chapter 19

Povero Papa

'But I know her, and in fact have met her. She is just a common woman who makes potions from roots and herbs. She certainly won't know more than the doctors. What if she doesn't want to come? She probably hasn't ever been outside of the village.'

Il Conte looked serious and stubborn. 'I don't care how good she is, or isn't. La Contessa wants her here and if it makes her feel more relaxed and less worried then that is all I care about. The doctors will still be here to make sure this woman does no harm. If she won't come of her own accord, then drag her.' He handed me an envelope. 'Here, Eleanora has written her a letter. Go now, so I can tell la Contessa that you are on your way and then maybe she will sleep.'

I wasn't happy about going on what I considered to be a fool's errand, but though il Conte had made it sound like a request, it was, of course, an order. I took nothing with me; I had clothes at the Villa De Lorenzo. There were horses there too, so we would have fresh ones for our return. I rode as fast as I dared and stopped only when it was too dark to see the road in front of me and restarted as soon as the sun cast its first rays over the sleeping world. I slept wherever I could find shelter, wrapped in a blanket, my saddle for a pillow. It was cloudy, cool and dry - perfect weather for riding. When I reached Montalcino, I didn't go to the villa but rode straight up the side of the hillside. I remembered the route I had taken when I had first come across Sofia. I rode past where I had so inexpertly crossed the river until I saw the entrance to the wood, which I now knew led to her cottage. I hobbled the horse and walked along the path.

She didn't hear me coming. She was crouched down feeding the chickens making a soft, clucking sound as if talking to them in their own language. I called her name and she turned, a look of surprise on her face, then a scowl, which seemed to be her perpetual expression.

'You! What do you want? Are you lost again, signore?'

'It is not I who want anything, signorina. It is la Contessa. She has need of you. Here, she has written you a letter.'

Sofia got slowly to her feet and looked at me angrily. 'Do you mock me? You know full well that I cannot read.' She put her hands on her hips. 'You must read it to me.'

I was reluctant to open the letter. 'It may contain something personal that it would not be proper for me to hear.'

Sofia laughed contemptuously. 'Ha! You have no embarrassment to enter her most private places and deceive her husband, but you are squeamish about reading words on a page? Get on with it, signore.'

So, I tore open the envelope and read the few lines out loud.

Sofia, my friend,

Please come to me as quickly as you can. I cannot feel my baby move and there have been drops of blood for the last few mornings. I am frightened. Please come and make everything well.

Your friend in need,
Eleanora, Contessa De Lorenzo

I read it again to myself, my stomach churning at the words.

'Is all this normal? For the baby to stop moving, for there to be blood? Is it, witch lady?'

She ignored my insolence. 'Sometimes the baby quietens down before the end, but she is not ready to give birth for a number of months yet. It might still be perfectly alright, though. Have you brought me a horse?'

'Not here, no. I need to get them from the villa. Can you ride?' She nodded. 'I'll go and fetch them whilst you put together whatever you need to take. I won't be long.'

Before I had even turned to go she had disappeared inside and I heard her banging about, muttering to herself. Within an hour I had collected two fresh horses and I was loading the panniers with bottles that Sofia handed to me, along with a bundle of clothes. I realised that I had forgotten to change my own whilst I had been at the villa.

'Why do you need so many bottles,' I grumbled.

'I don't know what is wrong, if anything. I need to be prepared. Stop complaining, they are not heavy.'

When she had finished packing, rather than mount the horse, she went back into the wood.

'Sofia, where are you going now? Do come on, we need to go.'

I couldn't see her by now, but I could hear her angry words. 'I am going to say goodbye to my animals. I have never been away from them before. They need to know what is happening, that they will be looked after and that I will be back soon.'

I waited impatiently and when she returned I almost threw her onto the back of the horse and led the way down, without either of us speaking further. Just as we were leaving the village she stopped, dismounted and disappeared into one of the rough houses. I restrained from screaming after her and when she returned just a few minutes later she was nodding. 'That's good. Her daughter will go and stay at my house and look after the animals until I am back. Come on, what are we waiting for, let's go?'

It was Sofia herself who suggested that, as the evenings were still quite mild, that we sleep in barns or sheltered spots, rather than having to find taverns. We spoke little throughout the journey, neither of us interested in each other, only in our own thoughts. Just five days after being sent on this mission, I was back at the Villa Bouganville, presenting Sofia to il Conte, who took her hands gratefully.

'Thank you for coming, signorina. My wife and I are indebted to you. Do you want to freshen yourself before seeing her?'

'No, Conte De Lorenzo, please take me to her straight away.'

Before leading her away il Conte turned to me and wrinkled his nose. 'Philippe, you need to go and bathe and change your clothes. Aren't those the clothes you left in?'

He didn't wait for my answer but took Sofia's elbow and led her towards his wife's bed chamber. After I had washed my body of five days' worth of sweat and grime and changed my clothes, I followed in their footsteps. I found il Conte sitting on a marble bench. He sat hunched forwards staring intently at one of the floor tiles. I almost felt sorry for him. I sat down next to him and studied the same floor tile.

'The signorina is with Eleanora now. *Dottore* Sacchi is also in attendance. They won't let me in there. She is my wife, Philippe, I should be with her.'

'It is not the way, *mio signore*. Husbands are superfluous at these times.' And lovers.

I shifted my concentration to a picture on the wall opposite; it was of the Virgin Mary holding the infant Jesus. She looked at me serenely, a contented smile on her face and I mouthed a prayer to her, asking her to keep my love and my child safe. The knot in my stomach, however, remained.

It was not long before the doctor came out, shutting the door quietly behind him. He remained with his hand gripping the knob facing away from us. He stood like that for what seemed an interminable period, before pushing his shoulders back and turning towards us, his face sorrowful.

'Conte De Lorenzo, it grieves me to say this but the signorina and I are in total agreement that the child has not survived.'

There were seconds of total silence as we both absorbed his words, then il Conte cried out, or perhaps it was me. I felt the bile rise in my throat and I had to put my hand to my mouth to stop myself vomiting. Il Conte stood up, his fist clenched tightly and I was worried he was going to punch the bearer of this awful news.

'How can you be certain? Are you sure?'

'There are ways of telling, signore, and the signorina and I are both quite sure.' He hesitated and took a deep breath. 'We need to get the baby out, or your wife will be in danger of losing her life also. I am so terribly sorry, signore, so terribly sorry.'

'No!' Il Conte shouted, 'No! You must save her. Do whatever you have to, but she must live. Do you understand, she must live!' His whole body shuddered and his voice fell to a hoarse whisper. 'I cannot lose another one.' He turned, his face frozen into an expression of total despair and he stalked out of the hallway.

I wanted to scream after him, 'It is *my* child, do you hear me? *My* child!' I wrapped my arms around my chest to prevent myself from falling into pieces.

The doctor was still standing there. 'It is noble of you to empathise with your master's grief, but you need to be strong. He will need you more than ever now.'

I don't know what made me ask, but if I couldn't be with her I wanted to know what she was having to go through. 'Does Eleanora, la Contessa, know that the baby is dead?'

'We have not told her. It is best if she thinks she is giving birth to a live one. The signorina is giving her a tonic of pennyroyal to induce the birth. This is going to be a very long night for everyone. Your prayers will help, signore.'

He re-entered the room too quickly for me to see inside, but I imagined my Eleanora lying in her bed on white satin sheets, her black hair spread out on the pillow. Sofia would be whispering words of comfort into her ear, whilst holding a cup of her poison to her lips. Oh, my poor Eleanora. What a terrible, terrible ordeal to have to endure and for what? For a dead baby. How would she cope with the grief?

I suddenly rushed outside and disgorged the contents of my stomach into the flower bed. I went into the kitchen to get some wine to freshen my mouth; all the kitchen staff looked solemn and there was none of the usual banter. News travelled fast.

How I longed to be with Eleanora. I would mop her brow, stroke her hand, tell her how much I loved her and how we would have more babies, as many as she wanted. I couldn't bear to be so far from her so I went back to my seat to keep vigil.

The screaming started some hours later, a primitive, bestial sound that made my hairs stand on end. I rushed to the door, but stopped myself just in time. If husbands were not allowed in, then certainly the husband's secretary would not be. Oh, my God! What agonies she must be going through. I paced, relaxing only slightly when the screaming stopped, but it was short-lived. I could hear murmurings from within, perhaps Sophia encouraging Eleanora, promising her it would soon be over, maybe even lying to her that there would soon be a baby for her to hold.

Mary, mother of Jesus, looked down and mocked me.

At some point il Conte joined me, pacing by my side.

'You need not stay, Philippe. There is nothing you can do. Go and get some rest.'

'I am here for you, signore. You should not be alone.'

So, we paced together, hands clenched behind our backs, treading the same tiles: red, white, black, black, white, red, over and over again. Then in the early hours, when night is at its blackest there was a final scream and then absolute silence. No slap, no baby's first howl.

Nothing. Then a yowl of pure anguish and denial, followed by great wrenching sobs that tore at my heart.

We both stopped in our tracks.

'Do you think I should go in, Philippe?'

Il Conte seemed to have grown smaller, uncertain of himself and what to do, how to behave. 'Not yet, signore, not yet.'

So, we restarted our pacing. I noticed il Conte wipe his eyes and I felt genuinely sorry for him. The door opened and Sofia came out, carrying something wrapped in a white cloth in her arms. Her hair was plastered to her head and her face was wet with sweat and perhaps tears. She held the bundle out to il Conte.

'It was a boy, signore. Would you like to see him?'

The man who had faced death as a soldier many times and who had been by the side of his men as they died from the most horrible wounds, could not bear to see the face of his dead son. He shook his head and quickly walked away to grieve in private.

Sofia looked at me, for once her expression one of compassion. 'Would you like to see him?'

I hesitated then held out my arms and she placed my son into them.

My son.

His lips were blue and his wrinkled skin was almost purple, smeared in blood and covered in soft down. I was relieved his eyes were closed; I could not have born it to look into his soul. I felt such immense sorrow and I could not stop the tears from coursing down my cheeks and splashing onto his. I wiped away the wetness, surprised at the warmth and softness of his skin.

'Are you sure he is dead? He looks as if he is just sleeping. Have you tried to rouse him?'

'He is dead, signore, I'm so sorry. Now, I must go back to la Contessa. She is bleeding heavily.' She took the baby off me and went back into the room.

Eleanora was bleeding heavily? That did not sound good. I restarted my pacing, praying over and over that she would recover soon. We would not have to wait so long now before we could run away. Oh, selfish man! How could I think of that when my own son was still lying in the next room? Eleanora would need time to grieve. We both would.

I heard raised voices from the bedroom; Dottore Sacchi and Sofia did not agree about something. Should I go in? Oh, how I longed just to hug Eleanora to my breast, to squeeze out all her misery and squeeze in all my vitality. I heard more sobbing, different from before and then the door opened and the doctor came out, head hung down, shuffling like an old man. He looked around and saw only I was present.

'Where is Count De Lorenzo?'

Before I could answer a voice came from the shadows. I don't know how long he had been standing there. 'I am here, Doctor. She has gone, hasn't she?'

The doctor nodded and began to explain but I didn't hear his words. She's gone? What did he mean, she's gone? Gone where? To Corsica? She wouldn't go without me. We were going there to live with Eduardo and I was going to work in administration and we were going to be happy!

I didn't stop to think; I just rushed into the bedroom, to Eleanora, who I was so relieved to see was just sleeping.

She was sleeping, wasn't she? She looked so serene, a gentle smile on her lips, her black hair as I had imagined it, spread out like a fan on the white pillow. She looked so beautiful.

'Wake up, my darling, wake up.'

I shook her gently, then more strongly as she failed to open her eyes.

'Signor Agostini, remember yourself. Beware of what you say!'

I looked at Sofia in confusion. She had trails of tears down her face; it must have been her I had heard sobbing at the end.

'She is gone, signore, We couldn't stop the bleeding and when she knew there was no baby, she just seemed to give up.'

'Did she say anything?'

'Not for your ears, signore.'

I felt the blood rush to my face but before I could say anything il Conte came slowly into the room, supported by the doctor. He stood at the foot of the bed, somehow looking both young and old at the same time.

'Leave us. Please, just leave us.'

We left and as I closed the door I heard dry, wrenching sobs that told of his loss and despair. He had loved Eleanora as much as I had.

I too needed to be alone with my grief. I left Sofia and the doctor standing in the hallway, ran out into the rose garden and threw myself onto the seat where Eleanora and I had dreamt our dreams, ignoring the dew that wetted my clothes. I wept as I had never wept before, not even at the death of my parents. The sun was just peeping over the wall, its beams lighting up the roses. Would such a sight ever give me pleasure again?

I suddenly felt exhausted. I staggered into my room and fell onto my bed and immediately into a deep sleep, a baby's chuckle and a woman's quiet laugh just beyond reach.

When I woke the sun was at its zenith and I lay wondering what I should do. In the end my sense of duty prevailed and I went in search of il Conte. There were things that needed to be done. I found him in his study. He obviously hadn't slept. Isabella was sitting at his feet. She was stroking his hand and her head was resting on his knees. When I entered she smiled at me sadly; il Conte didn't seem to notice me.

'*Povero, povero*, Papa.'

My mouth was bone dry and I had to force out my words. 'I offer my condolences, signorina Isabella. This is a sad, sad time for everyone.'

She was only eight and she had already lost two mothers.

'Papa is too distraught so I think I need to arrange the funeral. Will you help me, signor Agostini? I wondered if those boys would sing at the funeral. She would like that.' Her voice broke and she hid her face in her father's lap and sobbed quietly. As I left I noticed il Conte was stroking her hair.

Chapter 20

The return

Despite Isabella's faith in me, I didn't know what to do, so I went to see my good friend, Monsignor Mazzini. His smile of greeting disappeared as he took in my appearance.

'What has happened, Philippe? I got you message a week ago that you would be away, but you look terrible. What has happened?'

'They are both gone, Monsignor, Eleanora and our child. Gone. I prayed and prayed that they might live but He didn't hear me.'

Monsignor was quiet for a while, absorbing what I had said. 'Eleanora? You mean la Contessa? And your child, Philippe? She was expecting *your* child?'

The words came tumbling out. 'We were going to run away to Corsica when the child was born. It is, was, all planned. We loved each other, Monsignor, we truly loved each other and have done so for the last four years.' I put my head in my hands and sobbed as the sense of loss and what might have been threatened to overwhelm me.

Monsignor poured a couple of glasses of wine. 'Does Count Lorenzo know of this?'

'No! He thinks the child was his. Maybe it was, now we will never know. I held his poor lifeless body in my arms last night. The baby had apparently been dead for sometime and after giving birth la Contessa lost too much blood and died early this morning. Just a day ago we had our dreams to hold onto and now I have nothing, nothing and no-one.'

Monsignor looked at me sternly. 'The Count deserves our pity. He has lost a wife and he thinks he has lost a child, whose ever it really was. He lost his first wife in childbirth, didn't he, but the child lived?'

'Yes, Isabella. She is a sweet thing, the same age as Roberto and Fabio, but she has an old head on her young shoulders. She has asked me to help her arrange the funeral as she doesn't think her father will be able to. Oh, God! How can I arrange a funeral for my own love and son and hide my grief? I can't do it.'

Monsignor stood and came round to my side. I thought he was going to pat my shoulder in sympathy but instead he slapped my face.

'Philippe, control yourself. You have deceived everyone for the last four years so you can continue to deceive them for a bit longer. You must act as if la Contessa was merely your master's wife. You must never tell him that she was your lover and might have been carrying your child. You must never tell him that you were going to run away together. Do you hear me? You must never tell him; it would destroy him and he has done nothing to deserve that. What you did was wrong and now you must suffer alone and grieve in private. Do you understand?'

I was shocked at his anger and lack of compassion but I nodded. 'Will God forgive me? We loved each other so much, surely that cannot be wrong? God is love, he will understand, won't he?'

Monsignor sat back down and sighed. 'I suggest you pray for forgiveness and from this very moment live a righteous life. If you are truly remorseful, God will forgive you. Now, the funeral, I can help with that.'

By the time I left I had a list of things to do and I remembered with a pang the list Eleanora had helped me with just a few weeks earlier. When I returned to the villa I asked for the whereabouts of Sofia and I was told that she had left, taking the horse she had ridden from Montalcino. The next few days were filled with preparations for the funeral and I thankfully had little time to think, falling exhausted into bed each night, too drained to grieve.

Il Conte remained in his study. He didn't change his clothes, didn't shave, didn't sleep, didn't touch the food that was left in front of him. He looked haunted and although I had been going to steal his wife and child from him, I realised that I cared for him and hated to see him in such a state.

The evening before the funeral I went to the study but he wasn't there. I went in search of him and found him in the rose garden, our rose garden, sitting on our seat, a half empty bottle of wine in his hand.

'Ah, Philippe! Care to join me?' He thrust the bottle at me. I took it but put it on the floor, untasted.

'Signore, I speak to you as a friend, not as your secretary. This cannot go on. You must sleep, wash, change your clothes, eat and sober up. You cannot attend your wife's funeral in this state.'

He pouted as if he were a small child. 'I don't want to go to my wife's funeral.'

I crouched before him and made him look at me. 'I know, *mio signore*, but you must. Your wife and child are dead; nothing will change that. You could not live with yourself if you did not attend their funeral, did not say your final farewell.'

173

'How dare you tell me what to do? You have no idea how I feel.'

I did know how he felt but I could never reveal my true feelings to him. 'Of course I don't know how you feel. All I know is that everyone expects you to be at the funeral, and you can't go looking like this. Surely your wife deserves the utmost respect? What do you think she would say if you turned up in this state?'

His shoulders slumped. 'She would chastise me, wouldn't she? Oh, Philippe. I know I wasn't the husband she wanted and deserved but I loved her in my own way. Did I ever tell her? I don't remember, what if she died never knowing that I loved her?'

'You can tell her tomorrow. She will hear you.'

'She gave me new life after Regina died. She was too young really, but I think she tried to be a good wife to me and a good mother to Isabella. What am I going to do without her?'

He started to sob and I found myself sitting next to him, holding him close so that his tears wet my shirt, and mine his. 'I will help you through each day, *mio signore*, and each day will be slightly easier than the previous one, until one day you will be able to face the future alone. Until then, I will always be here.'

His weeping finally subsided and he pulled away, embarrassed. 'Forgive me, Philippe, that was weak of me. You are a good man and a good friend. You are right, I need to pull myself together for Eleanora, for Isabella and for myself. I thank you for your support and for arranging the funeral. You are a good man.'

I attended the funeral in body, though not in spirit. I can remember little and I don't want to remember more. I know the church was full of mourners; I know a choir of castrati, including Roberto and Fabio, sang as the coffin was carried into and out of the cathedral; I know the heat of the candles and the smell of the incense made me feel nauseous; I know Isabella shivered by my side as she cried for the only mother she had ever known and the brother she would never know; I know that il Conte stood as rigid as only a military man can, neither singing nor praying, all his energy focussed on staying in control.

Il Conte hadn't had time, of course, to purchase a vault so they were buried in a plot on the side of the hill overlooking the Arno. The trees were bare now but in spring they would be full of blossom and the ground would be dappled in sunlight. Eleanora was buried with our son in her arms.

I left with all the other mourners, leaving il Conte sitting alone by his wife's grave. I went into the city and drank all day in an attempt to obliterate all my memories and my dashed dreams, All I succeeded in doing was getting thrown out of every tavern and spewing into the street like a common peasant. At dusk I started to make my way back to the villa but ended up in the cemetery. There was no-one else there; il Conte had left so I lay by the grave of my lover and my son and wept into the newly turned soil.

The cold woke me. There was a full moon that peeped out from behind the clouds that raced across the sky as if late for some assignation. I imagined Eleanora lying asleep beneath me, holding our child, and I kissed the ground over her head and said my goodbyes.

Later the following morning, il Conte called me into his study. He looked haggard, but clean and sober; he didn't mention the funeral.

'I need to go back to the Villa De Lorenzo. There are things that need to be done. We will take Isabella, and I thought we might take the two boys along. Isabella was rather taken with them and keeps talking about them. She needs friends at the moment but hasn't made many here, and certainly none we can take with us. Tell Monsignor to release the boys for a few weeks. Tell him also to send a priest to make sure they continue with their lessons. Arrange it, please Philippe. I want to leave tomorrow.'

So, it was that we set of the following day, Isabella, Roberto, Fabio and Brother Marcus in the carriage with Davide at the reins, whilst il Conte and I rode our horses. The journey was slow, we were in no rush. We stayed at taverns each night; il Conte and Isabella taking rooms, whilst the rest of us slept in stables or outhouses. Even in deep mourning my master was still careful with his money.

The boys appreciated the need for seriousness but I could see their growing excitement at going home by the brightness of their eyes as they looked out at the passing scenery, and their constant whispering together. They became more and more agitated as we neared Montalcino and as soon as we entered the village I suggested to il Conte that we let them out. They leapt from the carriage and ran towards their homes, unable to resist yelling, 'Mama, Papa, we're home!' It was good to see their unrestrained joy and for a few seconds I shared it.

Having breakfasted the next day I spent a few hours with il Conte writing letters to relatives and friends informing them of the death of his wife and son. The cold words on the page did not reflect the emotion with which they were dictated and written. The letter to Eleanora's cousin Tommaso could never be sent, of course, and I burnt it in the grate in my bedroom. I would write my own later on, carrying on the pretence of my marriage to Eleanora and thanking him for his offer of hospitality.

Afterwards, I wandered down to Montalcino to pick up the boys for their lessons. I expected that I would have to go in search of them and drag them away from the loving arms of their families, so I was surprised to find them both sitting morosely on a stone at the outskirts of the village. I noticed that their shirts were dirty, as if they had been rolling in the mud and Roberto had a cut lip.

Before I could even ask what had happened, the boys stood up and started walking along the path I had just come down. They said nothing and didn't look back. It was when I heard one of them sniff that I quickly overtook them and stood in front of them, barring their way. 'What has happened?'

They looked at each other as if seeking permission to tell. Then Roberto spoke.

'Mama and Papa were pleased to see us at first. They hugged and kissed us and showed us how they had spent the money Count De Lorenzo had given them. We told them what life is like at the conservatoire and we had a lovely evening. Fabio and I slept together in the hayloft like we used to do. This morning we went outside to piss and one of my brothers asked to see where we had been cut. So, I showed him, why wouldn't I? And he brought others and they stood in a circle and stared, then jeered, then threw stones. They were our brothers and cousins and they laughed at us.'

Fabio chipped in, 'I saw Papa standing in the doorway. He didn't try and stop them. He wasn't laughing but he looked, I don't know, sad? No, not sad, more like ashamed. He had his arms out, stopping Mama from coming out. He just stood and watched as we tried to fight back. But we were two against eight and they were our brothers and cousins, signor Agostini! Why were they so cruel, why?'

This is why Monsignor Mazzini said he never lets his *castrati* return home within the first six years. 'Because, I'm sorry to say this about your family, but they are ignorant, and ignorance breeds cruelty. They don't understand what has happened to you or why, so they resort to being bullies. I am so sorry this has happened.'

I felt such anger. What had we done to these boys? They had lost so much and what had they, what had anyone really gained? As we neared the villa my anger grew and grew and I knew I couldn't sit and teach them their letters or watch them play ball with Isabella, so I left them in the care of the good Brother Marcus and went for a walk. I found myself ranting out loud about the unfairness of life, the selfish ambition of il Conte, the cruelty of the boys' families, the loss of my beloved.

Sofia, the witch! Why hadn't her potions worked? Had she given the wrong one? Had she in fact killed Eleanora?

Chapter 21

The need for forgiveness

Before I knew it, I was standing outside the witch's house, banging on the door and shouting, 'Open up *tu strega*! I know you're in there, open up!'

The door opened and Sofia stood, a spoon still in her hand from whatever concoctions she had been brewing.

'Why are you shouting, signor Agostini? I am not deaf. What's the matter?'

I pushed her out of the way and stormed into the house.

'What's the matter? What's the matter, you dare ask? Why, only that my son and my beautiful Eleanora are lying in the ground, rotting, because you meddled and failed!'

'I did not fail, signore.' She spoke calmly against my bellowing. 'There was nothing to be done. The baby had been dead for a while by the time I arrived and Eleanora's body just couldn't take the birth and her mind couldn't take the death. I did everything I could, as did the doctor, but in the end she just didn't have the will to carry on.'

'What do you mean? That's wrong! She still had everything to live for. We could still have gone to Corsica, made a new life, had babies. She wouldn't have given up on our dream.'

She looked at me sadly. 'That is indeed what it was, signor Agostini, nothing but a dream. I think you know in your heart that she would never have left her husband, would never have willingly given up her status and wealth to live as the wife of a mere secretary.'

I didn't want to hear her opinion and I swept my arm across the table, knocking the bowls and bottles onto the floor, where they shattered into tiny fragments, my howls of frustration and torment echoing round the room.

Sofia continued to stand just in front of me, calm before the storm of my anger, grief and guilt. I took her by the shoulders and, God forgive me, shook her, over and over again, sobbing 'It's your fault, it's your fault they're dead.' She suddenly managed to wriggle away from me and slapped me hard, once on each cheek.

I was shocked into silence and immobility and then I slumped to my knees and found myself weeping uncontrollably. She squatted down in front of me and took me in her arms, whispering, 'I know, I know, it is hard to bear, I know.' She rocked me and I felt the warmth of her breast on my stinging cheek. She stroked my hair, still murmuring words of comfort. Her hand moved down my back and her touch, gentle and meant to console only, made me harden. I turned my face and kissed her hard, her mouth tasted of honey.

The dog, Pepe, growled, bringing me to my senses. 'My God, forgive me Sofia.' I tried to pull away but she held me close and continued to stroke my back. I had not had a woman in over a year and I groaned. I pushed her onto the floor and lay down on top of her. Her skirt had lifted, revealing her nakedness underneath. I tugged down her bodice and took an erect nipple into my mouth. She moaned and pulled at my shirt, the buttons popping off under her impatient fingers. She put her legs round me and squeezed so hard that I feared she would break my ribs.

It was over in just seconds and at my climax it was just my own cries that reverberated off the walls. I rolled off her and lay face down. I heard her breathing slow back to normal then she stood and pulled down her skirt. I remained lying on the floor, wishing it would open up and I could fall into a bottomless pit. I felt so ashamed at my weakness, at my disloyalty to Eleanora. I didn't know how to face Sofia; I didn't know what to say.

'We will never speak of this. You should go.'

I heard the dog whimpering. Sofia went over to him and spoke quietly. She came back to where I was still lying prone. Her tone to Pepe had been reassuring, to me it was contemptuous. 'Call yourself a man? I felt sorry for you but *sei patetico*. Get up and get out before I cut you up into little pieces and feed you to the pigs.'

I felt something sharp against my neck. I got slowly to my feet, avoiding looking in her direction. I tucked my shirt into my britches and brushed off the dust from the floor. I plucked up the courage to look at her, but her back was to me as she swept up the broken shards of glass and pottery. I left a pile of coins on the table, enough to replace the bowls and bottles a hundred times over.

No further words were exchanged and I closed the door quietly behind me.

I don't remember walking back down into the village; my head was full of images of Eleanora, the baby and Sofia whirling round and round each other, all looking accusingly at me and weeping tears of blood. When I reached the little church where we had first heard the boys sing, another image came to mind. It was of me at about eight, the same age as Roberto and Fabio, and I was skipping down the path of the church in the town where I was born. I was holding Mama's hand and she was laughing; she looked so happy. Papa had his arm round my elder brother, listening to his amusing account of some event that he had doubtless greatly exaggerated to make it all the more amusing. I could see the roundness of Mama's belly so it must have been about four months before my world had begun to disintegrate.

How I longed to be that boy again; still believing that life was good; still enjoying the warmth of a loving family; still looking forwards to tomorrow, next month, next year, the rest of my life. How and when had I become such a man as I was now, one who could break up another man's family, one who could take a woman only days after his beloved was laid to rest? I had to sit on a rock until the spasms that shook my body ceased.

I needed to be forgiven.

When I arrived at the villa I found the boys in the music room, practising their scales, whilst Isabella listened raptly, clapping whenever they reached the high note and gave a dramatic trill to impress her. Brother Marcus was listening too, nodding with pleasure at their skill.

I left without anyone seeing me and went to find il Conte. He was in his study, staring into space. I stood in front of him for quite a while before he realised I was there.

'You look terrible, Philippe, are you ill?'

'Yes, no, *mio signore*. Not physically but spiritually. I wondered if you would allow me a few days to go and visit the graves of my parents. It is the anniversary of my mother's death,' I lied, 'and I feel the need to be with her, to speak with her again.'

'You loved Eleanora,' Il Conte said in a matter of fact way. I gasped and looked at him sharply, but he continued, 'Everyone loved Eleanora. I know that I am not the only one grieving. One person's death reminds us of others who have gone before. Of course you must go home. Brother Marcus can look after the boys; he seems to be able to control them.'

I remembered what the boys had gone through with their families. 'Thank you. It would be better if the boys slept here from now on. Their families have cast them off and it would not be safe to send them back.'

Il Conte merely nodded, not acknowledging his part in their rejection. I bowed my farewell, packed some clothes and left without telling the boys. I had such a desperate need to leave that I could not countenance even a short delay to say goodbye.

It took just over a day to get to Siena, spending the one night in a dense wood, protecting myself from the cold and damp with a thick horse-blanket I had taken from the stables. I arrived at the outskirts of the town, where we had once lived, in the late afternoon. I left my horse at a tavern and then walked along the familiar streets towards the house where I was born. I argued with myself about the sense in revisiting it, but my curiosity won, but I wish it hadn't. The building itself was unchanged, but the garden that Mama had loved and nurtured had been completely re-designed and her well-stocked herb garden had been covered in lawn. There was evidence of young children in residence; a ball and piece of rope discarded on the path, a rag doll left half in and half out of a pram. It was the same house, but no longer my home.

I made my way to the church; this at least would be the same. There would be new occupants in the graveyard, but they would be invisible to me and I knew that the atmosphere of the place would remain unchanged until the day of the final resurrection.

I visited Papa's resting place first. Although in unconsecrated ground, the priest had allowed me to mark the grave with a simple wooden cross. He had known the family for years and he and my father used to play chess together once a week. If he had had his way he would have buried Papa next to Mama, but rules are rules and he feared to break them. He did, however, bury him feet away from Mama on the opposite side of the dividing wall. I tidied around the cross, kissed it and then clambered over the wall to where Mama lay in her eternal sleep. There was a small marble headstone with an engraving of angel's wings over Mama's name and date of birth and of death and the simple words '*molto amato e molto mancato.*'

I sat on the damp soil and stroked the words, repeating them out loud. 'You are indeed much loved and much missed, Mama. Life was never the same after you left us, and now there is only me.'

I believed in life after death and that whatever her form, she could hear me.

'You must be so disappointed in me, Mama. I have not turned out the way you would have wanted. I have made such a mess of things; I feel I have sunk to the very bottom of the cess pit.'

I waited for a sign from her, to show that she heard me, understood me and forgave me. Instead a male voice said, 'Philippe? It *is* Philippe, isn't it?'

184

It was our priest, Father Joseph. He must have been well into his fifties by now but he had changed little, specks of grey in his hair and an extra chin. I nodded but found I couldn't speak. He studied my face, then said most gently, 'Do you wish me to hear your confession?'

I suddenly wanted to tell this man everything and through him obtain God's forgiveness. I nodded again and we went together, side by side, into the dimness of the church and into the little confessional box. It was here I used to tell this same priest all my sins, from swearing to hiding my elder brother's toy soldiers. He had been a good listener then, as he was now.

I started with my seduction of Eleanora when she was eighteen and had only been married to il Conte for just over a year. I told of our affair that had only ended with her death; of the years of deceit; of our plans to run away to Corsica; of the child we had made together and whose dead body I had held in my arms. I told of my part in the boys' castration and of my mistreatment of Sofia. The words kept tumbling out and I didn't stop until I had told him every sordid detail.

When I had finished I was exhausted and sat with my head bowed. We were in the shadows and I sensed Father Joseph next to me, rather than saw him.

'Are you sorry for what you have done, Philippe?'

'I am sorry for the deception, for the hurt it would have caused il Conte, for what we have done to the boys, for what I have done to Sofia. But I cannot be sorry for loving Eleanora. How can something so wonderful be wrong?'

'It was not a pure love, Philippe; the Devil whispered lies into your ears and blinded your eyes to the truth. La

Contessa had made her vows to Count De Lorenzo before God and it was wrong of her to break them. Your love made you happy, yes, but at what cost?'

'Will God ever forgive me, Father?'

'Of course, my son, if you truly repent. Do you?'

I felt an overwhelming desire to purge myself, to vomit out my sins and shed my skin of depravity. I wanted to be as clean and pure as a new-born babe, as my Eduardo had been.

'How can I show that I repent, Father, tell me what I must do?'

'You will know, Philippe. I cannot give you a list of things to do after which you will be forgiven. Pray, read your Bible, go to Communion and listen for God's voice. Stay here for a while if you wish.'

We left the confessional box; he shook my hand and left me standing, with just a couple of candles keeping back the blackness. I sat in the pew that the Agostini family had once sat in and I prayed as I had never done before. Then I sat and waited. I wasn't aware of hearing God's voice but as I stood to leave I realised I understood what I had to do. I needed to continue to serve il Conte as his secretary to the best of my ability; to be his prop as he suffered the loss of his wife; to be as a father to Roberto and Fabio and ensure that their lives were blessed and not ruined; and, hardest of all, to seek Sofia's forgiveness. I would start all of these tasks right now, apart from the last one - that might take some time.

Chapter 22

A visit to the opera

No-one wanted to stay at the Villa De Lorenzo for longer than necessary but neither did they want to rush back to the Villa Bouganville; at both places there were too many memories that were still vivid and painful. Our reluctance slowed us to almost walking pace but even so we turned into the gates two weeks after initially setting out. One good thing about our sojourn was that Isabella, Roberto and Fabio had become good friends and they managed to take each others' minds off the realities that haunted their young lives. When the carriage stopped they bounded out like gazelles released from a pen and ran straight onto the lawn and just chased each other round and round until all their pent up energy had been expended. Il Conte stood on the path and watched them, his face devoid of expression, apart from a slight tic in the corner of one eye.

'Take them back, Philippe. Take them back now.' He beckoned to Isabella and she immediately came to him, turning and blowing a kiss to the boys in farewell. She took his hand and together they slowly walked into the gloom of the villa.

I took the boys back to the conservatoire and for a small treat we stopped for supper at a tavern en route. As we sat waiting for the wench to serve our food, Fabio started taking bits and bobs from his pocket and lining them up on the table. There was a perfectly oval, pale grey stone with a seam of white through the middle of it; a few coins; a shard of dark green glass that made my heart quicken at the memories it invoked; three small pink pearl buttons and a silver thimble. I pointed at the latter items. 'Where did you find those?'

Fabio looked me straight in the eye. 'I didn't steal them, signore. Signorina Isabella gave them to me. She took them out of her sewing basket.' He seemed to lose his confidence. 'They were hers to give, weren't they, signore?'

'Yes, Fabio, they were hers to give. These are all splendid items to add to your collection. It must be getting quite large now, where on earth do you keep it?'

Fabio looked away and his mumbled answer was drowned out by the clatter of bowls as our food was served.

As I had promised myself in the presence of God, I endeavoured to execute my duties to il Conte with as much energy and enthusiasm as I could muster. It was not an easy task but I listened patiently as he reminisced about his years with Eleanora, his memories became more like the stories of a saint as each day passed. How I longed to share my own recollections but I bit my tongue and said nothing to disabuse him.

Each morning I taught at the conservatoire and returned there in the evening to share supper and the recreation period with *i castrati*. One afternoon per week Roberto and Fabio were allowed to come to the villa to play with Isabella. It amused me to watch them suffer the indignities of being dressed up in lace, gauze and pieces of fabric and invited to a banquet of stones, mud and grass. Il Conte stood watching them with me one afternoon. 'They make good playmates for her, Philippe. There is no risk of anything,' he seemed to search for the right word, 'anything untoward.'

'They are just innocent children, *mio signore*.'

He shook his head. 'No, Philippe. Only our beloved Lady was conceived free from original sin.'

We all grieved for what we had lost, but the boys at least seemed happy and to have put their humiliating familial experience behind them. Mixed with my grief for the loss of my lover and my son, was the guilt I felt towards Sofia. I tried to put her out of my mind but she sat in a dark corner, waiting to come shrieking into my dreams, her eyes sending out bolts of accusation; her claws ready to tear me apart, her teeth devour me. These nightmares left my sheets sodden with sweat and my body bruised.

It is an undeniable fact that for the living time marches pitilessly onwards and before we knew it, it was May and Isabella's eighth birthday. Her father was too engrossed in his own grief to remember the date and we were only reminded of it on the day we all went to the cathedral to hear the boys singing during Pentecost Sunday. It was a beautiful service and the choir was magnificent. Isabella mouthed the words that the boys had taught her and as they sang joyously of the descent of the Holy Spirit she took my hand and squeezed it hard. I could see that she was overcome with emotion and trying hard to control the tears that threatened to spill over. I glanced at il Conte to see how he was coping; his expression was stern and he was staring unblinkingly at something no-one else could see. As the voices reached their glorious crescendo the tic at the corner of his eye started its steady throb, as if beating in time with the music.

I think we all felt a certain amount of relief when the service was over; it is exhausting to keep one's emotions in check for a long period. It was a slow journey home in the carriage as we manoeuvred our way along the busy roads. Isabella sat with her head out of the open window, giving a running commentary on the outfits worn by both male and female pedestrians, as they sauntered along in the spring sunshine.

'Look at that lady over there, Papa. She really shouldn't be wearing yellow, not with her hair colour. A blue or green would be far more becoming.' Il Conte merely smiled indulgently at his judgemental daughter; she expected no response from him and continued with her prattle. We stopped for a few minutes to allow another carriage to join the stream. Something caught Isabella's eye and she leaned further out for a better look. 'Oh, look at that advertisement for an opera!' Before we could stop her she had leapt out of the still stationary carriage and run to the shop window, upon which a poster had been pasted. Her father sighed, 'Go after her, Philippe. See what she is so excited about.'

The poster proclaimed in large letters that in a week's time the *Teatro della Pergola* in Florence would be the venue for one night only of a performance of Baldassare Galuppi's comic opera, *Le nozze di Dorina*, featuring the newly discovered castrato, Gaspare Pacchierotti. Isabella jumped up and down when she read the date and rushed back to the carriage, sat down opposite her father, took both his hands in hers and pleaded that we might go and be entertained.

'And Papa, we must take Roberto and Fabio. It would be wonderful for them to see a castrato singing on stage and being applauded. Do say we may go, Papa, please? For my birthday?'

How could any loving father refuse such a plea? Il Conte was no exception.

A week later I picked up the boys and could not help smiling at how uncomfortable they looked in their stiff, white shirts and black velvet britches that Isabella had insisted were bought for them. Their faces looked as if they had been scrubbed with a brush and their hair had been washed and combed to remove the nits and tangles that all eight-year old boys seemed to nurture.

We returned to the Villa Bouganville and picked up il Conte and Isabella. They had dressed in their finery for the occasion; he in a splendid turquoise and gold brocade jacket, with black lace around every edge, and she in a pretty multi-layered pink satin frock with matching slippers. Her maid had pinned her hair up in the style that Eleanora had worn and when her father held her hand as she stepped gracefully into the carriage I had a lump in my throat.

The theatre entrance was full of people when we arrived and it took us a while to wend our way through the crowd until we could enter the relative quiet of the De Lorenzo box. The experience of going to the theatre was new to the children but I still found it fascinating and all of us, apart from il Conte, leaned forwards in our seats in order to enjoy the entertainment within the oval shaped auditorium, before even the opera had begun. There were three tiers along the semi-circular walls with each tier containing twenty private rooms, where the aristocracy could flaunt their wealth, see and be seen. I knew how much il Conte paid annually for his box and it was the income from these purchases that paid for the majority of the costs of putting on performances. Atop the third tier ran the *piccionaia*, the pigeon-loft, where people sat who couldn't afford a box but who also didn't want to sit in the pit.

There were no seats provided in the pit but people were quite happy to bring their own or sit on a blanket on the floor. There was constant motion as everyone wandered around greeting friends and family, sharing food and drink, even playing cards. A fight suddenly broke out and there were insults and fists thrown about for a few minutes until their attention was caught by something else and the small crowd dissipated and the two fighters shook hands and went back to their respective families. I watched guiltily as a couple copulated right under us; I glanced at the children but saw that they were too busy watching the antics of two men who were dancing a jig as another played a flute.

A steady stream of visitors came to pay their respects to il Conte, to share a glass of wine or sample the food that was offered. Il Conte always introduced all of us to each guest and I was proud of my boys as they bowed but kept silent. I had bought a résumé but, despite the candles, it was too dim to read, although I knew that if it was a comic opera about *le nozze*, a wedding, then the plot was bound to entail a husband, a wife, a lover, a servant and a multitude of misunderstandings. I was sipping my second glass of wine and wishing that Eleanora was there when I glanced at the stage and saw that the play had started. None of our party, indeed it seemed no-one in the theatre was watching, apart from Roberto, who was leaning on the balcony, resting his chin on his arms, staring intently as the characters cavorted about and sang their inane words.

It was only when Gaspare Pacchierotti, a seventeen year old castrato, came onto the stage that the audience hushed and everyone's eyes were on him. He wore an elaborate gown of pale green and silver, shoes with such high heels that he pranced rather than walked; his lips were blood red and his cheeks powdered until they were as white as his tall wig. A sigh of appreciation rippled throughout the theatre, absolute silence as he sang his aria and thunderous applause at its conclusion. Then attention was returned to the eating, drinking and conversation as the other characters played out their ridiculous parts on the stage.

Only Roberto was transfixed throughout the whole time and when the opera was over and Gaspare came back on stage to take his bow he stood to his feet, applauded and shouted '*Bravissimo!*' at the top of his voice, along with the rest of the audience. A shower of roses and coins rained on the young man's head and I gave the three children a few coins apiece so that they too could show their appreciation. Roberto and Isabella took them eagerly but Fabio shook his head and I recognised the stubborn set of his mouth.

Isabella was beside herself with excitement. 'Oh, Papa! Wasn't that wonderful? Wasn't she, he I mean, magnificent? Roberto, Fabio, that could be you one day, just think of that!'

Roberto laughed gleefully and he struck a pose as Gaspare had done, throwing back his head and holding his arms out as if to embrace the world. 'Did you see how everyone loved him and threw money at him? One day that *will* be me and I will be rich and famous! He sang well, but I, we, can sing better!'

Fabio said nothing.

Il Conte wanted to stay longer to discuss a few things with some business associates so I accompanied Isabella home first and then the boys back to the conservatoire. I let Roberto go through the gate and then took hold of Fabio's arm. 'Is there something wrong? It didn't seem as if you enjoyed yourself.'

I was surprised at the vehemence of his reply. 'It was embarrassing! He looked ridiculous and everyone laughed at him. I am here to learn to praise God and that is what we should be doing, singing to the glory of God, not entertaining the rabble.' With that he stalked away, catching up with Roberto but not joining in his excited chatter. I let him go, not saying out aloud that he should remember that he was one of the rabble. On the way back to the villa I pondered on Fabio's words. I couldn't help but agree with his opinions of the opera singer, but I was worried that he would dampen Roberto's enthusiasm and destroy any motivation he may have to excel. I need not have been concerned; thereafter both boys worked even harder, both seeming to want to prove something to themselves and to others.

Life settled back into its normal rhythm although Il Conte still grieved for his wife, as I did for my lover. It was soon early November, a year since the death of Eleanora and our child, and my exploitation of Sofia.

Chapter 23

Tabitha

Il Conte announced that he did not wish to be in Florence during November; he did not want to be in the same place where the memories of that dreadful time were still too real. So, once again I asked Monsignor if he would release Roberto, Fabio and Brother Marcus and we set off for Montalcino just two days shy of the anniversary. The journey was a repeat of the previous year, although we were not so morose. The youngsters especially were lively and entertained il Conte and me with their constant chatter. I, however, carried the additional burden of knowing that I would have to take this opportunity to go and visit Sofia, to make my peace with her and beg for her forgiveness for my weakness.

It took me two days to pluck up the courage and to run out of excuses not to go, so after our midday meal I made my way up the now familiar path to the little house in the wood. As I approached I saw smoke coming out of the chimney and I heard singing from within. I stopped in my tracks. What if she refused to see me? What if she attacked me with teeth and nails, as she still did in my dreams? I almost turned back but I heard the voice of Father Joseph after my confession to him, telling me that I would know what I had to do. And I *did* know what to do, if only I was man enough to do it.

I took a deep breath, strode to the door with an air of confidence I did not feel and rapped on the door. The singing stopped.

'*Chi è là?*'

I wondered if she would refuse entry if I said my name, but said it anyway. 'It's Philippe Agostini. I, I would like to speak with you if I may?'

There was a silence broken only by the scratching of the chickens and the grunting of the pigs.

'It's open.'

I went in and shut the door behind me and stood inside still holding the handle. I did not want to go any further into the room until I knew how she would react to my presence; she had, after all, said we should never speak of our last meeting. Sofia eyed me suspiciously and as she did so I studied her. She was sitting in a rocking chair by the fire, the little terrier curled at her feet. The dog raised his head to glance at me, then rested it back onto his paws; he didn't seem to remember me. Sofia had a colourful shawl wrapped around her shoulders and around something that she was holding in her arms. It made a mewling sound and Sofia moved the bundle slightly until there was the sound of contented suckling. The shawl fell and revealed a baby's head, a halo of auburn down glowing in the firelight, the same colour as its mother's hair.

'Ah, signor Agostini. I had hoped never to see you ever again. But now you are here you might as well come in. And you can close your mouth, have you never seen a baby feeding before?' I sat opposite her and she looked me straight in the eye, 'Why are you here?'

The words I had rehearsed now seemed inadequate and hollow, but they were all I had. 'I wanted to apologise for my behaviour a year ago. I regret my actions more than I can say and more than you will ever know. I am so terribly, terribly sorry and want to know if you could ever forgive

196

me?' Her dour expression didn't change. I found her silence disconcerting and I said the first thing that came into my head. 'Whose baby is it?'

She gave a brittle laugh. 'She is mine. Whose did you think she is?'

'I apologise. I just meant, well, did you get married?'

She cocked her head to the side and looked at me half pityingly and half contemptuously. 'She is three months old. You work it out, signor Agostini.'

Sofia swapped the baby to her other breast as I did the simple arithmetic.

'She's mine?'

'No, as I said, she's mine. You had a very minor role and are of no significance to her or to me.'

I should have felt relief but instead I felt disappointment and a stirring of something akin to pride. 'What is her name?'

'Tabitha, after my grand-mother.'

'May I hold her? May I hold Tabitha?' I tentatively held my arms out.

'Certainly not, not whilst she is feeding.' I put my arms back down by my side and waited patiently whilst Tabitha continued to suckle until she was so sated that she fell off the nipple. Only then did Sofia hand the sleeping baby to me. I took her and instinctively rocked her gently. I remembered the last time I had held my child, but what a difference. Tabitha was white and pink, with red lips that were puckered up, still searching even as she slept. I put my little finger into her mouth and she opened her bright blue eyes, stared at me and started to suck. She was so full of life and I could feel my heart melting. She didn't flinch as I stroked her plump cheeks.

'She's beautiful.'

'Why wouldn't she be? Out of your weakness, as you call it, God has created something wonderful for me to love and care for.'

'You can't mean to bring her up by yourself? Here?'

She threw back her head and gave a throaty laugh. 'And why not? My mother brought me up here alone, and her mother before her. Men have never been part of our lives. They are good for their seed only, then we have no need of them. Tabitha will grow up learning how to make use of God's bounty for the good of herself and others, as I did, as my mother did, and as her mother did before her.'

For a brief moment I wondered whether it was I who had been used a year ago rather than the other way round. But no, it was not Sofia who had seduced me; it was I who had succumbed to temptation and lost control. It was I who had taken advantage of Sofia's attempt to comfort me. Tabitha had fallen asleep again as we spoke and I watched her in fascination. She did not sleep peacefully; she gave little frowns, her mouth would give a smile then purse into a perfect round, her nose would twitch. I laughed at her expressions.

'What can she be so cross about at just three months? She looks very like you when she scowls.'

I thought I had been too presumptuous but Sofia gave a ghost of a smile and held out her arms for the baby. 'Give her back to me. I haven't finished feeding her yet.'

I noticed that the milk was squirting out of her breast in a fine spray. Tabitha latched on quickly and there was the noise of her snuffling with satisfaction. I watched mother and daughter with as near a feeling of contentment as I had felt for over a year. When Tabitha had been lain in a wicker basket, Sofia covered herself and looked at me enquiringly. 'Well, signor Agostini, why are you still here?'

'I really do want to apologise. I wanted to explain, not to justify, just to explain. I had held my dead son in my arms, buried my lover and my two boys had been ridiculed by their own families. I was angry, grieving and I hurt so much inside. I needed a release, but I am so ashamed of how I got it. I went to confession the next day and I sat in the church afterwards. I knew God wanted me to come back and ask for your forgiveness. I'm just sorry it has taken so long.'

She surprised me by admitting, 'I sometimes go to church.' She got up and poured two cups of wine and handed me one. 'I know the priest there; I give him something to ease the aches in his old bones. I don't understand much of what he says, I just like to sit and listen. A phrase he once used has stuck with me: 'God moves in mysterious ways.' I like that, 'moves in mysterious ways.' He has blessed me with Tabitha despite our weakness.'

'Our weakness? No blame lies at your door.'

Sofia stiffened. 'I said then that we should never speak of it again and yet here you are, talking of nothing else. If you are waiting for me to say "I forgive you," then you will have a long wait. Please go now, you have outstayed your welcome.'

I stood to go. 'Can I come again? I know you don't need me in your lives, but I would so like to see Tabitha again. I won't interfere, I promise. I would just come and visit when

I am at the Villa De Lorenzo. Would that be too unbearable for you?'

She pondered a few minutes and I felt inexplicably nervous. 'No, I suppose not. But mind what you promise, I'll not have you interfering. You have said what you came to say, now go, I have things to do.'

I peeped once more at the babe, now in a restful, deep sleep and took my leave. Half way down I realised I should have left some money, but with the little I knew of Sofia, I suspected she would have thrown it in my face and accused me of treating her like a whore.

And so began my visits to Sofia and Tabitha. I managed quite easily to arrange to go to Montalcino every two or three months, there was always something that I needed to do regarding the management of the estate. I intended to tell il Conte about my daughter, but there never seemed to be the right opportunity.

Each time I saw Tabitha I was amazed at how she had changed. I clapped when she rolled over, yelled '*urrà*' when she waddled from Sofia to me and bit my lip when she uttered the word 'Papa.'

'You are a very emotional man, signor Agostini.'

'I do wish you would call me Philippe, Sofia. I think we know each other well enough by now, don't we?'

She shrugged. 'Alright then, Philippe. Rather than waste your energy on emotions, perhaps you could help me repair the goat shed. It needs two people and clever though Tabitha is, she is not yet able to hold a plank of wood.'

I held the board whilst Sofia competently hammered in a nail. Out of nowhere, with no premeditation, I suddenly blurted out, 'Should we marry?'

Sofia missed the nail, hit her finger and uttered a peasant oath. She looked quickly across to Tabitha to make sure she hadn't heard, but she was sitting with a look of ecstasy on her face whilst five kittens clambered over her plump legs.

Sofia sucked her finger and glared at me. 'What rubbish are you saying? Why on earth would we marry?'

'I just thought we could make a proper family. I'm sorry, I didn't realise that the idea would be so repulsive to you.'

'Well it is! I said you could come and visit once in a while as long as you do not interfere. I think getting married is the biggest kind of intrusion, don't you? I keep telling you, we don't need a man in our lives. I am happy here and so is Tabitha. We have a good life, we want for nothing and the villagers are grateful for the potions I make. Were you thinking you would come and live here and still work for Count De Lorenzo? Or did you think I would leave all this and go and live in the city of sin?'

I had to admit it, 'I wasn't thinking at all.'

'I didn't think so. Now, hold up that wood so we can finish this and then you should go.'

Over the months, Sofia allowed me to stay a little bit longer each time and to do small jobs for her around the place. She had quite a collection of animals and I enjoyed helping feed or clean them out. One of my favourites was a little pony called, for obvious reasons, Piccolo. Some old man had given him to Sophia when she had eased his poor wife's last few days. The pony was quite content to stand for hours whilst Tabitha just sat on his back and stroked his mane whilst she played with her doll or made a necklace of flowers to put round the horse's neck. There were also the more useful chickens, goats, pigs and many generations of a cat family. Sofia, as most of the villagers did, grew her own vegetables and people would often show their gratitude by leaving a basket of food. Sofia was right, she was resourceful, independent and had no need of me, or indeed any man.

Once Tabitha was old enough to walk more than a few steps Sofia took her into the woods or up the mountain, teaching her about the flowers, roots and herbs that she needed to be able to identify if she were to be as good a healer as her mother. After quite a few visits, Sofia allowed me to accompany them so that I could carry either the produce or Tabitha when she got tired. I began to recognise some of the plants, especially when they flowered, but I was never confident enough to pick mushrooms, having once made myself violently ill after taking just a bite, without first checking with Sofia. On one occasion, Sofia asked me to take Tabitha to the river to collect some water cress. The look of pride on Tabitha's face as she held out the wilting bunch of carefully picked leaves and Sofia's look of love and tenderness was almost too much to bear.

I could never tell Sofia when I would be able to visit and she never asked, merely shrugging when I left, and nodding her head at me when I arrived. I now always put some coins into a glass jar, telling Sofia it was just in case she had an urgent need. The jar was never emptied.

Chapter 24

The wedding

Tabitha wasn't the only one growing and changing, so too were the boys. Slowly but surely their bodies were transforming into the recognisable form of a castrato. By the time they were eleven they had shot up and were a head taller than any of the *integri*. They both looked plumper in the face and torso, their arms were disproportionately long, and no lump disfigured the smooth line of the throat. Their voices too were becoming richer and purer, whilst still maintaining the unnaturally high pitch.

I was very proud of my boys and now that they were part of a choir I went to listen to them when I could. Isabella continued to adore them and when they were all together Roberto and Fabio would run around like any others boys and not be laughed at for their strangely shaped bodies and voices like girls.

Time is indeed a great healer and my grief at the loss of Eleanora and the future we had planned together waned in proportion to the joy I experienced at sharing some of Tabitha's life. Il Conte too came out of the black sorrow he had wrapped himself in and began to accept invitations to social events. It was at a dinner given by a minor court official that he found himself seated next to Signora Bellini. She was a mature woman, nearly the same age as il Conte, and had been widowed for two years, as he had. She didn't have the youth and beauty that Eleanora had had, nor the wealth or title, but she had intellect, compassion and a sense of humour that immediately endeared her to him. She also had almost as great a love of horses as il Conte. They were unaware, I suspect, of the hostess's match-making machinations that provided them with the opportunity to form a friendship. Over the following months their friendship deepened and il Conte's musings were less and less of Eleanora and more and more about how Isabella needed a mother, especially now that she was nearing the age where female guidance would be required. He never once, I noticed, mentioned that he needed a rich wife to improve his standing in society.

The winter of 1760 was long, bitterly cold and damp. I had been to the Villa De Lorenzo for a few days, carrying out some business for my master and, of course, visiting my little girl. On my return to Florence, there was a note waiting for me from Monsignor Mazzini asking me to go to the conservatoire as soon as I could. I went to find il Conte to tell him of my summons and found him entertaining la Contessa Bellini.

I apologised for interrupting their conversation, gave il Conte a brief report on my visit to the Villa De Lorenzo and then told him of the note I had received from Monsignor. Il Conte only seemed to be half listening but he nodded his assent to my leaving to go to the conservatoire immediately. He glanced at Signora Bellini, who bobbed her head slightly and then put his hand on my arm to prevent me leaving. 'Before you go, Philippe. It may not be socially acceptable for me to tell you before any of the family, but after what we have gone through together these past years I feel happy that you are the first to know my good news. I am proud to say that Catherine has agreed to be my wife.' I did not resent il Conte's new relationship, for didn't I have one myself, and my congratulations to them both were heartfelt and sincere. I left the two of them smiling at each other and holding each others' hands like two lovesick youngsters.

There was nothing specific in the note from Monsignor but I sensed I needed to get to the conservatoire as quickly as I could, so I rode there rather than walked, as I would normally have done. Monsignor wasted no words in greetings. 'I'm sorry to bring you over here, but I'm afraid Roberto is unwell. He has caught a chill and bad throat. His life is not at risk but I think it would be better if he was taken away from here and nursed in isolation. Do you think Count De Lorenzo would agree for him to stay at the villa until he is well? He will have a much better chance of a full recovery if he is somewhere warm and dry and has more dedicated care than we can provide. There are twenty other boys in the infirmary and Father Simon is doing the best he can but, well, he is only human.'

Perhaps I should have gone back to the villa to get il Conte's permission but I answered without hesitation. 'Of course, Monsignor, I will take him back. Is Fabio alright or should I take him as well?'

'No, Philippe, Fabio is quite well and it would be better if he remained here. He needs to practise for his solo at the cathedral in a few weeks' time. Roberto was going to give one also. It is such a shame that he won't be able to now, but he needs to recover his strength and his voice. Come, I'll take you to him.'

Within but a few minutes, I had literally picked Roberto up from his sweat sodden mattress. There was barely room to walk so cluttered was the floor with the small wooden boxes in which the sickly boys lay. The air was humid and filled with the smell of camphor and lemon and the sound of sniffs and coughs. As I bore Roberto to the horse, I remembered how I had carried him into the room where Il Barbiere had executed the irrevocable operation. Roberto was a lot heavier now and his length made him more awkward to hold. By the time I got to where Brother Pietro was holding the horse I was sweating, despite the chill air.

Having notified il Conte of the situation, I put Roberto into my bedroom, laying him on a truckle bed that I pulled out from under my own bed, not used since the time servant boys used to sleep at the foot of their master. I decided to stay with him myself that night, not wanting anyone else in the household to catch his symptoms. I tried to sleep but couldn't, as I listened to him tossing and turning and making low moaning sounds. I could feel the heat of his body from where I lay, so I stripped him and wiped him all over with a cool, damp cloth. Before I had left the infirmary Father Simon had slipped a bottle of medicine into my pocket, telling me it would ease poor Robert's inflamed throat, so I tried to pour some of it down his throat. I don't know whether he managed to swallow any; it seemed to me that it jut dribbled down his neck leaving a sticky trail. I wished Sofia were here with one of her salves; she would know what to do.

Eventually, Roberto quietened and seemed to sleep, albeit fitfully. I was just dropping off myself when I was startled awake by a loud laugh. It was early morning and in the dawn light that was seeping into the room through the edges of the curtains, I saw Roberto sit bolt upright in bed. He opened his arms wide, threw his head back and with a wide smile on his flushed face, enthused, '*Grazie, grazie.*'

He seemed to be imagining himself on stage, receiving the accolade of an adoring audience. As quickly as he had sat up, his body collapsed and he fell back into a restless sleep, mumbling incoherently and thrashing his arms as if fighting off a swarm of wasps.

The next few days Roberto remained semi-conscious and although I felt beholden to stay with him, il Conte sent one of the house maids to sit with him for a few hours during the day whilst I carried out my duties. Each morning Isabella popped her head round the door to see if she could come in and each morning I said, 'No, not until his fever has broken.' On the third night both Roberto and I had our first uninterrupted sleep and when I felt his brow it was cool and dry. When I heard Isabella's slippered feet on the tiled floor I called out to her, '*Entra, entra*, Roberto's fever has broken. It is safe to come in.' She skipped in, carrying a box of toys, which she placed heavily at the foot of the bed, pulled up a chair and settled down to entertain him.

'*Buongiorno*, signor Agostini, I am so glad Roberto is better. You can leave him to me from now on; I will take care of him. '

'*Grazie*, signorina. He needs to get his strength back, so don't tire him out, but I know I will be leaving him in good hands.' I hadn't had a chance to speak with her since knowing of il Conte's impending re-marriage. 'Are you pleased that you will be getting a new Mama?'

She nodded and looked genuinely pleased, 'Oh, yes! I like Signora Bellini very much. She makes Papa happy.' That was evidently sufficient for Isabella to accept her.

Roberto was still groggy and when I left the room he was looking slightly bemused at the tin soldiers, cups, wooden bricks and rag dolls that Isabella had emptied from the box for his amusement. From then on Isabella took over the nursing and within a couple of weeks Roberto was sufficiently well enough to return to the conservatoire. Isabella would have preferred him to stay there for much longer; their friendship had deepened and they both enjoyed being in each others' company, even if it was merely to throw a ball to each other, or for Isabella to read him a fable from Giambattista Basile's *Il Pentamerone*. The marriage of il Conte and signora Bellini, however, was only a few weeks away and Father Guiseppe wanted Roberto to practise for a duet with Fabio to sing at the wedding.

I will always cherish the memory of Isabella standing at the gate waving and shouting, '*Addio*, Roberto,' as he, one hand in mine, waved the other frantically and shouted equally loudly, '*Ciao*, signorina Isabella!'

The day following Roberto's return to the conservatoire was Fabio's solo at the cathedral. Due to his illness Roberto had to be content to being just one of the choir. Fabio looked so young and small and I was worried that his voice would be lost in the immense cavern. My mouth was dry as he opened his but I soon relaxed as the notes filled the dome and entranced the congregation with their resonance. My own sense of pride at Fabio's rendition, however, was dulled by Roberto's scowling expression throughout. 'He's jealous,' I thought. I knew that it was Roberto who yearned for fame and fortune, rather than Fabio, and I surmised that it must have been galling for him to see Fabio being the centre of such intense attention, even for the duration of a short hymn of praise. As it was a church service there was no applause when he finished, of course, but a wave of appreciation rippled through the pews. I saw Roberto's mouth turn down even more and the furrow in his brow deepen.

The next time I was in *Il Duomo* was for Il Conte's and Catherine's wedding. They had seen no reason to wait a long time before getting married and had asked for the first available Saturday, this being the traditional day for a widow to be remarried, and so the date was set for the third Saturday of March. The early spring day dawned bright; the sky was a clear pale blue, just dotted here and there with white lumpy clouds that skittered across the sky. I had no responsibilities and was merely one of the household who escorted il Conte as he paraded slowly from the villa to the cathedral. He was in his dress uniform, his boots polished until they shone like glass, the silver buttons on his black jacket glittering like stars in the night sky. A barber had attended him that morning and his clean-shaven face gleamed with oils. He marched slowly through the streets, smiling his thanks at the well-wishers who hung out of the windows, stopped to watch the procession or joined our group. Isabella, in her excitement, darted first to me, then to one of her maids, then to her Papa, then back to me. All the staff were part of the happy procession, apart from those who needed to prepare for the banquet.

Our timing was perfect, for as we reached the steps of the cathedral, so did Catherine and her small wedding party. The two walked up the stairs together and down the aisle to the front whilst the guests filled up the pews, whose ends were all decorated with magnificent floral decorations. I escorted Isabella to her seat near the front, then asked her to excuse me so that I could go and be near the boys when they sang their duet.

'Tell them I wish them luck, signore.'

One of the ushers pointed out a small wooden door and I climbed the steep, stone steps to the balcony where the choir was ensconced. I leant over the marble balustrade and had a good view of the proceedings. Catherine's dress was of a dark blue satin, covered in layers of pale blue organza and was the one she had worn for her first wedding, over ten years previously. Although not considered to be a beauty, she looked beautiful, as all brides do, so I am told. She was not as slim as Eleanora had been but she held her figure proudly, looked the bishop in the eye and spoke clearly when she made her promises. During one of the hymns she turned to seek out her step-daughter and winked at her, which made Isabella giggle uncontrollably and made me feel confident that Catherine would be a good mother, despite her inability to actually bear her own.

The hymns were joyful and sung by the congregation with great gusto. The conservatoire had provided a choir of boys, both *castrati* and *integri*. Their voices rebounded off the curved dome so that it seemed as if we were surrounded by a choir of angels. When il Conte and Catherine were officially man and wife, they turned towards the congregation and started their walk back down the aisle. As they did so I saw the choir step back, leaving just Roberto and Fabio at the front. My skin tingled and the hairs on the back of my neck bristled as the most exquisite sound wafted above the heads of the congregation. I smiled to myself as everyone looked up, even the bride and groom, but none of them were able to see Roberto and Fabio as they sang their duet. Their being nick-named as nightingales had never been more appropriate and I imagined two such birds high in a cypress tree, singing their praises to God.

The notes got impossibly higher and higher as the song reached its climax and then suddenly it was as if one of the nightingales had transformed into a rook, for one of the voices changed from being a pure, sweet sound to a coarse, tuneless screech. The whole congregation gasped and I saw a fleeting look of fury cross il Conte's face. I stepped towards the boys and saw with a sinking heart that it had been Roberto's voice that had failed. He looked at me in anguish and mortification. I tried to smile encouragingly at him and nodded to him to start again. I was the only one facing the boys and I was the only one who saw the smirk of satisfaction on Fabio's face as, with a last desperate look at me, his cousin fled past and down the stairs.

It had all happened in the beat of a bird's wing. I turned to follow Roberto but was stopped in my tracks as the singing started again, but just the one voice, the voice of a nightingale. It was still pure, still exquisite and now being a solo, somehow more poignant.

Chapter 25

A dream dashed

I desperately wanted to go after Roberto, but I also didn't want to cause a disturbance, so I waited impatiently as the couple made their way sedately down the long aisle, the bishop gave a final blessing and the congregation was dismissed to the sacred music of Fenaroli. As soon as people started to move the boys of the choir rushed to Fabio, patting him on the back and praising his singing and his splendid recovery from the near disaster. Before I could take my leave Father Guiseppe saw me and rushed over, twisting his hands in his anxiety. 'Oh, Philippe, *che catastrofe, povero, povero* Roberto.'

'What in the name of God happened?'

'His voice has failed a couple of times since his illness but over the last few days it has been perfect and I hoped that it had regained its former strength. I did suggest to him that it was perhaps too soon to perform in public but he was so determined and he worked so hard. Oh, that this should happen, today of all days.'

'I need to find him, father.'

'Yes, go, go and find him, Philippe. He needs you now more than ever; you must handle this situation with care.'

I went to the conservatoire, first of all, but Brother Pietro shook his head when I asked if Roberto had passed through the door. I then raced to the villa. It was a hive of activity, for the staff had returned from the church and were now completing the preparations for the festivities that very afternoon. I asked a few of the passing maids whether they had seen a young, tall boy but the shake of their heads confirmed my own suspicion that he would not have gone there to lick his wounds. The only place I could think of where he might have gone was the river. I knew it brought back memories of his childhood, when he and Fabio were content to milk goats and look for shiny things on the river bed.

He was sitting with his back against the gnarled trunk of an ancient olive tree, hugging his knees. His shoulders shook as he sobbed. He didn't hear me until I sat down next to him. He turned his tear-stained face to mine and I have never seen such an abject look of misery.

'Have you come to tell me off for ruining the wedding?'

'Oh, Roberto, of course not. Firstly, you didn't ruin the wedding and secondly it was not your fault.'

'Of course it was my fault! It was my voice that failed, *my* voice. It's the only thing I have that makes me special, that gives me a chance of making something of myself and it's broken.' His voice wavered and ended in a sob.

'It's not necessarily permanent, Roberto. It is the illness that has weakened it; you just need more time to build up your strength. Take it slowly, keep practising and you will soon be as good a new.'

He wiped his runny nose on his sleeve. 'What happened afterwards?'

'Fabio finished by himself.' I regretted the words as soon as they were out of my mouth.

'So, Fabio got to do a solo. Again.' He almost spat the words out.

'He did well for carrying on, Roberto. You are both such wonderful singers and you both have the potential for great things. I know you feel ashamed and frustrated now, but you have to pick yourself up and carry on, and show the world what you can do. *Capisci?*'

Roberto said nothing for a while, just stared at the flowing waters of the River Arno.

'I want so badly to be like that opera singer, signor Agostini. People respected him, they admired him, they adored him and they threw money at him!' His lips began to tremble again and I had to lean in close in order to hear him whisper. 'I have had so much taken from me, is it too much to ask that the one thing I am good at is not also taken from me? Have I done something so bad God is punishing me?'

'No, Roberto. If anyone should be punished it should be me, for agreeing to take you from your family in the first place. But we cannot go back, only forwards. You will face many obstacles in life, Roberto, this is just one you must overcome. You can do it, I know you can.' I stood up and held out my hand. 'Come on, let's go back to the conservatoire. Don't be embarrassed. Congratulate Fabio, for he did carry on beautifully, apologise to Father Guiseppe for running off, and then tomorrow is a new start.'

'Was il Conte very cross?'

I smiled at him as I helped him to his feet and lied. 'Of course not, it was his wedding day! How can a man be cross on his wedding day?'

I accompanied him back to the conservatoire and saw him through the gate, then returned to the villa to join in the celebrations, which went on into the night and early morning. I drank far too much wine on an empty stomach but didn't embarrass myself any more than the other intoxicated male guests. I danced and flirted and forgot, for a few hours, about Roberto's pain.

Everyone slept late the next day so I missed giving my lessons; in fact I didn't go to the conservatoire for the next fours days, as il Conte insisted I give all my time to him and the tasks he found for me to do. On the fifth day I arrived at the conservatoire just as the boys were returning from church and sleepily making their way to the refectory in order to break their fast. The group of *castrati* were easy to see, distinguished as they were by their height and falsetto chatter. I waited for them to come alongside and then walked with Fabio, who was trailing at the back, head down.

'Where's Roberto?'

Fabio shrugged; he didn't make eye contact.

A cold hand squeezed my heart. I grabbed Fabio by the arm hard enough for him to yelp out and pulled him away from the other boys. 'Fabio! Look at me, where is Roberto?'

He shrugged again, then lifted his eyes to mine and I saw a coldness in his eyes that bode ill. 'He has gone, signor Agostini. He told me not to say anything until after breakfast to give him a chance to get away.'

'Get away? What do you mean, get away?' Fabio shrugged again and in my anxiety I grabbed him even tighter and shook him. 'Where has he gone, Fabio, tell me now!'

'You're hurting me, signore. Please, I don't know where he's gone, he wouldn't tell me.'

I released him, then stroked the marks I had left on his arms, trying to erase the evidence of my unintended brutality. I pushed him in front of me and guided him to Monsignor's study. I knocked but went in without waiting for an invitation to enter. Monsignor looked up from his writing, an expression of surprise then concern on his face as he took in the scene before him.

'Tell Monsignor what you just told me, Fabio.'

He looked down at his shuffling feet and mumbled 'He's gone.'

Monsignor leaned forward in an attempt to hear. 'Speak up boy, I can't hear a word you are saying.'

My impatience got the better of me and I answered for him. 'Roberto has gone, Monsignor. After the church service this morning he told Fabio to say nothing until after breakfast to give him a chance to get away.'

Monsignor got up from his desk and walked around to us. He took the boy's chin gently in his hands and lifted it so that he could look him full in the face. 'You are not in trouble, Fabio, but we need to find Roberto and you will be helping if you tell us exactly what he said.'

'He just said he couldn't stay any longer because his voice is ruined. I don't know where he's gone, honest I don't!' Fabio started to snivel and wiped his nose on the sleeve of his tunic. I remembered that Roberto had done exactly the same thing a few evenings ago when I had found him by the river.

Monsignor patted him on the shoulder. 'Stop crying now, go to the refectory and ask Father Guiseppe to come to my study. You stay and have your breakfast and then continue with your lessons as normal. Don't worry, we'll find Roberto.'

I paced up and down impatiently waiting for Father Guiseppe's arrival. As soon as he entered and before he even had the chance to ask why he had been summoned, I grabbed him by the arm and blurted out, 'Roberto's run away, did you know?'

Father Guiseppe removed my hand, carefully sat himself down and indicated that I should also. His voice, though controlled, had a hint of anger.

'No, of course I didn't know. Do you honestly think I would have just let him go?'

Monsignor calmly intervened. 'Has anything happened since the wedding, Father?'

Father Guiseppe sighed and his shoulders drooped. 'Poor Roberto. He was very brave after the debacle at the cathedral and practised so very hard but his voice kept breaking more and more frequently. He would be singing perfectly one second and then the next, well, you heard what it was like. It was heart-breaking to hear, it really was.'

I felt so angry. I gripped the arms of the chair until my knuckles were white. 'But how can this have happened? The voice of a *castrato* doesn't break, that is the whole point of their existence!'

'I know, Philippe, but very occasionally, if the castration was not done properly, then the voice breaks as for a normal boy. However, in Roberto's case, I think it is down to his throat infection and something was damaged. I told him this and said that if he rested it for a while he may recover his voice. He wanted me to promise he would be able to sing again and I couldn't. I did tell him he could train as an alto and still be part of the choir but he said he wanted to be a *castrato* in an opera or nothing. I didn't keep on at him; I thought it best to leave him to think things over. I never dreamt he would run away.'

He gestured out of the open window and we all followed his pointed finger, as if we would see Roberto in the distance. I remembered how even his own family had made fun of him and I groaned. 'We need to find him and bring him back, how will he survive out there? They'll destroy him. All they'll see is a strange-looking boy with a girl's voice. They won't see a frightened child in need of protection. We've got to find him.'

I got to my feet to leave and Monsignor said he would send messages to all the priests in Florence and ask them and their flocks to keep their eyes open for Roberto. 'Don't worry, Philippe, he'll soon be back with us.'

But I was worried. Florence was a big city and Roberto a small boy. I went back to the villa and told il Conte what had happened. I asked for his permission to go looking for Roberto and was shocked at his response.

'What's the point? He's no good to me now if he cannot sing as a castrato. I'll not pay for him to be just an ordinary singer. No, we need to focus our endeavours now on Fabio and make sure he is the best he can be. I was very impressed with him at the wedding. No, I'll not countenance you spending your time searching for Roberto.'

I was speechless for a few seconds then spoke as calmly and firmly as I could, biting back the anger that bubbled just under the surface, threatening to boil over. 'We took advantage of their family's poverty by tempting them with gold in exchange for their sons. We had the boys' bodies mutilated in the pretence that it was all for the glory of God, but really it was purely for your own advantage and ambition. We have used these boys and up until now they have given you everything you demanded of them. They are boys, signore, just boys, not automata; they have feelings, dreams and nightmares. Fabio, I am sure, will go from success to success and you will achieve your ambition and rise in society as a result of your patronage. But Roberto's dream of being an opera singer is dashed and we need to find him and help him build and realise a new dream, one that doesn't depend on a voice that God never intended him to have for ever. If you don't give your permission then I resign, here and now, for I *will* go and look for Roberto and I will help him start a new life, with or without your support.'

I glared defiantly at il Conte, who looked intently back at me, his expression one of interest rather than anger. 'You would really resign for the sake of the boy? You have become fond of Roberto, I can see that. Go and find him, then, and we'll see if we can find him a job here, maybe in the kitchens or the gardens. I'll give you a week, no more. If you haven't found him by that time then he obviously doesn't want to be found and you can either return to your duties or, if you insist on continuing the search, I will be obliged to accept your resignation, although I would rather not.'

I nodded my thanks. I went in search of Isabella and, finding her practising the piano in the music room, told her about Roberto and asked her to keep her eyes open around the villa just in case he decided to hide in one of the outbuildings. I suspected he wouldn't come near the place but it made Isabella feel as if she was helping in the search.

'Poor Fabio, he must feel awfully worried. He will miss Roberto terribly.'

I had to admit that I hadn't given Fabio's feelings a moment's thought and I doubted very much that he was worried. 'You're right, Isabella, it is kind of you to think of him. Perhaps your father would let you invite him here; I know your friendship means a lot to Fabio. Now, I am going into the city to look for Roberto.'

For the next three days I scoured every road, track and path and asked everyone I met, from prince to pauper, whether they had seen a young boy, tall for his age, round in face and torso. Always there was the shake of the head and the shrug of the shoulders. I walked up and down the banks of the river, looking under bushes, behind trees and inside the crude dwellings that seemed to grow out of the ground like infectious sores. I visited every tavern, church and even whore houses to no avail; I never heard nor saw anything of him.

It then occurred to me that he might try and get home. Although his last visit was mortifying for him, they were still his family and surely they would welcome him back if he was in need? It was a slow journey to Montalcino, as I stopped to look in every outbuilding, and knocked on every farm door. It was a fruitless search and in the afternoon of the fourth day I arrived in the village and went straight to the family home. I dismounted and knocked on the door. Roberto's mother stuck her head out of the window and asked '*Chi è?*' She recognised me and her near smile changed into a grimace. 'What do *you* want?'

'Is Roberto here?'

Roberto's father's head joined that of his wife through the window. 'Why do you ask, signore? We have not seen him since that time you brought him just after the Contessa died.' They pulled their heads back in and slammed the window shut. They didn't ask what had happened or why I was looking for their son. I felt nothing but contempt for them.

I knew he wouldn't be there, but I went to the Villa De Lorenzo and told the small number of staff that were still there to be vigilant and to let il Conte know as quick as possible if he turned up. I then made my way up to the house in the wood. When I arrived Sofia and Tabitha were inside; Tabitha was playing with a doll I had bought her from Florence and Sofia was at the table grinding roots in a bowl with a pestle that had belonged to her grandmother, if not her great grandmother.

As soon as she saw me Tabitha rushed over and hugged my legs so that I couldn't walk. I picked her up and twirled her round and round, her hair, auburn like her mother's, swinging out like a skirt. Her squeals of delight lightened my heart but her mother must have seen something in my expression for she waited for me to put Tabitha down and then she said, 'Let's all go and look for truffles.' Tabitha and Pepe scurried through the woods, looking amongst the roots and carpet of leaves for the tubers, not realising that it was the wrong season to harvest them. It gave the two adults, however, a chance to talk.

'So, Philippe, tell me what is wrong.'

Chapter 26

'These are my family now'

I don't know whether it was because I couldn't find Roberto or because of Sofia's uncharacteristic gentleness, but I was overcome with emotion and it took me a few minutes before I could tell her everything that had happened at and after the wedding. 'I have searched everywhere, Sofia, places I didn't even know existed. I left a coin with everyone I could and asked them to tell Monsignor at the conservatoire if they have sight of Roberto.'

'Maybe someone has already told him and Roberto is safely back there.'

'Maybe.'

'But you don't think so?'

'No. His looks are so distinctive and yet no-one in the whole of Florence had seen him. If he can stay hidden for three days, he can stay hidden for three weeks, three months, three years. God, I wish we had never heard them singing at their cousin's wedding. I wish il Conte hadn't taken it into his head to enhance his reputation by sponsoring *castrati*. I wish their parents had refused the gold. I wish the boys had run away before the operation, like the others, whose names I can't even remember.'

I expected a sharp retort from Sofia as was her wont, but she said nothing and just took my hand in hers and squeezed it gently. 'We don't live in a fairy tale and there is no such thing as a magic wish. All you can do is to keep looking and to be there for Fabio; he will miss Roberto very much. Il Conte has only Fabio left to bring him glory and that is a huge responsibility for his young shoulders to bear. Come, the sun is sinking, we need to get back. Do you have your book of poetry with you?'

I was surprised at the change in subject. 'Always, why?'

'You can read some to me after supper.'

She kept hold of my hand as we returned to the house, the basket empty but my heart full.

Having put Tabitha to bed, Sofia sat with me before the fire and reminded me of her desire for me to read to her. She didn't like the courtly love poems that Eleanora had insisted I proclaim to her, instead she preferred the works of Margherita Costa, dead for a century, but whose humorous mocking of politics and attitudes towards women resonated with Sofia's own opinions. She also liked to hear *Bacco in Toscana*, Francesco Redi's long celebration of Tuscan wine and she usually joined in with gusto, especially the verse that started:

Hah! Montalcino. I know it well, -
The lovely little Muscdel;
A very lady-like little treat,
But something, for me, too gentle and sweet;

Even having heard it a number of times she still laughed at the last verse:

At these glad sounds,
The Nymphs, in giddy rounds,
Shaking their ivy diadems and grapes,
Echoed the triumph in a thousand shapes.
The Satyrs would have joined them; but alas!
They couldn't; for they lay upon the grass,
As drunk as apes.

Tonight though, I had only just started reading when she slipped off the chair and came to sit at my feet, her arms around my legs and her head resting on my lap. I was so distracted that I read the same verse twice. She giggled, a sound I had never heard her emit before, and when she started to stroke my thighs, the smile she gave me when I stumbled on my words was both mischievous and inviting.

I was two years since I had taken her and the memory of my actions at that time made me tentative and nervous this time. It was Sofia who guided my hands to disrobe her and then she slowly removed my boots, shirt and britches. We lay down, the fire keeping us warm and the rush mat on the earthen floor protecting our nakedness. We explored each others' bodies, leisurely at first but very soon with increasing passion and our joint climax echoed round the room, causing the bottles on the table to jingle, Pepe to let out a surprised yelp and Tabitha to cry out in her sleep.

I stopped the night for the very first time and slept with Sofia in her bed. As Tabitha was in a cot in the same room our love-making was, by necessity, more gentle but also more intense and oh, so satisfying. As we lay in each others' arms I spoke when I should have remained silent, 'Now will you marry me?' All I got was a hard poke in the ribs, a muttered, 'Don't be ridiculous,' and Sofia's back.

I woke the next morning, the sole occupant of the bed and the room. I could hear movement outside and guessed that Sofia and Tabitha were feeding the animals, and going about their normal daily routine. I lay for a few minutes, feeling deeply contented but then, with a stab of guilt, I remembered Roberto. I leapt out of bed, dressed and went outside to take my leave. Tabitha was squatting in the pig pen, ensuring that all five piglets got a fair share of their mother's milk. She came running when she saw me, hugged and kissed me in childish abandon, then returned to her task.

Sofia was throwing scraps for the chickens; they came running from all directions, clucking their appreciation. I wasn't sure how I should behave, like a lover or as if nothing had happened between us? Sofia answered my unspoken question by merely glancing unsmilingly at me, raising a hand in acknowledgement, or perhaps dismissal, then continuing to scatter the stale crumbs and pieces of wilting vegetables with intense concentration.

I shook my head at her attempt at nonchalance and decided it was time to take more control of the situation. I strode over to her, took the bowl from her, put it on the ground, hugged her hard, planted a kiss on her open lips then handed her back the bowl. I shouted, '*Ciao* Tabitha, *ciao* Sofia, *arrivederci!*' as I mounted my horse and rode away. I heard Tabitha chirp '*Ciao*, Papa, *ti amo!*' and smiled at Sofia's quieter and more restrained, '*Ciao*, Philippe.'

I rode as quickly as I could back to Florence, aware that by the time I arrived at the Villa Bouganville I would have exceeded the deadline il Conte had set by quite a number of days. I had threatened to resign if he hadn't allowed me to search for Roberto, and in the heat of the moment I would have done so. Now, however, the thought of no longer working for il Conte and having to find other employment filled me with trepidation. It was true that I had made some tentative enquiries about opportunities at the new secular school that had recently opened in Florence. I knew that there were posts available for teachers in a number of subjects that I could fill, but I would prefer to make such a big change in my life from choice, rather than from necessity.

As soon as I got back to the villa I sought out il Conte and blurted out my apologies. '*Perdonami, mio signore* but I felt I had to go back to the village to see if Roberto had returned home. I rode as fast as I could but I know I have still gone over the week you kindly allowed me. I meant no disrespect and I hope that you will be as generous as you have always been and forgive my small insubordination.'

'I assume you have still not found the boy?'

'No, signore. I called at the conservatoire before coming here and they have had no messages left by anyone who has seen or heard of him.'

'Then he obviously doesn't want to be found. You need to let him go and get back to your duties. In fact, sit down as I have some things I need you to do today.'

So, daily life returned to normal but in the evenings, rather than go to the conservatoire to sit with *i castrati*, I continued to wander around the streets and alleys of the city, still hoping to find my boy. Some five weeks after Roberto had run away, I was on my way home over the Ponte Vecchio. Although it was nearly dusk, the shop keepers still displayed their wares on tables outside their shops, hoping to attract custom from the throngs of people strolling in the balmy evening air. I was hot, tired and down-hearted after another unsuccessful evening's search and I slipped between two shops and leant against the stone balustrade, looking into the waters that swirled beneath me on their way to the sea.

A piece of cloth of indeterminate colour was caught on a branch that had got stuck in the mud. The sight triggered two simultaneous thoughts: The first was a vivid memory of the piece of red kerchief that had marked the spot of little Luigi's demise and the second was a notion that made me gasp. What if Roberto had decided to end it all by throwing himself into the Arno? I knew that many a suicide had leapt into these waters, the turbulent currents being too strong for even the best of swimmers. In fact, I remembered a time when I and the boys had been walking along the river bank at the same time as a body was being hauled out of the water. We had crossed ourselves and I had pushed the boys on ahead of me, but not before they had seen the white, wrinkled face of the corpse and the black, empty eye sockets looking up to a heaven he would never attain. I looked more intently at the flow and imagined a small body being carried in its watery arms. Would it be carried out to sea or might it get stuck in the weeds like the corpse we had seen or on a branch, like the piece of cloth that seemed to wave mockingly at me.

The next day, in between giving my lessons at the conservatoire and paying a visit to il Conte's banker, I made a detour to a building on the banks of the river that was the offices of the river authorities. It was here that one went to purchase a license to sell wares, offer transportation or to fish on the banks of the River Arno. Or to see if the body of a loved one had been plucked from the waters.

'Have you found any bodies over the last five weeks or so?'

The river master was a grizzled old man who grinned toothlessly at me, as if I had made a huge joke. 'How many do you want?'

'I don't want any! I want to know if the body of a young boy has been found. He has dark hair, a round face, taller than average.' I held my hand to show how high.

'By the time we get to them, the fishes have nibbled them so that their own mothers don't know them. We make a note of the bodies we find. Here, see for yourself.' He went behind a counter and brought out a large, leather-bound ledger. He opened the pages and turned to the ones dated from May 1761. He turned the book around so I could see the list, in a writing that was surprisingly neat and well formed:

May 22   male, unidentified
May 22   male, unidentified
May 23   male, unidentified
May 23   male, priest?

The list went on and on. There was nothing that gave any indication that one of the bodies found was that of Roberto and then I remembered something that might help identify him. 'He was a *castrato*. He wouldn't have had any balls.'

'Ha! Those bits are the first to be eaten. Most of them found would sing with high voices, if the dead could sing.'

'What happens to the bodies?'

'They get wrapped in a cloth provided by the do-gooders of the city and they are dumped in a field. They don't get a proper burial and there isn't nothing to mark the spot. There must be hundreds of bodies by now. If your boy was picked up, you'll never know.'

I had nothing to prove it, but I convinced myself that Roberto had ended his own life and he was now either at the bottom of the sea or at the bottom of a pit, surrounded on all sides by other poor souls whose life they had thought was not worth living.

I felt desperately sorry at such a sad and lonely end, one I felt partially responsible for, but I also felt relieved that I could stop searching. That evening, rather than scour the city streets I went to *Il Duoma* and prayed for Roberto's soul and the following evening I went back to the conservatoire to sit with *i castrati*. I shared my understanding of what had happened with them and they all nodded, agreeing that this was the most likely scenario. I put my hand on Fabio's shoulder, thinking I could offer some comfort.

'I am so sorry, Fabio. I know you were very close to Roberto and loved him like a brother.'

He shrugged my hand off and looked at me clear-eyed. 'We were not that close, not recently. To take one's own life is a sin. I do not mourn a sinner.' He looked around at the seated boys. 'These are my family now.'

I was speechless at his cold-heartedness and with it came a realisation that it had always been Roberto that I had loved the best and all I now felt towards his cousin was antipathy. That night I begged God's forgiveness, for I had promised Him to look after the two boys as if they had been my sons, but I had let one die and now I couldn't bear to be near the other. I never went back to the conservatoire in the evening, the thought of sitting with *i castrati* with their effeminate bodies and hearing their unnaturally high voices, made me shudder.

Chapter 27

Berti

Encouraged by Catherine, il Conte had bought the Villa Bouganville and was now having extensive work done to increase its size by having an additional wing built. This gave me a lot of work to do in ordering supplies, hiring and firing builders, dealing with questions and minor disasters. I grieved for Roberto privately and wished I could share my pain with Sofia. I longed to return to my haven in the wood and one evening, at supper with the De Lorenzo family, I asked if he needed me to go there soon.

'As it happens, yes, Philippe. I think it is about time I sold the place. Prince Caspar says he is interested in buying it, so I need you to go there and close the villa down.'

'You can't!'

Il Conte looked at me quizzically. 'I can't? I can't sell my own villa?'

'Forgive my rudeness, *mio signore*. It's just, well,' I had to tell him the truth, 'I have a family at Montalcino, a woman and a daughter. The only time I get to see them is when I go to the villa to do business for you. If you sell the villa ...' I didn't even want to put the consequences into words.

Catherine, who had been listening, clapped her hands in glee. 'Bravo, Philippe, but you must bring them here!'

'*Scuse*, Contessa, but Sofia is very independent and she will neither marry me nor move away from her home. She is a healer and much respected by the villagers. To live in a city, even one as beautiful as Florence, would kill her.'

Il Conte frowned then his brow cleared. 'A healing woman, you say? Not the one you fetched for poor Eleanora?'

'Yes, signore. That was Sofia. We became friends.' I couldn't tell them the circumstances of our first physical union. 'We have a little girl, Tabitha. She is four years old now. I go and see them whenever I am at the villa.'

A look of concern crossed il Conte's face. 'You are not going to leave us and go and live with her, are you?'

'No, signore. As I said, she won't marry me; I think my visiting every few months suits her. I don't want to make more demands in case she stops me going altogether. I couldn't bear it if I wasn't able to see my Tabitha.'

'Of course not!' Catherine looked sternly at il Conte, an expression which almost made me laugh out loud. 'Carlos, put the poor man out of his misery.' Before even her husband could draw breath, she continued, 'Oh, I will, if you won't. Carlos is only selling the villa to the Prince, he will be keeping ownership of the vineyards, the produce and the villagers. So, he will still need you to go there every few months to make sure everything is running smoothly.' She sat back smiling contentedly at her good news. I returned her smile, a feeling of relief washing over me.

'Thank you, Catherine. So, Philippe, you will indeed still need to go there and I was thinking you could start to bring back the rents, rather than Pedro. He hates making the journey and will be happy to hand over the responsibility to someone else.'

It wasn't until I returned to my family some four months later that I noticed the slight swelling of Sofia's belly. She saw where my eyes were fixed and she smiled at me, something she had been doing far more often over the last few months.

'We've made another one?'

'We have indeed. This one will be a winter baby.'

She allowed me to hug her and I felt the tightness of her stomach against mine.

'Is it moving yet?'

'No, he's concentrating on growing.'

'He?'

'He or she, but certainly not it. I am not *La Strega*; I can't tell the sex of a baby before he or she is born.'

I had only had the experience of Eleanora's pregnancy and I remembered how ill and tired she had always been. I tried to make Sofia sit down and offered to go and pick her plants and feed the animals so that she could rest. Sofia gave her habitual laugh of contempt that made me feel as small as a mouse.

'Having a child is not an illness. I am feeling perfectly well and quite capable of living my life as normal. I certainly don't want to lose all my patients because you have mixed up hemlock with parsley.'

I must have looked hurt at her rebuff for her face softened and she gave another laugh, this time a genuine one. 'I'm sorry, Philippe, but I do not need looking after and I do not need your help, not yet anyway. But thank you for your concern.'

I had a lot to do at the villa and stayed almost a week. Each evening, after a long day of instructing the staff what needed to be done to the villa and its contents, I would walk up to the house and share supper and Sofia's bed. The evenings were light until late and we would often go and sit in a nearby glade, where Sofia would sit and mend whilst I and Tabitha made up stories. Tabitha was always the heroine and there was usually an animal to be saved from the clutches of a witch, goblin or *Lo dragone*. This was a happy week and I was loathe to leave and for the first time Sofia clung to me before pushing me away, her cheeks flushed with embarrassment.

Whenever I returned to Florence, I tried to time it so that I would spend the night in the deserted village before entering the city the following morning. I always slept in the same house that we had all stayed in the very first time, as it still provided sufficient shelter, regardless of the weather. I had never seen anyone else there and this time also I was the only inhabitant, but I did see evidence of others: ashy remains where fires had been left to die down; the earthen floors churned by more feet than just mine and areas of compression where bodies had obviously lain to sleep. It didn't worry me that other travellers took advantage of the dwellings and I thought it might be nice to have company if our stays coincided.

When I got back to the villa I saw il Conte and Catherine taking a stroll round the rose garden. Catherine had moved the seat where Eleanora and I had sat and made our plans into a sunnier position and I no longer felt guilt or remorse when walking past it. Any memories of those times had been washed away by the winter rains and bleached by the summer sun. Il Conte beckoned to me to approach. We exchanged greetings and I handed my report to him.

'So, Philippe. You saw your little family?'

'Yes, thank you, Contessa. It was a very pleasant week.' I felt I needed to reassure il Conte. 'I stayed no longer than

233

was necessary. I am happy to say that we are expecting another child in about another four months time.'

'Oh, Philippe, that is wonderful news. We are very happy for you, aren't we, Carlos?'

Il Conte grunted his assent and looked up from the report and at me over his spectacles, which he had started to wear when reading. 'Does this change anything?'

'No, *mio signore*. It changes nothing.'

'Then I offer my congratulations, also.'

I don't know whether it was Catherine's influence or just il Conte's unexpected good-heartedness but thereafter I was sent back to the Villa De Lorenzo more frequently and managed to see Sofia and Tabitha once a month or so. During my next visit, I felt the baby kick against his confines and thought they were stronger and more impatient than Eduardo's had been, but maybe this was just wishful thinking. Our night-time stories now included Tabitha saving a baby from the lair of a wolf or the nest of an eagle.

Sofia and I continued to have sex right up to the end. I was never the initiator because I was concerned about causing damage to the baby but Sofia always assured me that making love was the most natural thing in the world and she taught me ways we could both be satisfied without harming the waiting child. I didn't ask her how she knew such things.

As her time neared, I marvelled at how well she looked. She was not pale and drawn as Eleanora had been, but rather glowed with good health and vitality. Her hair shone like polished copper and I wondered whether the new baby would have his mother's colouring, as Tabitha did, or have my dark locks.

I wanted desperately to be at the birth and I shared my desire with Catherine, who I knew would gently bully her husband into letting me stay away as long as was necessary. He pretended to be cross at the inconvenience and dictated a long list of tasks I needed to do whilst there. The villa now belonged to Prince Caspar but I still needed to check the books, the storage, production and sale of the wine, and ensure the villagers had no complaints that the estate manager was not dealing with. In addition, this time I would bring back the half-yearly rent that had been collected from the villagers. As I finished writing he came to my side of the desk, shook my hand and hoped the birth went well. I was so surprised I forgot to thank him.

I had been with my family for but three days when early in the morning, before even the sun had risen, I was prodded in the back and told to go and fetch signora Ricci from the village. It was December and cold but I rushed out without my coat and so shivered as I waited for the old woman to prepare and as she walked at a leisurely pace up the hill. She refused to mount the horse and I didn't want to leave her in case she got lost, so I walked with her, resisting the temptation to throw her onto the horse and gallop the rest of the way. When we arrived Sofia was sitting serenely in bed.

'Thank you for coming, signora. Now, Philippe, take Tabitha up the mountain and go and pick a basketful of nettles. Not the ones in the wood here but go up to the source of the stream, where it gushes out of the rocks. I will then boil them and the liquid will help me produce more milk. The baby won't be born until this evening so you have all day.' She must have seen me still shivering. 'Make sure you both wrap up well.'

I made sure Tabitha wore her sheepskin boots and coat and donned my own outer clothing and we spent a happy day climbing up the mountain side, stopping for lunch sheltered from the cold wind behind a huge rock that we agreed must have been hurled there by a furious giant. We picked a basketful of nettles; they looked exactly the same to me as those that grew outside the front door, but Sofia was the expert and she wouldn't have sent us all this way for no reason.

Being a winter month, the days were short and we got back to the house just as dusk was falling. As we entered I held Tabitha's hand and squeezed it gently, half expecting to hear Sophia's screams, but I could hear nothing and my heart lurched at the thought of what might have happened. My fear must have passed to Tabitha for we both stood stock still, listening for a sound, any sound, to indicate that there was life in the house. Then I heard something that I recognised, the suckling of a nipple. I rushed over to the curtain and pulled it back to see Sofia sitting comfortably in bed, her nightgown and sheets spotlessly clean, her hair brushed and a small head locked onto her nipple. It had a mop of black hair.

'You minx! You sent us away on purpose. The nettles in the wood would have been just as good.'

Sofia merely smiled at me, took my hand and put it on the baby's head. 'Say hullo to your son, Philippe.'

I didn't know whether to laugh or cry, so did both. I sat on one side of Sofia and Tabitha on the other, and we just stared and stared at the little head that refused to pull away so that we could have a better look.

Eventually he fell asleep and let go of the nipple and Sofia turned him so we could see his face. His cheeks were red and his lips swollen, so strong had been his sucking. He had long, black lashes that fluttered on his cheeks and I was mesmerised by the perfection of his tiny ears. Tabitha stroked his downy head. 'What are we going to call him?'

Sofia looked at me. 'You choose, Philippe.'

I hadn't given it a thought, assuming that Sofia would name him, but I didn't have to think for long. 'Alberto, after my father; a kind and honourable man. Would you mind?'

'Alberto is a fine name.' Sofia kissed the top of his head and whispered, 'Welcome little Berti, welcome to your family.'

Chapter 28

I banditi

I stayed for another couple of days, trying to help so that Sofia could concentrate on Berti, but she was constantly telling me what to do and what not to do. She wouldn't let me chop herbs, telling me I was holding the knife all wrong; she wouldn't let me milk the goat, saying I didn't have the touch, which was true; she wouldn't even let me feed the chickens, claiming that I wasn't distributing the morsels fairly, overfeeding some, and starving others. I very soon realised that I was not needed and wasn't surprised when Sofia handed me a bag containing some bread, cheese and slices of cooked chicken.

'You need to go now, Philippe. You still work for il Conte and he won't stand for this long absence for ever.' She gave me time to kiss my children goodbye then pushed me firmly out of the door, without even offering her cheek.

Before making the return journey I stopped at the vineyard and picked up the monies that had been collected over the previous six months. Pedro, despite his advanced age, still had enough of a threatening presence to be more than capable of carrying on collecting the rents from the villagers for many a year yet. He had the body and constitution of an ox and I don't think anything scared him apart from, perhaps, the thought of getting too old to do his job. The only thing I was aware of that unsettled him was having to leave his beloved Montalcino to travel to the sinful city of *Firenze*. He was, therefore, very happy to share a glass of wine with me, fill my saddle bags with the coins and wave goodbye as I rode away.

My horse knew the route so well now that I was able to dream the day away without worrying about getting lost. I wondered what sort of man Berti would become; I wondered whether he would be a man of letters or of action; I wondered whether I would be able to pass on my love of poetry to him; I wondered whether he would be a country or a city lover. It had not occurred to me before, but I also wondered how his being a boy would disrupt the matriarchy that had endured in the little house in the woods for at least three generations.

By the time I reached the empty village outside Florence I was saddle sore and weary. I had eaten a quick supper at a tavern a few hours earlier so once I had hobbled the horse I wrapped myself in a blanket and was soon fast asleep. I have noticed before that whatever I was thinking of just before sleeping had a tendency to infiltrate my dreams, often in a grotesque manner, and this night was no exception. I dreamt not of one baby, but of many, all so small they fitted in my pockets, sat on the brim of my hat, clung onto the tops of my boots and swung from my collar. One of them bizarrely held a giant hat pin in his tiny hand that he proceeded to stick into my neck. I cried out and knocked the baby to the ground but the pain continued.

I woke with a start to a deep, throaty whisper in my ear, 'Make a move and I'll slit your throat.' I had no reason to disbelieve him. 'Empty your pockets.' He prodded the point of the knife in harder; I felt a drop of blood roll down my neck.

I felt strangely calm. 'I need to sit up.' He eased away to give me room to move but kept the blade in position. I emptied my pockets onto the floor. There was no moon and

I hadn't lit a fire but one of the men who was standing in the doorway was holding a lantern, which gave enough light for it to be clear that I carried no treasure on my person. There were a few coins, which were greedily snatched up, a wooden block that Tabitha must have slipped into my pocket and my book of poetry. My assailant picked up the book and flicked through it one-handed, the other hand being preoccupied with still holding the knife steadily against my throat.

I wondered if he was a reader himself; whether there was a bond, however tenuous, that I could use to my advantage. 'Do you like poetry, signore?'

He laughed, a guttural sound that held no humour. I couldn't see him as he was crouched behind me, but through the doorway I could see the others, some six or seven of them milling around the horse. Half were grown men but the others were just boys. One of the men opened one of the saddle bags and let out a yell, 'Ha, look what we have here!' He took a handful of the coins and held out his palm, the gold glittering in the lamplight. They all cheered and looked at each other excitedly.

'You are foolish to carry so much money,' the voice whispered behind me. For some unfathomable reason I felt obliged to explain.

'It is the rent from the villagers of Montalcino.'

Another bleak laugh behind me and he put his mouth to my ear and croaked, 'How very appropriate that we should take it.'

I didn't know what he meant but when I tried to turn to question him the point pierced even deeper. One of the men, the leader perhaps, stood at the entrance, looked over my shoulder at the man behind me and silently dragged his finger across his neck in a slicing motion. The instruction was clear and I tensed myself in preparation to fight back.

'Be still, signor Agostini. I will not kill you, not this time.'

Who was this man, this whisperer, who knew my name? Then I realised he must have read the P. Agostini that I had written in the front of the book. The man must therefore be educated. 'Who are you? Why are you doing this?'

The whisperer waited until his fellow *banditi* were on their way, taking my horse with them, and then growled into my ear, 'Sometimes there is no choice, signore. Life does not always turn out as hoped.' With that he gave one final jab, which made me gasp with pain then loped away.

There was still some light cast by the lamp that was fast disappearing and I saw a tall man, with disproportionately long arms striding away. There was something about him, but no, how could it be? I nearly called out to him, but I hesitated and then it was too late, for he was engulfed by the blackness. I could hear the *banditi's* chatter getting quieter as they moved away but I'm certain that I heard the name Roberto. Not an uncommon name, I know, but his form and his walk had seemed so familiar. Was it possible? Had he known my name because he recognised me rather than having read it in my book of poetry? Had Roberto not drowned himself after all? Had he instead joined the only people that would take him in - a gang of murderers and thieves?

I sat in the pitch black and very soon the small thrill of excitement that had fluttered down my spine at my happy conjecture turned into shivers of delayed terror that wracked my whole body. I was cold too, and the only warmth came from the blood that was dripping down my neck. At least the *banditi* had left me my blanket so I wrapped myself in it and lay, staring into the night and waited for the dawn.

I must have dozed for I woke to the sound of rain on the roof tiles. I was chilled to the marrow and hungry but they had taken my horse and all my money; all I could do was to start to walk down the steep path to the river and onto Florence. I warmed myself with the thought that Roberto was still alive and of the sympathy that il Conte would feel at my plight and his relief at my survival.

'In the name of God, Philippe, couldn't you have stopped them?'

Catherine and Isabella spoke at the same time.

'Carlos, have a heart! There was only him against how many?'

'Papa! Poor signor Agostini could have been killed and there were hundreds of them!'

'There were seven plus the one with the knife at my throat, the one I believe was Roberto.'

Il Conte huffed. 'Well, if it was Roberto he wasn't going to kill you, was he? You should have used that to your advantage.'

'I didn't realise until they had left, by which time it was too late. I think like *un segretario, mio signore, non un soldato.*'

'I know, I know. I'm just annoyed that they took so much gold. Next time you will need to be armed. You can at least defend yourself?'

'I was only in your army for a few weeks and if you recall you found me in the library, not on the battlefield. I am a man of words, signore, not of the sword.'

'Words never killed anyone! I suppose I am going to have to hire an armed guard. More expense I can ill afford!' Catherine tutted her displeasure at him and then herself cleansed the wound in my neck, which was swollen and sore, whilst il Conte stared out of the window. I saw his jaw clenching and unclenching and then he sat upright and banged on the table with his fist. 'I will discuss this with some others and propose we form a militia, find these *banditi* and remove them from the face of the earth.' He didn't ask for our opinion of his plan but strode out of the room, a spring in his step as if he relished the thought of killing again.

After Catherine had bound my neck she indicated that I stay seated.

'You are sure it was Roberto?'

'Yes, Contessa. The more I think about it, the more certain I am. It is not just that I recognised his distinctive gait but also that he knew my name. I am sure that he recognised my book of poetry for I always have it with me and I would sometimes read to the boys from it. After all, how many *banditi* can read? I am also sure I heard someone say his name as they were leaving.'

'But his voice was different, you say?'

'Yes, it was a hoarse croak like this.' I spoke in a fair imitation of the voice that had whispered in my ear the previous night.

Catherine looked troubled. 'He is trying to erase everything of who he was.'

I nodded in agreement. 'There is little left of the boy who dreamed of being an opera singer.'

Isabella, who had been listening intently to our conversation, suddenly smiled. 'At least he is not dead. We must tell Fabio, signore, he will be so pleased.'

I waited for Isabella to leave for her morning lessons before sharing my fears. 'I am worried, Contessa. You heard what il Conte said about raising a militia, finding and killing these *banditi*. They won't be inclined to search out one boy and spare him.'

'No, I'm afraid you are right, Philippe. You need to join them, try and find Roberto first and prevent them from hurting him. Or indeed, any of the boys; they are just children, desperate and dangerous maybe, but still children. Yes, you must join them. Explain the reason to Carlos, make him understand. He is not cruel. It is the leaders they will want, not their minions.'

I went in search of il Conte and found him in the stables, ready to mount his great black horse, Maximillian. I explained why I, a man of words, wanted to join his men of war.

He glowered at me. 'You are too soft, Philippe. I won't risk giving you a weapon; you are more likely to kill me than one of the *banditi*. I won't be able to look out for you but if you manage to find Roberto you will need to get him away quickly for I cannot guarantee that the others will understand or share your sensibilities. I'll let you know the plan when we have one.'

It was only when I watched him ride out of the villa gates that I realised I hadn't told them about Berti.

Although it was too late for me to give my lessons I walked to the conservatoire to tell the good news about Roberto. Monsignor Mazzini and Father Guiseppe were, as to be expected, initially pleased that he was alive but then almost immediately anxious about his current predicament. The fact that I would be joining the militia in an attempt to save Roberto did not appear to appease their concerns.

Fabio's response was not totally unexpected, bearing in mind his attitude when he thought Roberto had killed himself. He spat out the words. 'He is a fool! He may be my cousin but I no longer recognise him as such.'

'Fabio, you are too cruel. Have you forgotten how much you loved each other? How do you think you would have coped if it was you whose voice was ruined? You know singing was everything to Roberto. He needs our care not our condemnation.'

Fabio sneered. 'I would have accepted God's plan for me and whatever role He offered to me, be it as a singer or otherwise. It is not my place to question Him but I would have continued to praise Him in any way I could.'

He bowed to me stiffly, turned and went back to his lessons.

I wondered whether he had been born such a pompous and heartless prig.

Chapter 29

The rescue

I continued with my daily routine but I walked around with a hard knot in my stomach as I waited for il Conte's summons to outline his murderous plan. It came a week later.

'All the men I have talked to support my scheme and we are agreed that we are going to spread word that there is a lightly guarded bag of gold being transported from a Florence bank to Pistoia in the early morning the day after tomorrow. I have surveyed the road and there are just two places which *i banditi* are likely to choose for an attack. We will have both places staked out ourselves. We will be better armed and ready for them.'

'But which group should I be in, signore? What if I am in the group that is in the wrong place? How will I save Roberto then?'

'Ah, Philippe. I have thought of that. You will be one of the guards. Then you will be wherever the attack takes place. It is a perfect plan!'

'Me? You want me to be the bait? Every ruffian in the whole of Florence will be there; they'll kill me before anyone has a chance to blink. It's a terrible plan!'

Il Conte actually laughed. 'Fear not, my little *segretario*, you will have Davide by your side and he does know how to fight. And you will be surrounded by seasoned soldiers who will be more than ready to wipe these *banditi* from the face of the earth.'

'But...'

'There are no buts, Philippe. If you want to protect Roberto then you will need to be there when the gang attacks and the only way you can guarantee being in the right place is being with the gold.'

'Yes, but what if Roberto's gang doesn't attack? What if it is another gang or more than one, but not his?'

'Then what do you lose? You will still be doing your bit to rid Florence of dangerous scum and protecting its inhabitants. You will be a hero!'

The picture in my head showed very clearly what I would lose, and that was my life. Another thought occurred to me. 'What if they attack somewhere else?'

'They would be fools to attack anywhere else. These two locations are the only places ideal for a surprise attack but they are also ideal for us to defend as long as we get there first.'

I bit back the retort that it was quite likely that these men were fools and would not necessarily recognise an advantageous strategic military position even if they were looking for one.

I went to the stables in search of Davide and found him sharpening a long knife on a whetstone. I sat down next to him and watched as he honed the edge. I didn't want to break his concentration so waited until he had finished and tested the sharpness by effortlessly slicing a thin blade of grass down the middle.

'So we are to be the lures.'

'So it would seem, Philippe, but there will be plenty of men waiting to attack once the robbers show themselves. Here, this is for you, just in case.' He handed me the knife, its blade shining in the sunlight. I pushed it away.

'I don't want it. I could never stick that into anyone's flesh.'

'Take it, Philippe. You may not want to use it, but no-one else will know that. Just thrust it out so,' I backed away as the point came dangerously close to my chest, 'and they will assume you mean to use it in earnest.'

I suddenly had an image of the knife in Father Stephen's chest and I shuddered. Davide held the knife out to me and I took it tentatively. I placed the edge very gently on my finger tip and it sliced through my flesh as if it were butter softened by the sun. I grimaced and sucked the blood. Davide grinned and handed me a leather sheath.

'Here, you need to keep the knife in this. Wear it across your chest so that you can get at it quickly if need be. But I wager you won't have to.' That was a bet I was happy for him to win.

I felt anxious all that day and the next. My imagination ran wild and each of my imminent deaths was more bloody and gruesome than the last. I was almost relieved when it was time for me and Davide to set off on the road to Pistoia, with leather saddle bags full of stones. It was still dark, just before dawn, but Catherine and Isabella were there to wave us off and wish us good luck. Il Conte had already left to get his men into position at one of the two likely attack sites.

As we rode through the street of Florence I felt unseen eyes watching us from the dark alleyways and the shadowy doorways. I looked around me nervously but there was no-one else yet abroad. Davide grinned at me. 'There is nothing to worry about, not yet anyway. I'll tell you when to be on your guard.'

We rode on as the sun climbed slowly over the edge of the world and by the time we left the city I could see the blackness lightening in the gaps between the banks of rolling clouds that threatened more rain. There were still homes here, albeit humble and run down, but I appreciated that this would not be a good place for an attack and I relaxed slightly. As the road rose up into the hills and the dwellings petered out, however, my stomach started to churn. I found myself gripping the handle of the knife, which was safely sheathed under my jacket but was easily accessible.

'Not yet, Philippe, it is too open here. There is nowhere for anyone to hide and we would see them before they had time to get anywhere near us. You see those trees over there? That is the first of the places we need to be careful.'

The wooded area was still about an hour's ride away but I kept my eyes riveted on it in case I could see anything to indicate that there was anyone hiding, defender or attacker. I saw nothing and heard only the clip clop of the horses' hooves. As we neared the wooded area my body tensed and my breathing quickened. I gripped the horse hard with my thighs and clenched the knife handle, gaining some comfort from the feel of the smooth wood in my hand.

It took but a quarter of an hour for us to travel through the wood. Only once the trees were behind us and we were in more open ground did I relax my hold on both horse and handle and allow myself to breathe more normally. Davide grinned at me, his tanned face creasing in his amusement. 'Did you see any of the militia men?'

'No! Not one, did you? Were they there?'

'I spied five or six but there would have been many more; they were mostly well hidden. They are professionals. I bet they were disappointed we were not attacked.'

I felt no sympathy for them and began to hope that perhaps we wouldn't be attacked at all. We had no idea if the rumour of the transportation of the gold had reached the right ears or if they would decide to try and take it. We rode for another hour and when I saw another wooded area I looked quizzically at Davide and he nodded in agreement. As we neared the edge of the trees this time I gripped the handle of the knife and unsheathed it.

'Be careful with that, you might cut yourself, or even worse, me!'

I glowered at his attempt at humour but continued to hold the knife out in front of me in the hope that it would frighten off a band of desperate men. I noticed that Davide had also released his own knife and was holding it almost casually across the pommel of the saddle.

As we got further into the wood the winter daylight lost its battle and we could barely see more than a few arms' lengths ahead of us. The air seemed too thick to breathe and, despite the cold air I felt sweat trickling down my back. Suddenly there was a hoot of an owl from my right, and almost immediately, as if in response, there was a howl of a wolf from the left.

'This is it, Philippe. They are calling to each other.'

I found it difficult to swallow and I almost dropped the knife from my trembling, sweating hand.

'Keep alert. Remember, our men are out there too.'

The next two minutes were the longest in my life. I suddenly saw something move in the undergrowth, just a pale flash, perhaps the hind of a deer, or a man's face. I could hear Davide breathing heavily and he was holding his knife for action.

Then it was absolute mayhem as men and boys ran out from the trees from all sides, whooping and screeching and running in circles around us. The whites of their eyes stared crazily at us from their mud smeared faces. We stood stock still as they continued to circle us, making terrifying undulating noises like a herd of wild beasts. Some had knives, others pikes but most just their bare hands. I had to fight hard to stop my horse from rearing in panic. I knew that we two didn't stand a chance.

Suddenly, as one, they stopped their capering and stood in a large circle facing us. The horses nervously pawed the ground, their ears laid flat and their nostrils flared. There were well over twenty men and boys; two or three gangs must have joined together. I tried to count exactly how many there were but my attempt was interrupted by one of the men stepping forward and looking up at me.

'Well, what have we got here? Where are you travellers going on this cold winter's day?'

I tried to speak but I had no saliva and my mouth was bone dry. It was Davide who answered, in a friendly tone. 'We're just on our way to Pistoia, to court two lovely sisters.' Everyone sniggered at his lie.

The leader, for I assume that is what he was, eyed the saddlebags on Davide's horse and, with a leer, started to open it. I glanced quickly at the men and boys who were within the range of my sight and immediately recognised

Roberto. He returned my stare, a puzzled look on his face. He would have recognised both Davide and myself and would have known full well that we were unlikely to be carrying gold from a Florentine bank, nor were we likely to be courting two sisters.

I could tell the very instant when he realised that this was a trap. His eyes opened wide and he opened his mouth to shout a warning but it was lost in the noise that suddenly erupted when an army of men hurled themselves out of the woods, led by il Conte. Some had spears, some pikestaffs and some even muskets, all of which were pointing at a different *bandito*. Every rogue was covered by at least three militia men. The gang remained perfectly still, as if turned to stone, continuing to look inwards as the soldiers began to circle silently around them. No-one uttered a sound, which I found more threatening than the cries of the attackers had been. I took my eye off Roberto for a few seconds when il Conte caught my attention and gave me a wink, but when I looked back at the boy he was glaring at me with absolute hatred burning from his eyes.

'*Bastardo*' he mouthed. He then raised his clenched fist and shouted, '*Bastardi.*'

It was as if this was a sign, for *i banditi* turned outwards as one and surged towards the militia men, knives slicing wildly into surprised flesh, sticks splitting heads, fists breaking noses. The hooligans didn't have a chance, of course, and the militia men soon regained the upper hand. I had to struggle to keep control of the horse amidst the cries of anger and pain, the mud that splashed under the trampling feet and the smell of blood that tainted the air.

I looked for Roberto and saw him in hand to hand combat with a man I knew to be a trained soldier. Roberto was easily pushed to the ground and a knife poised over his throat. I screamed, 'No!' and forced the horse forwards through the mass of heaving bodies. 'Leave him, he's mine.' The soldier looked at me with eyes full of madness, his chilling grin never leaving his face. With as much authority as I could muster I said, 'On Count De Lorenzo's orders.' The soldier's mouth and knife-hand twitched and I thought he would ignore my command but after a few seconds he withdrew the knife, but still stood with one boot on Roberto's chest, pinning him to the ground. I dismounted, as did Davide, who pushed the militia man off Roberto, telling him to go and fight a different battle. We manhandled Roberto onto the back of Davide's horse and tied his hands and feet loosely to make it look as if we were taking him prisoner. Davide mounted behind Roberto and I climbed onto my horse and we turned around and slowly walked back the way we had come.

I have never taken part in a war but surely this was what it looked like at the end of a battle? There were bodies carpeting the floor, mostly those of *i banditi*, their meagre clothing covered in mud and blood. The faces I could see, especially those of the young boys, had death masks of terror that chilled my already frozen heart. The militia men were dragging the bodies and loading them like sacks of grain onto the back of a cart that had appeared from I don't know where. My master was directing the clean-up operation and didn't acknowledge our leaving. I waited until we were out of sight before slipping off my horse and emptying my stomach onto the woodland flora.

Davide had dismounted also but only to remove the false shackles from Roberto. He shook his head sadly. 'They had the bloodlust. It is a good thing we managed to get Roberto out.'

I looked up at the boy, not knowing what to expect, thanks or derision? He sat with his head bowed, tears streaming down his cheeks, leaving tracks in the caked mud. He sensed my gaze and raised his eyes to mine. They were filled with such pain, 'They were my family, signor Agostini, my family,' he had forgotten to disguise his voice and he sounded like a young girl. He started to sob. He sat slumped like a wooden puppet whose strings had been cut. I reached up to try and comfort him but he pulled away as if my touch would burn him.

'Roberto, il Conte has said he can give you a job. Maybe in the stables with Davide? You'd like that, wouldn't you, working with horses? Or in the gardens?'

He lifted his face and his look of despair had been replaced with utter contempt. 'No, I would not like that.' His voice was a gruff whisper again. Before I could grab him he had slipped off the back of the horse and ran into the trees and immediately out of sight.

'Roberto, come back!' I went to follow him but Davide held me back.

'You won't be able to find him, Philippe, Leave him be. You tried your best. At least we know he is alive. Come, let's go back.'

I didn't want to leave but I knew Davide was right. Roberto had gone again and I had failed, again.

Chapter 30

The apprentice

We both remounted and made our way slowly back to Florence. I forced myself to think of something pleasant and tried to imaging the weight of Berti in my arms, the feel of Tabitha tugging at my hand, the smell of Sofia after she had been rooting in the woods. Each image, however, was interrupted with a blade piercing soft flesh or the surging cry of a man lusting for blood or the sound of sobbing.

When we got back to the villa the courtyard was filled with an army of militia men, laughing and slapping each other on the back. Those men who had lain siege to the first wood were easily identified by their unmarked clothing, whereas those from the second were spattered with mud, blood and worse. I didn't want to join in their celebrations; all I wanted to do was to strip off my own clothes, wash my body from head to toe and fade into a dreamless sleep.

Before I could make my escape, however, il Conte saw me and Davide and strode over to us and put his arm around our shoulders. He smelled of blood and wine.

'Well done, men, well done! We got them all. We've brought the bodies back and we're going to hang them from the bridges as a warning to any others who decide to intimidate us and take what is not theirs.' He thrust a cup of wine into each of our hands than raised both his high into the air. '*Evviva*! Hooray for justice! Well done, men, we showed them!' Everyone raised their cups and shouted '*Evviva*!'

I had to clamp my mouth shut to stop myself from vomiting again.

I slipped away but as I entered the villa Catherine, who was reading in the salon, saw me and beckoned me in. 'Did you find him?'

I sat down opposite her, put my head in my hands and nodded.

'They didn't kill him, did they? Please don't say they killed him.'

'No, Contessa. I was able to take him away before they slaughtered him, as they did every other man and boy. He ran away again.'

'But why? You saved his life! Surely he was grateful?'

'No, he was not grateful, he was traumatised. He looked on that gang as his family and he had just seen them hacked to pieces. Why would he be grateful to me, who had been a principal player in that horror?' Catherine bit her lip and I was sorry I had spoken so graphically. 'We have ruined his life not once but twice. I want to help him but I am probably the last person alive who he would ever turn to. God knows where he will go now. Forgive me, Contessa, but it has been a tiring morning and I need to freshen up and sleep awhile.'

She stood with me and put her hand on my cheek. 'None of this is your fault, Philippe. You are a good man, with a good heart.'

I did not feel good and my sleep was that of the damned.

The next morning I went to the conservatoire. I hadn't taught a lesson for a while and needed to return to some semblance of normality. My route today took me over il Ponte a Rubaconte and the first I saw of the grisly warnings that il Conte had boasted about was the flock of rooks that dived and rose along the whole edge of the bridge where the stripped bodies hung. A bird would survey the array of

256

tempting tit-bits before it swooped to grab a tasty morsel, a moist eye-ball or tantalising shred of pink flesh perhaps and then fly to a quiet spot to savour the treat. I put my hands to my ears so I wouldn't have to hear the ghastly cawing sound and ran as fast as I could over the bridge.

When I got to the conservatoire I went straight to my first lesson. Even though my attendance was irregular at best, one of the brothers usually took the class in my absence so that the boys did not suffer from my unreliability. I still enjoyed teaching the younger boys and for a few hours I lost myself in helping them with a frieze of all the letters of the alphabet. This was a project I had started many months ago and which they had continued during my absences, with the help of the assistant brothers. None of the boys were *castrati*, they were just normal boys, some serious, some mischievous, all who would rather be outside than stuck in a room learning letters. Nonetheless, we spent a light-hearted few hours and by the end I felt more relaxed than I had done since leaving my family in the woods.

Fabio, of course, attended classes at the conservatoire but since his solo at the wedding il Conte had suggested that he join Isabella in some of her afternoon lessons. Il Conte considered Fabio to be his stepping stone to the higher echelons of society and was willing to pay for his talented protégé to be better educated. So it was that most afternoons I would see Fabio at the villa, going to or from the school room or often in the company of Isabella. They had outgrown the games they used to play when the had been younger and now would sit in the same rose garden that Eleanora and I had frequented or they would sit in the library and read poetry to each other.

I rarely spoke to Fabio. I had never forgiven him for his reaction to Roberto's supposed suicide or to the discovery that he was in fact alive. I assumed that Isabella would tell him about Roberto's escape from the annihilation of *i banditi*, for I didn't want to hear the scorn in Fabio's voice or see the contempt in his eyes.

That May Isabella was thirteen. She was turning into a lovely young woman and it heartened me that she still treated me as a friend, but only when she was alone with me. When she was with Fabio she only had eyes for him and the pair of them walked around as if they were inside a bubble, whispering together and acknowledging no-one else. I thought it was a strange relationship and said so to Catherine one day when we were both walking to the stables and caught sight of the two youngsters ambling towards the rose garden, hand in hand.

She repeated what her husband had said to me a few years earlier. 'It is the best sort of friendship as he is neither male nor female. There is absolutely no risk of them growing physically attached to each other so nothing unsavoury can occur. Didn't they used to have eunuchs in the East to guard the women of the harem because they were not a threat?'

It was true that Fabio was neither strictly male nor female. He didn't wear a dress and yet his whole demeanour when he walked, talked and gestured was that of a female. He giggled and tossed his head like a girl and his complexion and lack of facial hair belied his masculinity. Catherine was right and my concerns were groundless; Isabella obviously just looked on Fabio as a female-like companion.

One afternoon in June I was crossing the lawn when I heard Isabella shouting hysterically, 'Stop it! Both of you, stop it!' I ran towards the rose garden, where the cries were coming from. When I raced through the entrance I was surprised to see Fabio tussling with someone on the pebbled path. Fabio was tall but not strong and his opponent, who was taller and stronger suddenly got the better of Fabio and threw him on his back, sat astride his chest and started to pummel him relentlessly, screaming '*Bastardo*!' over and over again.

I rushed over to the pair and pulled off Roberto, for he was the assailant, pinning his arms so he couldn't lash out at me. His face was contorted with rage and he struggled like one possessed until Isabella stalked up to him and slapped him hard across the face. He froze in surprise and watched as she went over to Fabio and helped him to his feet. His nose was bleeding and I imagined that he would have a few bruises from Roberto's pounding but I suspected that it was his pride that was hurt more than his body.

I maintained my hold of Roberto. 'What happened?'

Fabio glared at Roberto and spat at him, the mucus sliding slowly down his cheek. I tightened my grip but Roberto didn't react. 'He was spying on us from that tree.' The same tree that I had climbed all those years ago in order to escape from il Conte discovering my liaison with Eleanora. 'We were just sitting on the bench and he suddenly leapt on me, started beating me and shouting disgusting things. He took me by surprise, that's all.'

259

I glanced at Roberto but he was staring unblinkingly at the ground and I knew he wouldn't give me an explanation in the presence of the other two. Still grasping him fast so that he couldn't run away, I told Isabella to take Fabio back to the villa and clean his face.

When they had gone, Roberto sagged in my arms. I didn't release my hold for I didn't trust him not to run off and I didn't want to lose him again. I was shocked at the feel of bones under a thin layer of flesh; all his former chubbiness had disappeared. 'Do you want something to eat?'

Roberto seemed surprised at this turn of conversation. He reverted to his hoarse whisper, 'Not here.'

'No, we'll go to a tavern. Do you promise not to run off again?'

He nodded but I wasn't convinced so I continued to hold his upper arm and led him out of the garden and villa and along the street to the nearest inn. I sat him in a seat then positioned myself to obstruct his exit. I ordered the food and a flagon of wine then sat silently, waiting for him to speak. He fidgeted under my stare but managed to keep mute until the meal was served. He must have been ravenous for he tore at the bread and barely chewed a piece of meat before putting another into his mouth. I ordered a second helping for him, which he still finished before I had emptied my bowl, but he ate slower and seemed to be savouring the taste this time. When he had finished he gave a satisfied belch and sat back, his expression and stance more relaxed.

'Well?'

He bit his lip, a habit of his when he was unsure what to say. I decided to find out why he had been at the villa before enquiring about the fight with his cousin.

'Why were you up the tree?'

'I wanted to catch you without anyone else being around. I know you like to go there to read so I have been going there and waiting for you but you never came.'

'How long have you been doing that?'

'For the last few weeks. Sometimes I would see you but you were always with il Conte or his new wife. I often saw Isabella and Fabio but they never saw me amongst the leaves. I was quite comfortable and I felt safe.'

'Alright, so you were up this tree waiting for me to appear alone when suddenly Isabella, your friend, and Fabio, your cousin, came into the garden and sat in the seat just below you. Then what happened?'

'They sat talking and then ...'

'And then what, Roberto? What happened that made you come out of your safe spot and try and beat Fabio half to death?'

Roberto, bit his lip again and he clenched his fists. 'He touched her.'

I felt my stomach tighten. I waited for him to say more but his mouth had become an uncommunicative thin line. I had to know. 'Touched her where?'

Roberto blushed and looked away. 'He put his hand up the skirt of her dress. I expected Isabella to push his hand away but she didn't. Maybe she was too shocked. So I jumped down and pulled him off. He's dirty; he shouldn't have touched her in that way.'

I suspected that Isabella hadn't pushed Fabio away not from shock but for an entirely different reason, but I didn't want to disillusion Roberto. 'But surely, Roberto, *castrato* don't feel the same, well the same urges as normal men?'

'Is that what you have been told, signor Agostini? Maybe my operation wasn't done properly but my cock still hardens at the sight of a pretty girl and Fabio's was certainly pointing towards his God when I jumped on him.'

'They're both of an age when they are learning about themselves and their bodies. They were just exploring, there is no harm done and no danger.'

He looked at me as if I had vilified the Virgin Mary. 'No harm done? No danger? No one should touch her there until she is married. He was taking advantage of her innocence. He deserves to be punished and never left alone with her again.'

'Roberto, it was good of you to try and defend her and I'll have words with both Fabio and Isabella, but you may have really hurt him, even damaged his voice.'

'Good.'

'You don't mean that. It is not Fabio's fault that your voice is damaged and hurting him won't alter the fact.'

'I hate him.'

I touched his arm. 'Don't say that. You are angry that your life hasn't turned out the way you dreamed it would. I can understand that. But that is no reason to hate Fabio. Won't you be a little pleased for him if he becomes a success?'

He looked at me as if I were a crazy man, shrugged then changed the subject. 'When you took me away from the wood that time, you said you would help me get work. Did you mean it?'

'Of course I did. Davide is always complaining that he needs more help in the stables. You like him, don't you?'

Roberto nodded hesitantly.

'But Roberto, I need you to promise me that you won't run away again nor fight with Fabio. Do you promise?'

He sighed and nodded again. He slumped in his chair and I saw that he was exhausted. I had him back again and I intended to take good care of him. 'Come on. Let's go back to the villa. What you need now is some sleep and feeding up.'

Although it was still early evening, I took Roberto straight to the stables and found him a place to sleep. He snuggled down with a light blanket pulled up to his chin and went to sleep instantly. I watched him for a few minutes and although he was not my son and I would never love him as I did my own offspring, my heart still contracted and a surge of love for him washed over me. Finally I had a chance to help him lead a better life, if he would let me. I went to find Davide and found him walking a young colt round and round to get it used to wearing a harness.

'I have found you an apprentice.'

He smiled appreciatively. 'Good, I need one.'

Chapter 31

The invitation

I went to the De Lorenzo family, who were sitting under the shade of a large tree in the garden. Since his marriage to Catherine, il Conte had found more time to spend with his family, when he wasn't butchering *banditi*. Isabella blushed when she saw me and concentrated hard on embroidering an initial on the edge of a lace kerchief. It could have been an 'I' or a nascent 'F'.

'Ah, Philippe, anything to report?'

'Not much, signore. Only that Roberto has turned up, asking for our help.'

Il Conte looked up, Catherine clapped her hands and Isabella embroidered.

'What sort of help, work or money?'

'Work, signore. He seems to be serious. I took the liberty of apprenticing him to Davide and I have made it clear to him that he won't get another chance. I hope that is acceptable?'

Il Conte nodded, Catherine smiled at me with real pleasure and Isabella embroidered. As I turned to leave Isabella looked up and I caught her eye. I shook my head very slightly, she gave the smallest of nods and continued with her embroidery.

I had promised Roberto that I would have words with Isabella and Fabio but such was my excitement at having Roberto back in my life that I forgot. When I did remember, many days later, the event had somehow shrunk in significance. I rarely saw them and I decided it wasn't my place to question them and that I would comply with the proverb, '*Non destare il cane che dorme.*'

I started to pop into the stables every day just to see Roberto and Davide at work. They had known each other, of course, from the very beginning but now they seemed to have formed a bond of friendship that required minimal talking, which suited them both very well. Davide only had to show Roberto how to do something a couple of times before he could trust the young man to execute the task without supervision. I enjoyed just sitting and watching Roberto as he cleaned out the stables or brushed down one of the horses. There was nothing effeminate in his actions and it was hard to remember that only a few years ago his dream was to don an elaborate frock and have roses thrown at him.

There was one horse that Roberto had a particular affinity to, il Conte's huge, black horse, Maximillian, that even Davide had to use all his strength and cunning to control. For Roberto, however, the horse was like a baby lamb and followed him out of the stable or stood still whilst he was brushed. Roberto would speak quietly to him and the horse would seem to listen and nod sagely. Roberto would stroke the velvety nose and the tension would flow from the horse's muscles and he would nuzzle Roberto fondly. Roberto didn't laugh much but he whistled a lot, so I surmised that he was, in his own way, happy. I started to join Davide and Roberto for supper and would sit with them in the stables, often saying nothing, just listening to the horses shuffling and munching contentedly on their fodder.

Time passed, as it does, and one early spring evening the following year, Roberto and I were sitting in the garden enjoying the balmy air. I was reading from a new book of poetry that had just arrived from Rome and I was trying to find a poem that would please Sofia when I next visited. Roberto had been whittling a stick but I realised that he had been silent for quite a while. I looked up to find him staring at me, biting his lip.

'Something wrong, Roberto?'

'No, signore. I was just remembering how much I used to enjoy your lessons at the conservatoire and I was wondering...' I raised an eyebrow. 'I was wondering whether you would have time to continue them. I would like to be able to read poetry from such a book as you have there.'

It is difficult to describe or explain the surge of joy that I felt. Roberto, who at one time I had believed to be so unhappy that he had drowned himself; Roberto, who in his desperation had become part of a gang of robbers and murderers; Roberto, who had lost his family not once but twice; Roberto, whose dream of becoming an opera singer had been cruelly dashed through no fault of his own; this same Roberto now wanted to learn to read poetry, to better himself, and he wanted me to help him.

'Of course, Roberto. I would be happy to. We can have a lesson each evening after supper. There's no time like the present, let's see what you remember.' And so daily life subtly changed yet again. Davide would often sit with us, although he didn't partake in the lessons; he was too old to learn his letters, he said, and what good would they do a man like him, anyway?

Since Roberto's arrival the previous year I had seen little of Fabio. I had had fond hopes that the two cousins would become friends again, but Fabio never came near to the stables and Roberto never strayed far from them. Neither one of them gave a hint that they were interested in reforming their attachment. By all accounts Fabio was continuing to excel at his singing and Isabella's tutors spoke highly of him. Maybe he had become less priggish but I never had the opportunity to find out.

I had, of course, still been going back to Montalcino every few months to execute my duties for il Conte but also to spend time with my family. That summer, out of the blue, il Conte suggested that I take Davide and Roberto for company and protection.

'Why do I need protection?'

'There is a rumour that the gangs have organised themselves again and have started to waylay travellers. Although you won't be carrying any gold they are likely to kill you first before finding that out. I would feel happier if you had someone with you who could wield a knife. I remember that Roberto has such skills.'

He gave me a rueful smile then handed me some papers I needed to take.

The ride to Montalcino was the most enjoyable that I remember. We three enjoyed each other's company, the weather was glorious, the horses fresh and full of energy. We slept in the open and Davide re-appropriated his role as rabbit catcher and cook. Farmers' wives provided us with eggs and bread and I made sure we paid for them all. Roberto never spoke to anyone other than myself and Davide and wrapped a red neckerchief around his elongated neck to hide what he considered to be his deformity.

On one of the evenings I asked Roberto if he would sing for us. He shook his head sadly. 'Never again, signore, never again. I would not mock God by trying.'

When we got to the village we rode straight through and Roberto didn't even turn his head to look at his old home. He looked straight ahead and I could see that his hands clenched the reins, but he didn't falter. I left Davide and Roberto to take care of the horses at the stables that had been built as part of the vineyard and I hastily made my way to the house in the wood.

As I entered the thicket I heard the most awful noises of screaming, banging and squealing. With images of butchery in my head I rushed through the trees to find Sofia and Tabitha beating the earth with sticks and trying to herd eight little piglets back into the pen from which they had obviously managed to escape. Berti was toddling about getting under their skirts and not helping one iota. I was so relieved at this domestic scene that I just stopped and howled with laughter. Tabitha saw me first, threw her stick down and raced over to me, her shouts of '*Entra, entra*,' changing with glee to 'Papa, Papa!'

Then Sofia saw me. No welcoming smile. She kept the stick in her hand and seemed inclined to start beating me with it in her frustration. 'Don't just stand there laughing, help me get these little wretches back in.'

I told Tabitha to get Berti out of the way and then it took just a few minutes of collaboration for Sofia and me to get the piglets into the pen. Sofia kept watch whilst I found some wood and nails to block any further attempts at freedom. Only then did I get my welcoming smile.

The first few hours were always spent catching up with each others' news. I had, of course, told her the saga about Roberto over the years but I had never told her about the theft of the rents, the massacre of *i bandito* nor the part I had played in these events. I just told her that Roberto had turned up one day and asked for my help. When I now said that he had asked me to give him lessons she was as pleased as I had been.

'I've actually brought him along with me at il Conte's suggestion, him and Davide.'

'Oh, you must bring them here tomorrow. Entertain the children and I'll do some baking.'

The next day I spent a few hours at the vineyard with Pedro going over accounts. He was another person I had never told the full truth to. He seemed to accept that il Conte preferred to send an armed guard to take the monies back to Florence rather than trust it to his secretary. I then went to the stables and invited both Davide and Roberto to accompany me for refreshments. Davide declined and I saw Roberto about to shake his head also.

'She has fond memories of you and Fabio. You had followed someone there from your cousin's wedding and she found you listening at one of her windows. Fabio stole a bottle. Do you remember?'

He grinned and nodded.

'I would like you to meet her again and my two children, Tabitha and Berti.'

He bit his lip, trying to decide and then nodded in agreement.

I told him not to mention his time as a *bandito* and then we walked to the wood together in companionable silence. I noticed he had put his neckerchief back on.

'Sofia knows what has happened to you; she completely understands. There is no need to hide anything, just be yourself.'

When we arrived Sophia was squeezing oranges into a jug whilst Tabitha was bouncing a chuckling Berti on her knees.

'Ah, you have arrived just in time. Tabitha, take Roberto and go and pick some mint please.'

Tabitha handed Berti to me, wordlessly took Roberto's hand and pulled him along until he took control of his own legs. He turned to me with a look of happy surprise on his face then loped into the wood with my daughter.

'I haven't said anything to Tabitha about what has happened to Roberto. However he decides to speak to her she will accept as being normal.'

I spent the next half an hour re-acquainting myself with my son who was, according to Sofia, just a smaller, plumper version of me. When Tabitha and Roberto returned they were both talking excitedly. They sounded like two girls, Roberto obviously having decided to talk in, what was to him, his natural voice. They were holding hands and laughing and I thanked God for the innocence and accepting nature of my six year old daughter.

The bunch of mint seemed a bit sparse but Sofia plucked a few of the leaves and dropped them into the jug of orange she had just made, poured us each a cup and handed us a slice of the cake she had made the previous evening.

Roberto whispered, '*Grazie*' then after a kick from Tabitha he said loud and in his high-pitched voice, '*Grazie signora.*'

'Do you remember coming up here with your cousin all those years ago?'

'Yes, signora. You gave us a drink and some biscuits.' He hesitated. 'Fabio took a bottle. He used to like shiny things. He probably still does.'

'Yes, Philippe told me. Do you know what Fabio did with the potion in the bottle?'

Roberto pursed his lips. 'I don't know. I thought it was empty. If it wasn't he probably threw it away, it was the bottle he wanted, not what was inside.'

I was surprised at the intentness with which Sofia searched Roberto's face. Then she nodded and handed him a second slice of cake.

Roberto was about ten years older than Tabitha but they played happily together all afternoon. She showed him the animals and Roberto tried his hand at milking the goat with more success than he had had with La Diavolessa before he had been torn from his family and had nothing to worry about other than the bad-temperedness of a she-goat. I yearned to stay longer but I felt I had to take Roberto back and we were leaving for Florence early the next morning. I held my family close and promised to return soon. Roberto looked away, scuffing his shoes in the earth. His blushed cheeks and wide grin warmed my heart when Sofia and Tabitha went over to him and hugged him tight, telling him to come again.

It was no longer safe to stay at the empty village before entering Florence and so we timed it such that we got back

271

to the villa during the afternoon. I was nonetheless glad to have their company and protection on the road and thereafter they always accompanied me when I made the journey to Montalcino.

Since that first visit to my family Roberto gained in confidence and lost his inhibitions. He still spoke rarely, but that was just his nature, and when he did speak he didn't try and disguise it by whispering. I felt so proud of him, prouder than I did of Fabio who was quite the star at the conservatoire and still a great favourite of il Conte. Fabio's fame had spread and he was now invited to sing in churches around Florence and beyond and at celebrations held by the top strata of society, even the Grand Duchess herself.

I didn't feel obliged to attend any of these events, he no longer needed my support and there was something about his pious expression and condescending smile at the appreciation shown that quite turned my stomach. My dislike of Fabio intensified one afternoon when I was strolling towards the stables. I saw Isabella and Fabio walking ahead of me hand in hand. Out of the corner of my eye I saw Roberto standing by the stable door. Suddenly he seemed to come to a decision and he put the broom he had been holding aside, put his shoulders back and walked diagonally towards Isabella and Fabio in order to intercept them. Roberto was dressed in his work clothes, a baggy white shirt over dark cotton britches held up by string. He was tanned and muscular and his black hair was tousled with bits of straw sticking out. Fabio also wore a white shirt but it was spotlessly clean; his hair, as dark as his cousin's, was smoothed down and neatly cut and his plump face was pale, protected from the sun under Isabella's lace parasol.

I didn't hear what was said but I saw Roberto mouth something and put out his hand. I saw Isabella laugh and Fabio's hand slap Roberto's face rather than shake his cousin's. I felt my face flush with anger and mortification on behalf of Roberto and I started to run to prevent him from killing Fabio. He didn't react as I expected, though. Instead, he said something more, which cut off Isabella's laughter, bowed mockingly and walked slowly away.

Chapter 32

The discovery

It was from il Conte that I heard that Fabio had agreed to sing a small part in an opera.

'But he hates opera. He used to speak of it as if it is the devil's work and condemned Roberto for ever wanting to be an opera singer. What a hypocrite he is.'

'Your tone doesn't become you, Philippe. I have persuaded Fabio that he can serve God just as well singing in an opera as he can in a church. If the vessel is Godly, then the setting is neither here nor there. It is only a small part but the Grand Duchess is attending and it will do my position no harm for him to be visible. The performance is next week, please join us.' It was a command not an invitation.

I hesitated to tell Roberto about Fabio's operatic debut but in the end I did; I preferred that he heard it from me than from gossip in the kitchens or stables. I told him as gently as I knew how and waited for a reaction of anger, jealousy, censure or all three, but all I got was a shrug of the shoulders and the ghost of a smile.

Isabella was as excited about going to the opera as she had been when she had been eight, perhaps even more so this time. We arrived early but rather than go straight to il Conte's box, as we had done on the previous occasion, the family stayed in the foyer and mingled. Il Conte made sure they were seen and made it known that his protégé would be singing, just a small part, of course, but from a tiny seed a tall cypress tree will grow! The Grand Duchess singled him out and gave him and Catherine a kiss on the cheek, which would do their standing on the society ladder no harm at all.

I stood in a corner and studied the attire of the aristocracy. How my tastes had changed. It now amused me to compare the flamboyant, corseted and highly embroidered outfits, worn by both the men and the women, with the simple dresses donned by Sofia. I wondered what she would wear if she were ever able to attend such an event as this; probably just one of her normal dresses and perhaps fresh flowers in her hair.

At the thought of Sofia and the children I felt a pang of what I could only think of as homesickness. Why was I stuck in this most unnatural of locations with people I considered to be fools, about to listen to a young man who was far from normal sing of lives that had never been lived and words that had never been said?

When we were seated in il Conte's box I was idly looking at the people in the pits when I gasped - surely that was Roberto? But the crowd was milling around so much that I couldn't be sure. The opera was a new one but not the plot. Some of the singing was passably good and the lead female part was played by a *castrato* well into his middle years. Even from where I was sitting I could see the make-up cracking and melting on his fleshy face. I found him quite grotesque although the audience applauded him loudly. It was nothing, however, to their appreciation of Fabio. He played the daughter, who wasn't really integral to the plot but had a solo praising the morning and the prospect of a lovely day and a long, happy life ahead of her. Fabio was almost unrecognisable in a pale blue satin dress with a hooped skirt and short puffed sleeves that revealed plump, white upper arms. He wore a white, powdered wig, not as tall as the leading lady's, but tall enough for me to wonder how he managed to keep it upright. His face was painted white and his lips bright red. But I forgot how ridiculous he looked when he opened his mouth. His unnatural body produced the sweetest, purest, most nerve-tingling sound that I had ever heard and I knew that Fabio was well on the way to becoming a superb *castrato*, one of the best in Italy, maybe the world.

When he finished there was a stunned silence, for no-one had had any great expectations from this new singer, and then the theatre erupted into clapping and cheering. Flowers saved for the finale were thrown onto the stage and much wine was drunk to Fabio's health. Isabella was beside herself with excitement and delight at his success, as was il Conte and Catherine, although they were more restrained.

The rest of the opera was dull in comparison and the audience didn't listen, they were merely waiting for the end so that they could see Fabio again and hopefully persuade him to sing again, which he did. I don't know whether Fabio had prepared for this eventuality but he chose well. I thought he might sing a popular ditty that the audience would enjoy but instead he chose a hymn in Latin, praising God and all his bounty. Most of the audience didn't understand the content but they recognised a thing of beauty when they heard it. It seemed incongruous to hear these words surrounded by such opulence, falseness and raw ambition, but for just a few minutes, I was back in the wood with Roberto and Fabio when they had sung so beautifully just after the operation. I thought for a moment that there was hope for Fabio, that he would not be swayed by the applause and adulation but when he finished and had bowed to the audience he turned to our box and made a deep bow and blew a kiss to Isabella. The theatre went wild.

The following evening I went to the stable as normal to share supper and to give Roberto his lesson. Davide asked about the opera and I told him that the story was ridiculous but that Fabio had sung magnificently and had been well received. Roberto pretended not to listen.

'I thought I saw you there, Roberto.'

'Me? No, you are mistaken, signor Agostini. You will never get me back in a theatre. You are mistaken.' I caught a look at his expression before he lowered his head to his bowl; it was one of mild amusement.

The next morning I was surprised to see Fabio coming out of il Conte's study. He had a triumphant smile on his face that slipped when he saw me. We wished each other a polite '*Buongiorno*' and I watched him walk away with a heavy heart.

'Ah, Philippe, did you see Fabio just now? I've decided he is too valuable to remain in the conservatoire, where he might catch a chill and some disease. His voice needs to be properly looked after so he will be living here from now on. I want him to have his singing lessons here each day from now on.'

'Is that wise, *mio signore*?'

'Wise? Are you questioning me, Philippe?'

I didn't have any real evidence for why I didn't think it was a good idea for Fabio to be living under the same roof as Isabella. 'No, of course not, signore. I am sure Fabio will flourish here.'

'Be so good as to call on Monsignor and tell him the new arrangements. Work out a timetable so that the Father that trains the singers comes here once a day. I will pay handsomely for the lessons; that will keep Monsignor happy. And tell him that I want Fabio to sing in public more often, especially at important events. He is a real asset and I want to make the most of him.'

I made my way slowly to the conservatoire not looking forward to the conversation I was going to have to have with Monsignor Mazzini. I hadn't seen him for quite a while and as I sat opposite him and shared a glass of his best wine, I realised that over the seven years that I had known him, he had grown into an old man. His back had become more hunched and the flesh hung from his jowls and neck. His skin was dotted with age spots and, I noticed for the first time, he couldn't stop his hands from trembling. When I passed on il Conte's message, Monsignor looked relieved.

'I was worried you had come to tell me that Conte De Lorenzo was removing Fabio all together. At least the conservatoire will continue to benefit from his success. He's the best *castrato* we've ever had under this roof, Philippe. The Archbishop himself made a point of congratulating me the other day and hinted that, young though he is, Fabio might be asked to sing when His Holiness himself comes to Florence later in the year. Imagine that, Philippe, one of our boys singing before il Papa!'

'Il Conte's cup will indeed runneth over.'

Monsignor smiled at my biblical reference and we shared another glass and some small talk before I returned home.

Fabio quickly settled into life at the villa. Father Guiseppe came every morning and he and Fabio locked themselves in the music room until midday and we all got used to the most beautiful sounds wafting out of the window, from scales to hymns to Gregorian chants. Most afternoons Fabio and Isabella had lessons or just spent time in each others' company. They never went near the stables and although I often saw Roberto watching them from the shadows, neither he nor they made any attempt to re-tie the bonds of their friendship. The relationship between Isabella and Fabio made me uncomfortable, although I never witnessed anything untoward between the two of them. I put my uneasiness down to my own prejudices and intolerances.

March and April passed and soon it was only a week or so away from Isabella's sixteenth birthday. Catherine was organising a party thankfully and all I had to do was to ensure that the invitations went out to the right people. I was due to go to Montalcino directly after the party and I was looking forwards to seeing my family again. Every night I knelt and prayed for them, asking God in His mercy to keep them safe.

One night I had had a busy day and I had fallen into a deep sleep as soon as I snuffed out the candle and closed my eyes. Almost immediately, or so it seemed, I was being shaken awake and told to get up, quickly.

'What is it, what's happened?'

'Signor Agostini, you must save her. Please, get up!

'Save who? Is that you Roberto?'

'Si, signore. There is someone in Isabella's bedroom. I was passing her bedroom on the way back to the stables and I heard her moan then cry out, once then twice. Please, signore, someone is hurting her.'

I leapt out of bed, dragged on a pair of britches and raced down the corridor towards Isabella's bedroom, imagining all sorts of things being done to Isabella, from rape to murder. I didn't question what Roberto had said, nor wonder until later why he hadn't gone into the room himself. As I ran, I shouted to Roberto to fetch il Conte and then hurled myself into Isabella's room but rather than finding Isabella being abused I found her being caressed. She and Fabio were lying in each others' arms, the groans and cries that Roberto had heard explained by the look of contentment on their faces, a look that turned quickly into surprise and then horror.

I was standing speechless at the foot of the bed trying to think how the situation could be saved, when I was pushed unceremoniously aside and il Conte bellowed in fury, pulled the cowering Fabio out of bed and flung him onto the floor. He then turned to his daughter and roared angrily, 'Explain why I should not kick this piece of shit to a pulp.'

'Oh, Papa, don't hurt him, I love him!'

'Love him? What do you know of love? He's not a man and never will be! No one can love such a freak, such an abomination.' He turned to Fabio, who was eyeing il Conte with terror, whilst trying to cover the manhood that had just been so harshly belittled. Into this little scene of domestic discord stepped Roberto, who spoke almost apologetically.

'Not only has he defiled your daughter, signore, but he has murdered two men: Il Barbiere and Father Stephen.'

'No, you lie!' Fabio attempted to get up but il Conte's baleful stare pinned him down. 'I did not kill anyone, signore, you have to believe me, it was Roberto. And I have not defiled your daughter, I love her and she loves me; we want to get married as soon as she is sixteen.'

'Married?' Il Conte almost choked on the word. 'People like you don't get married, and certainly not to my daughter!' He grabbed hold of Fabio by the arms, pulled him upright and gripped his wrists so hard that Fabio grimaced in pain. 'Who do you think I'm going to believe? Hard-working, honest Roberto, or lying, deceitful Fabio?' Il Conte put his mouth to Fabio's ear and whispered loudly, 'You're going to hang for this.'

I gasped, Isabella screamed, Roberto smirked and Fabio wet himself.

Chapter 33

Capisco bene

The next morning, Fabio was released from the storeroom where he had been locked for the remainder of the night. He was allowed to dress but not to break his fast and once he had mounted the horse I tied his wrists behind his back and then sat in front of him. Isabella was left locked in her bedroom and as we rode away we could hear the sound of her hysterical crying. Il Conte led the way in silence and I only spoke when it was obvious that our destination wasn't the one I had thought it would be.

'Are we not taking Fabio to *carcere delle Stinche, signore?*'

'No, that place is just for debtors and the like, not for rapists and murderers.'

I felt Fabio tense behind me and warned him with my elbow to keep his mouth shut.

'Where are we going then?'

'You'll see.'

We rode through the bustling streets; our grim expressions and Fabio's bowed head and bound wrists causing people to move out of our way, like the parting of the Red Sea before Moses and the Israelites. At one point we stopped outside a tavern and il Conte indicated we should stay mounted. He was inside for just a few minutes and came out with a sorry specimen of a man. It was still only morning but he looked and smelled like he had been drinking continuously since the previous evening. His hair was unkempt, his eyes red-rimmed and his clothes creased and stained. He reminded me of a rat, with his pointed nose, wispy beard and sly countenance. He grinned up at us and revealed small, black, sharp teeth and I felt Fabio shudder behind me.

Rat Man had no horse so he scuttled alongside il Conte as we journeyed on, eventually reaching the outskirts of the city. Il Conte turned up a rough track that zig-zagged up the side of a hill, upon which stood an old, ruined *castello*. It must once have been a magnificent building, in a good strategic position to defend the burgeoning city. Now, however, much of the stone had been pilfered to build smaller, more humble dwellings and what did remain of the walls was carpeted in ivy. Il Conte led us round the back of the remains, where he tied his horse to a wooden railing that appeared to be but a few months, rather than a few hundred years in age.

Fabio seemed loathe to dismount and whilst I was trying to verbally persuade him, Rat Man reached up, pulled him to the ground and dragged him to where il Conte stood before a door. Unlike the rest of the building, the door looked new and after Rat Man had unlocked it, choosing a key from a bunch that hung from a leather lace round his neck, it swung open noiselessly on well oiled hinges. The door led into a small, empty room but from the daylight that filtered in, I could see that the three walls that limited the size of this entrance hall had only recently been erected. In each wall was a door, shut against my prying eyes.

Il Conte glanced around, but with no curiosity, so I surmised that he had been here before. He turned to Fabio and spoke to him as if his mouth were filled with rancid meat that he wanted to disgorge as quickly as possible. 'You will be kept here until I have decided what to do with

283

you. If I had my way you would be hung, drawn and quartered today and the pieces thrown into the Arno. My wife, however, has a bigger heart than I do and has persuaded me to let you live for a bit longer. You will therefore be kept here under the watchful eye of this man, who will act as *il guardiano*.' He flicked his hand, a sign for Rat Man to open one of the doors and push in Fabio, whose hands were still tied behind his back. All I saw when the door was opened was blackness; there were no windows to shed any light onto the inmate's solitude.

Il Conte quietly gave Rat Man some instructions, handed him a pouch of coins and then left, beckoning for me to follow. I turned as we started to ride away to see Rat Man leaning in the doorway, taking a swig from a flagon that he must either have had on his person or perhaps stored at the prison for when his services would be needed.

'What is this place, signore, and whose is it?'

'It doesn't belong to any one person but to a number of us who agreed that such a holding place would be useful. There are a number of *custodi* we can call upon to keep watch over the prisoner until their sentence is decided.'

'But who decides the sentence?'

Il Conte looked at me coldly, 'In this instance I will decide his fate. He has dishonoured me and my family and his punishment is mine to inflict.'

After that we rode in silence. I could not help but notice that il Conte looked ten years older than the day before; his back was stooped, his face pale and drawn, the lines in his face more deeply etched, the specks of grey in his hair more numerous. Il Conte stopped outside the tavern from whence he had plucked Rat Man.

'Let's have a drink, I need one.' He ordered a jug of their best wine and only after he had downed two cups straight down did he speak again. 'Did you know about all this, Philippe?'

My initial inclination was to deny it but I considered il Conte to be a friend more than a master and I felt obliged to tell him the truth. 'I didn't know it had gone this far but I have felt something was not quite right for a while. I should have said something but I had nothing specific to share, just a feeling of unease. Do you remember when Roberto came back into our lives and you let him work in the stables? Well, that was as a result of him spying on the two of them and seeing Fabio touch Isabella where no man should before he is married to her, to use Roberto's words. He was so incensed that he beat up Fabio. When he explained what had happened to me he had already convinced himself that Isabella was the innocent party but ...'

'But what, Philippe?'

'But when he said that Isabella didn't push Fabio away because she was so surprised, I did wonder if it was rather that she wanted him to touch her.'

Il Conte slammed his cup down so hard that the contents slopped over the table and then slapped me hard. 'How dare you! Are you calling my daughter *una puttana*?'

I felt sorry for him and wanted to choose my words carefully. I waited whilst he filled his cup again and for the smarting in my cheek to begin to fade. 'Forgive me, signore, I meant no disrespect. No, I don't think that Isabella is a whore, she is just a girl growing into a young woman and has been seduced by someone she believes she

285

loves. She has had no real experience of being in the company of normal boys and in her eyes Fabio *is* normal.'

'Are you saying all this is my fault?'

'I suppose I am, but only because you are her father and love her as a father should. In protecting your daughter and trying to keep her away from normal young men, she has not been able to make comparisons. In her eyes Fabio was a perfect companion and when she was ready to fall in love, as all girls do at this age, he was the only one available.'

'Last night,' Il Conte avoided looking at me and stared over my shoulder, 'last night.' He didn't seem able to continue.

'Last night, *mio signore*, it was clear that Roberto was correct when he told me that *un castrato* is still capable of performing sexually.'

He put his head in his hands and groaned, 'Oh, my God. I can't believe this is happening.'

'But Fabio is not able to produce seed, be thankful for that.'

Il Conte twirled his now empty cup. 'Isabella's reputation must be maintained at all costs. He attempted to rape her but did not succeed, do you understand?'

What choice was there? If I said 'no' and refused to support my master's story, then I would be blackening her name and she would never make a successful marriage. If I said 'yes' then her reputation would remain spotless but Fabio's life would be ruined.

'I understand, signore. What about Fabio's singing? Could he not just be sent away to Rome or Venice so that he could still continue?'

Il Conte shook his head. 'Do you not remember what Roberto said? He said Fabio has also killed two men. If he is a murderer as well as a rapist then he will hang.'

I did remember Roberto's accusation, but also his look of satisfaction when he saw the result of his announcement. I decided to keep my thoughts to myself for now. Il Conte ordered another jug of wine and we returned to the villa in the afternoon, both slightly inebriated.

Il Conte went straight to his wife's rooms. They shut themselves away and Isabella remained locked in her bedroom, her trays of food untouched. All the staff walked about with long faces and boots of lead. I went into the stable to find Roberto carrying on with his duties, whistling quietly to himself.

'You don't seem overly concerned with the fate of your cousin.'

Roberto continued to brush the rump of Maximillian. Only when he had finished and led the great horse back into his stable, did he come and sit with me.

'Fabio did wrong and should be punished.'

'He'll likely hang, or worse.'

'Yes, I heard il Conte say so last night.'

'Fabio will definitely be tried for rape, for which the sentence might be exile, but last night you accused him of murder, twice over, for which he will be certainly be put to death.'

'So be it.'

'Tell me about Il Barbiere.'

Roberto closed his eyes and hugged his knees. 'Do you remember the bottle he took from *la Strega's*? Well, he told me afterwards that it contained poison.'

'How did he know?'

'She had pointed out some bottles on a shelf that she said were dangerous in the wrong hands. They had a label with a cross on them.'

'There was no label on the bottle he showed me.'

'No, he took it off after he had emptied the contents into Il Barbiere's wine.'

'But why? Il Barbiere wasn't a bad man, he was just doing a job.'

'He killed Luigi.'

'Is that what you think? Il Barbiere didn't kill the boy on purpose, it was just bad luck.'

Roberto shrugged. 'I know that but Fabio said Il Barbiere was dangerous and shouldn't be allowed to kill any more boys. So, he had to die.'

I remembered my own sickness the day after we had left Murlo and I had handled the bottle. 'I swallowed some of that poison, that's why I was so sick the next day. For God's sake, I could have been killed as well!'

Roberto bit his lip. 'We thought there probably wasn't enough to kill you, so we said nothing.'

'Probably?'

'We couldn't tell you what was in the bottle. I know now it was wrong of Fabio but at the time I thought he was doing God's will by avenging Luigi's death.'

I shook my head in exasperation, 'And Father Stephen?'

Roberto's face tightened at the mention of the name. 'I told Fabio what *il padre* had done to me. He was furious and said such a beast didn't deserve to live. I know now it was wrong but at the time I agreed with Fabio.'

'But how did you do it? I can't see how he remained on his back.'

Roberto grinned, though the sight chilled rather than cheered me. 'I went in first and told *il grasso bastardo* that I was sorry I had got him into trouble and I offered to show my regret in whatever way he wanted.' Roberto gave a shudder at the memory. 'Whilst he was on his back and I was pleasuring him, Fabio crept in and stabbed him. Just the once but once was enough. His anger made him strong.'

I pictured the scene and I had to swallow the bile that rose in my throat. 'Both times you could have stopped him.'

'Not really. Fabio said he was the hand of God and who was I to challenge Him? He would have killed them with or without me. Now, forgive me, but I have work to do.'

I wandered back to the villa, troubled by my inability to believe Roberto. His story sounded feasible, but was it indeed just a story? There was something in the flatness of his voice and the cold look in his eye that worried me. As I walked to my room, Il Conte strode out of Catherine's rooms, nearly knocking me over.

'Ah, Philippe, just the man. I have discussed everything with Catherine and we are agreed on what we are going to do. We are taking Isabella to a cousin of mine in Venice. She will stay there, attend all the dances and soirees that she will undoubtedly be invited to, until a suitable marriage can be arranged.' He sighed heavily. 'I hadn't envisaged having to find a suitor quite so soon but she will be sixteen in just a few days so I suppose the timing is fortuitous. We will leave tomorrow and will stay for a few weeks. In my absence you will sort this mess out. Fabio is a rapist and a murderer and if he is still in Florence when I return I will

carry out the sentence of death. If he is not in Florence then
I can't. *Capisci*?'
'*Capisco bene.*'

Chapter 34

Accusations

'Oh, Philippe, what is to become of me?'

I was sitting in the rose garden, savouring the early summer evening, helped by a glass of fine wine. Isabella, released from her prison, sat heavily beside me. She took my hand idly in hers and studied first the front and then the back.

'Papa is taking me to Venice and is going to force me to marry an old man who I shall despise. He will make me have lots of horrid children and I will be so unhappy I will kill myself.'

She burst into tears and I had to control myself not to laugh. '*Mia povera* Isabella. Your Papa won't force you to marry anyone, I'm sure. He wants you to be happy.'

'How can you say that? How can I be happy ever again? I love Fabio, *he* made me happy but Papa is calling him all sorts of names and saying he is a murderer but he's not! Fabio told me what happened; it was Roberto who killed those men, not Fabio. Fabio tried to stop him but when Roberto is angry there is no stopping him. You saw how he beat Fabio and he was quite happy to join that gang of robbers and murderers. Don't they say that like attracts like? Fabio couldn't hurt anyone. We are so in love, please Philippe, can't you talk to Papa and persuade him to let us marry?'

'I'm sorry, Isabella but it would be wrong of you to marry Fabio even if he is innocent of the killings. You could never have children with him.'

'I don't care! I don't want children, ever!'

'You say that now, *mio caro*, but all women want children and I promise, when you are a bit older, you will want them too.'

'Catherine doesn't have children.'

'Have you asked her whether she doesn't have children from choice or necessity?'

'Well, no, but she is obviously perfectly happy.'

'Now, yes, she is. But only after many years of losing baby after baby before even it was born. She has suffered so much grief and pain and she is happy now because in your father she has found someone who loves her for herself and does not care that she cannot bear him children. But for many years she desperately wanted a child, as all women do.'

'Well, I don't.'

'Isabella, you are being a petulant child and proving to me that you cannot possibly make such a decision now. You say you love Fabio but you have no-one else to compare him with. You are old enough to understand that you are a count's daughter and as such you must do as he says and marry according to his wishes, not yours. That is the way of the world in which we live and you would be foolhardy to challenge it. You are nearly a grown woman, so act like one. Accept that you will never marry Fabio. You will go to Venice, meet new people, fall in love with a man your Papa approves of, get married, have children and live happily ever after. How do I know this? Because you are a lovely young woman with a great heart that needs to love and be loved.'

'I love Fabio and he loves me.' Her voice sounded less confident than it had.

I took her chin and forced her to look at me. 'No, Isabella, you have not known enough men to know whether what you feel is love or just friendship. I am sorry to say this, but Fabio was taking advantage of you and your father's wealth and position to further his own singing career.' She mouthed the word 'No' but made no sound. I brushed a tear from the end of her nose. 'I have only ever heard of one castrato who married, and it was a disaster; his wife left him after less than a year.'

'It is not Fabio's fault, he didn't ask for the operation.'

'I know, I know, but there is no going back, only forward. I'm sorry, Isabella, but if you want my advise then it is to let go of Fabio, go to Venice, heed your Papa and embrace life. Just because he wants you to have a successful marriage doesn't mean he doesn't want you to be happy, let him make you so. '

Isabella leaned forward and kissed me softly on the lips; I tasted the salt of her tears. Then she hugged me tight, like she used to do when she was a child, not so long ago. 'You are a good, kind man, Philippe. I will be a good, dutiful daughter but please promise me that you will do everything you can for Fabio. He didn't rape me and he didn't kill those men. *Promettere*?'

'*Lo prometto.*'

The next morning, before they left, Il Conte took me aside and handed me a ring emblazoned with the De Lorenzo coat of arms. 'When you wear this, you are me. People will act towards you as if I was standing before them. Do not abuse it.'

I took the ring and slipped it onto my middle finger, feeling inexplicably empowered. Having watched the family and their entourage disappear out of sight I went to the stables to confront Roberto. He was sitting with Davide finishing his breakfast.

'Roberto, please walk with me, I would discuss something with you.'

He looked puzzled, glanced at Davide, who nodded his consent, and followed me as I walked into the rose garden and along a meandering path.

'You knew full well that Isabella wasn't being attacked, didn't you?'

Roberto pursed his lips and nodded.

'Why did you pretend?'

'What they were doing was wrong.'

'It was, but that wasn't why you wanted to stop it, you were jealous. You have always resented Fabio's close friendship with Isabella, isn't that so?'

Roberto shrugged but didn't disavow what I had said.

'Whatever you thought of the situation, why couldn't you have just told me what was going on and I could have stopped it without Fabio being incarcerated and Isabella sent off to Venice.'

'You didn't stop them when I told you the first time I saw Fabio acting dishonourably. He needed to be stopped before he ruined Isabella's life.'

'Well, we can't undo what has now transpired. Roberto, look at me.' He lifted his gaze from the ground and looked at me from the corner of his eyes. 'Tell me to my face that Fabio killed Il Barbiere and Father Stephen.'

Roberto turned his face fully to mine and told me that Fabio had killed Il Barbiere and Father Stephen. He didn't blink, he didn't blush, he didn't hesitate.

'Alright. I am going to see Fabio now and you will come with me.'

'No, I don't want to see him; I want nothing more to do with him.'

'I am not asking you, Roberto, I am telling you. You *will* come with me. In il Conte's absence I am the master here, so if you want to continue working here you will accompany me.' Il Conte's ring seemed to make my voice deeper, my heart colder.

As it had been the previous day, the journey to *il castello* was done in silence. Roberto's lips were set in a thin, angry line and his eyes were fixed on the road ahead. We tied our horses to the hitching rail and he looked around with interest as we crossed the open ground to the door, newly set into the crumbling wall. It was ajar so I walked straight in. Rat Man was leaning back in his chair, his feet on the table, his head back, mouth open, snoring loudly, an empty cup on the table - the epitome of a drunkard. I slammed by hand on the table, causing him to almost leap out of his chair. He hadn't shaven, bathed or changed his clothes since the previous day and the smell of stale wine, breath and sweat was almost unbearable.

'I want to see Fabio, open the door.'

'Who the hell are you to come here and tell me what to do? I only take orders from Conte De Lorenzo and,' he looked around the room then grinned at me, 'he ain't here.'

I didn't want to get any nearer to him so I raised my voice and spoke slowly and clearly so that his befuddled brain could understand my words. 'I am here by the authority of il Conte.' I held out my hand and showed him the ring on my finger. 'By wearing this ring il Conte assured me that I would be shown every courtesy that he would have been shown if he were standing here. Was he wrong to think so?'

He twitched his mouth, like a rat, which I took to be a denial. 'So, you will speak to me as if you were speaking with Conte De Lorenzo himself. You will show me the respect that you would extend to Conte De Lorenzo himself. And you will open that door as if you had been asked by Conte De Lorenzo himself. *Capisci*?'

Rat Man glowered but nodded. I was the same man whom he had mocked the day previously but today, merely by wearing il Conte's ring, I had become of the class to be obeyed. He took a key from the bunch around his neck and walked the short distance to the prison door, his careful and studied gait a sign of the habitual inebriate. He flung the door open and snarled, 'You got visitors.'

I could see nothing inside and could not tell if the room was as small as the entrance hall or as large as an underground cave. 'Bring me a candle.' Rat Man made grumbling noises but did as he was bid and I was soon holding it aloft, illuminating Fabio's cell. There was nothing in it except a bundle of rags in one corner and a bucket in the other.

I went over to the rags and shook them carefully. Fabio raised his face, shielding his eyes from the brightness that had invaded the darkness. '*Chi è*?'

'It's me, Philippe. Philippe Agostini. I am here with Roberto.'

'Signor Agostini?'

'Can you stand up? You,' I gestured to Rat Man, 'bring in that chair so he can sit down.'

More grumbles but he dragged it in and helped me lift Fabio onto it, who, I could not help but notice, had soiled his britches and vomited down his shirt. His eyes were red from crying and he had a moustache of dried snot.

There was no point in further pleasantries. 'Fabio, you are accused on two counts, the first of rape ...'

'But I didn't rape her, signore. I love her and she loves me!'

'Hear me out, then you can have your say. As I said, the first is rape and the second is murder.'

'But that was not me, it was Roberto!'

'Fabio, be silent. I won't tell you again. If you say another unbidden word I will leave you here for il Conte to deal with.' I was wearing il Conte's harsh persona as well as his ring. 'I know from my own eyes that you did not rape Isabella.' Roberto shuffled behind me and I sensed he was going to say something. I looked over my shoulder. 'I don't want to hear from you either, Roberto. There is another cell across the way, which I am sure *il guardiano* will be more then happy to open up for you.' I turned back to Fabio. 'So, the accusation of rape is rescinded. Now, for the matter of the murders. Roberto, do you still accuse your cousin Fabio of poisoning Il Barbiere?'

'Si.'

Fabio slumped lower in the seat, moaned and shook his head. 'No, no, no.'

'Tell me your side of the story, Fabio.'

'I stole the bottle from *la Strega*, that much is true, but only because it shone so prettily in the sunlight and I wanted it for my collection. It was when we were at Il Barbiere's, after Luigi had died, that I told Roberto I thought it contained poison and I was going to throw it away. He said he knew just where to throw it and he took the bottle from me and poured it into the wine. It wasn't me, signor Agostini. I could have said something, yes, but I did not cause the death of that man.'

'You lie!'

Rat Man chuckled and jangled the keys. Roberto lowered his eyes to the ground under my angry glare.

'Roberto, do you still accuse your cousin Fabio of stabbing Father Stephen to death?'

'Si.'

'What is your story, Fabio?'

'It is no story, signor Agostini, I only tell the truth. It is true I stole Monsignor Mazzini's knife. He had left the study door open and there was a shaft of sunlight shining right on the knife that he had left on the table. It was as if God was pointing at it, so I took it. I had a hiding place in the jakes and when I told Roberto about taking it he would have known where I would have put it. I knew sometimes Father Stephen came into the dormitory and took boys away, including Roberto, but I didn't know why. The first I knew about his death was when Father Guiseppe told us all. It wasn't me, signor Agostini, I swear before God that it was not me.'

I studied Fabio's face. In the past few years I had come to despise him. He may have been a pious hypocrite and intolerant of his cousin's failings, but was he a murderer? I turned to look at Roberto, my erstwhile favourite. The reason I had loved him the most was because he was a passionate dreamer, but as such, was far more likely to kill someone than his cold-hearted cousin.

298

Il Conte had told me to either leave Fabio to be put to death or to make him disappear.

I made my decision.

'One of you is lying, maybe both of you. Maybe one of you killed Il Barbiere and the other Father Stephen. Maybe both of you were involved in the deaths, maybe neither of you were. You both blame the other and there is no way for me to know who is telling the truth.'

Rat Man chimed in. 'There is always the rack - that always brings the truth out.'

'*Grazie*, I don't think we need to revert to those days. No, God knows the truth and He will be the judge at the final reckoning. In the meantime, we will all return to the villa and I will tell you what I have decided.'

Before Rat Man could object, I flashed the ring at him. 'You would not challenge Conte De Lorenzo, do not challenge me.'

Chapter 35

The departures

It grieved me that the three of us, who not so many years ago would have been chattering and laughing together, now rode wordlessly. When we arrived at the villa I told Fabio to go and get changed into clean clothes and for them both to meet me in il Conte's study at midday.

I sat in my master's chair, still wearing his ring and felt confident in the plan I had devised. I waited until the boys were both settled in their seats and were looking at me expectantly. 'I have said this a number of times over the last few days, but we cannot undo what has been done, we can only control what will be. I honestly don't know which one of you is guilty of murder and I am not willing to bear the responsibility of making that judgement. I do know, however, that you are both guilty of distrust, jealousy, ambition and selfishness. I feel partly to blame for the part I have played in your younger lives but you are both of an age now when you must be accountable for your own actions.'

They both squirmed under my stern gaze. 'Neither of you can stay here. You will both be given enough money to make a new start but it is your decision what you spend it on. However, I need to make something very clear. Neither of you is to return to this villa unless invited to do so, neither of you is to attempt to contact Isabella in any way and if either of you smears the name of De Lorenzo or spreads rumours or gossip I can assure you that the words will hardly have left your mouth before your tongue is ripped out, along with your innards.'

The boys looked uncomfortable. 'Do you understand?' They continued to stare at their feet but both nodded. 'I suggest you spend the rest of the afternoon contemplating what I have said and tomorrow morning, after breakfast you will come to this study, I will hand you your bag of gold and you will leave.'

That afternoon, I walked to the conservatoire to spend an hour with Monsignor Mazzini then went to *il Duomo* for my own period of contemplation. I lit candles for my parents, Eleanora, Eduardo and for the two boys who had been, but who had died in spirit, if not in body, under the knife of Il Barbiere. I then went to the banker and drew out two bags of gold, the ring on my finger being sufficient authorisation.

The next morning I breakfasted alone and then went to the study to wait for the boys. I assumed they had been waiting in the shadows for they both turned up just a few minutes later, though separately. I invited them to sit down and I put the two leather pouches on the table in front of them.

'You have made your decisions?'

They both nodded.

I handed Roberto his bag. 'Tell me yours, Roberto.' He looked refreshed and clear-eyed. Was it because he was not guilty or because he was guilty but had got away with it?

'*Grazie*, signor Agostini. I want to go to school, have an education and maybe one day have a job like yours.'

'A good plan, Roberto. I wish you every success. And you, Fabio?'

He too looked rested; it is amazing what a good night's sleep and the promise of gold will do to one's physical and mental well-being. He seemed to have got over his grief at the loss of his beloved very quickly.

'I am grateful that you took me out of that dreadful place but I would like to say once again that I am wholly innocent and should never have been put there.'

Roberto snorted and I gestured for Fabio to continue.

'If I can't stay here then I will go to Naples. Prince Ferdinand has approached me a number of times wanting to be my sponsor. I have always said "no" before, but now, well, now I will say "yes."'

'I am sure you will be a great success, Fabio.' I held out the gold to them and as they took hold of the bags, just for a few seconds, my hands touched theirs. I had given their parents bags of gold in exchange for their sons; I was giving the sons bags of gold, in exchange for what? Their souls? My guilt? 'Remember what I said yesterday and may God forgive you for any wrongs you may have done. Now go.'

They both left without a further word, clutching their gold to their chests, avoiding eye contact with me and with each other.

I was shaking with emotion. I had once loved them both and now I felt nothing but sadness that it should all end like this. I was sure that Fabio would become a great opera singer and that Roberto would achieve his ambition of taking my job. But the cost was too high.

I continued to sit at the desk. I took off the ring and reverted to being a powerless secretary. The morning drew on and I continued to sit, pondering on the past and wondering about the future. I realised I was a weak man; maybe not a bad man, but certainly not a good one. I thought about Eleanora and saw her for what she really had been: young, manipulative, deceitful. I thought about the boys, my involvement in their lives and what actions I should have taken. I thought about all the things I had agreed to do for il Conte that I knew I shouldn't have done but did anyway, all for the sake of keeping my job and my so-called respectability. These people were my past.

I thought about Sofia, Tabitha and Berti. These were my future.

I knew what I had to do.

I took a sheet of paper, dipped one of il Conte's quills into the ink, wrote him a long letter and propped it against the ink well for him to see on his return.

I packed just my clothes, put the coins I had saved over the years into a pouch, which I tied around my waist and went to the stables. As I rode out I saw Davide standing in the shadows. We nodded to each other in acknowledgement of our friendship but we spoke no words of farewell.

I left the horse at the vineyard and walked home. When I arrived, I was tired, dishevelled and dusty and my stomach was growling with hunger. The door was open and I stood at the threshold quietly enjoying the domestic scene before me. Sofia was kneading bread and humming tunelessly, Tabitha was building a tower of wooden bricks that Berti was taking great pleasure in knocking down.

Time seemed to stand still and I was able to study Sofia's surprised expression as she noticed me standing there, Tabitha's look of pretend anger as her tower was destroyed yet again and Berti's flash of white baby teeth as he threw back his head and roared with laughter. I heard little Piccolo munching on the grass, the chickens clucking and scratching in the dust, the pigs snuffling, the goats bleating.

The birds were roosting and singing their evening chorus and just for a moment, I thought I heard a nightingale.

THE END

Bibliography

Barbier, Patrick. *The world of the castrati: The history of an extraordinary operatic phenomenon.* trs. by Margaret Crosland. London, Souvenir Press, 1996.

Hanlon, Gregory. *Early modern Italy, 1550 - 1800: Three seasons in European history.* London, Macmillan Press Ltd., 2000.

Marzo, Eduardo (Ed.). *Songs of Italy: sixty-five Tuscan, Florentine, Lombardian and other Italian folk- and popular songs.* trs. by Dr. Theo Baker. New York, G. Schirmer, 1904.

Vaussard, Maurice. *Daily life in eighteenth century Italy.* trs. by Michael Heron. London, George Allen & Unwin Ltd., 1962.

Woolf, Stuart. *A history of Italy 1700 - 1860: The social constraints of political change.* London, Methuen & Co Ltd., 1979.

Acknowledgements

I would first of all like to thank my sister, Adrienne, who suffered me e-mailing her chapter by chapter over many months. Her feedback was sometime hard to accept but it was always fair and invariably right. It was because of my sister that Sofia became a feisty, independent woman rather that the rather fey, drippy one I had originally created.

Then there is the Monday Wordsmiths: Ann Evans (leader), Margaret Mather, Maxine Burns, Mark Howland, Mary Ogilvie, Eleanor Simmons and Bec Woods. This is the writing group I attended, whose members only ever heard bits and pieces over the year but who always offered suggestions and encouragement. It was they who persuaded me that it was alright for humans to do horrible things to each other, but it was totally unacceptable for Philippe to kick the dog - so that bit had to come out.

And finally many thanks to Mike Linane, who has published all my novels and agreed to republish this book, that was originally called *Song of the Nightingale*, under its new title *Sold for a Song*.

ENJOYED *SOLD FOR A SONG?*

Thank you for taking the time to read Sold for a Song; I hope you enjoyed it. If you did, could you please leave a review on Amazon – you can do so even if you didn't buy the book from there but have bought other products. Write as little or as much as you like, but it will mean so much to me.

KEEP IN TOUCH

Follow me on social media:

Facebook: facebook.com/marilyn.pemberton.391

Blog: writingtokeepsane.wordpress.com

Website: https://marilynpemberton.wixsite.com/author

e-mail: marilyn.pemberton@yahoo.co.uk

Printed in Great Britain
by Amazon